He was her only hope…

She was his greatest temptation…

HIGHLAND PROTECTOR

"Lass, have ye gone to sleep?"

The hint of amusement in his voice caused her to lift her head and smile at him. Ilsabeth saw the way his eyes abruptly darkened. Her body responded to that look with a heat that nearly made her gasp. Suddenly she understood why some of her married kinswomen would blush when their men looked at them. They were seeing that look in their men's eyes.

Simon softly cursed even as he pulled her face closer to his, unable to resist the urge to kiss her, to taste that lush mouth that tempted him every time he looked at it. When Ilsabeth smiled at him, her eyes all soft and warm, his will crumbled. All he could think of was how much he wanted her to keep looking at him like that. It was madness.

She was his weakness, he thought with a touch of alarm. He had spent years hardening himself in heart, body, and mind, yet this small woman with big blue eyes easily cut through his armor with a smile. Simon knew he ought to run far and fast, but then his lips touched hers, and all his fears were burned away by the heat that flooded his body. . . .

Books by Hannah Howell

Only for You * *My Valiant Knight* * *Unconquered*
Wild Roses * *A Taste of Fire* * *Highland Destiny*
Highland Honor * *Highland Promise*
A Stockingful of Joy * *Highland Vow* * *Highland Knight*
Highland Hearts * *Highland Bride* * *Highland Angel*
Highland Groom * *Highland Warrior* * *Reckless*
Highland Conqueror * *Highland Champion*
Highland Lover * *Highland Vampire*
The Eternal Highlander * *My Immortal Highlander*
Conqueror's Kiss * *Highland Barbarian*
Beauty and the Beast * *Highland Savage*
Highland Thirst * *Highland Wedding* * *Highland Wolf*
Silver Flame * *Highland Fire* * *Nature of the Beast*
Highland Captive * *Highland Sinner*
My Lady Captor * *If He's Wicked* * *Wild Conquest*
If He's Sinful * *Kentucky Bride* * *If He's Wild*
Yours for Eternity * *Compromised Hearts*
Highland Protector

Published by Zebra Books

HIGHLAND PROTECTOR

HANNAH HOWELL

ZEBRA BOOKS
KENSINGTON PUBLISHING CORP.
http://www.kensingtonbooks.com

ZEBRA BOOKS are published by

Kensington Publishing Corp.
119 West 40th Street
New York, NY 10018

All Kensington titles, imprints and distributed lines are
available at special quantity discounts for bulk purchases
for sales promotion, premiums, fund-raising, educational
or institutional use.

Special book excerpts or customized printings can also be
created to fit specific needs. For details, write or phone the
office of the Kensington Special Sales Department. Kensington Publishing Corp., 119 West 40th Street, New York,
NY 10018. Phone: 1-800-221-2647.

Zebra and the Z logo are Reg. U.S. Pat. & TM Off.

ISBN-13: 978-1-4201-0463-9
ISBN-10: 1-4201-0463-2

First Printing: December 2010

10 9 8 7 6 5 4 3 2 1

Printed in the United States of America

Chapter 1

Scotland, summer 1479

"I bow in awe of the sacrifices ye are willing to make for our great cause, Walter."

"Dinnae bow too low, dear cousin, for my sacrifice will be but short-lived."

"How so? I do believe that anyone accused of murdering a king's mon is doomed to be, er, short-lived and treason brings one a most horrific death."

Ilsabeth halted, the words *murder* and *treason* stopping her dead in the act of sneaking up on her betrothed. She had left him an hour earlier, hidden away in the woods, and then slipped back to his home to see if she could discover why he had begun to act strangely. Another woman had been her suspicion. Sir Walter Hepbourn was a virile man and had not been expending much of that virility on her. Ilsabeth had begun to suspect that he was heartily feeding his manly appetites somewhere else, and even though they were not yet wed, such faithlessness was not something she could tolerate.

Murder and treason had never crossed her

mind. And the murder of a king's man? That was treason in and of itself. The mere thought of such a crime sent chills down her spine. Why would Walter have anything to do with such crimes, or even know enough about them to speak of them?

Keeping to the shadows cast by Walter's large stone house, Ilsabeth dropped to her belly and inched closer. Walter and his cousin David sat side by side on a large stone bench at the end of the garden Walter's rather overbearing mother took such pride in. Both men were drinking and enjoying the early evening, undoubtedly savoring the encroaching cool after a surprisingly hot, sunny day. It was a strange place to talk of such dark subjects as murder and treason.

"I intend to rescue my dearly betrothed, of course," said Walter. "She will have to flee Scotland but I have a fine wee house on the coast of France in which I can keep her. Her gratitude will keep me warm for many a night."

"Jesu, ye are nay still thinking of marrying her, are ye? T'was bad enough when she was just an Armstrong wench, but then she will be seen as the daughter of traitors."

The shock and disgust weighting every word David spoke stung Ilsabeth's pride like nettles but she hastily swallowed her gasp of furious outrage.

Walter gave a harsh laugh. "Still? I *ne'er* intended to wed her. I thought ye kenned that. She is an Armstrong, for sweet pity's sake. M'father would spin in his grave if I tried to mix his family's blood with that of one of those low reivers. My mother would soon join him. Nay, I but played the game.

Howbeit, she is a sweet morsel and I dinnae wish to see her in her grave until I have had a wee taste."

"Ye mean ye havenae had a wee taste yet?"

"I tried but it quickly became clear that someone taught her the value of her maidenhead."

"Ah, weel, I had thought ye had gotten betrothed to her so that ye could take that with ease."

"Nay, it was the best way to get close to her kinsmen, aye? I can see I erred in nay telling ye all my plans. We needed someone to bear the blame and I decided her family would serve. Now I will nay only be free of suspicion, but free of her cursed family as weel. If I step right, I may e'en get some of their land once our angry king rids this land of them. Or I shall get it when the new king is seated upon the throne."

"Clever. If it works. The Armstrongs being what they are, 'tis reasonable to think all blame could easily be shifted onto their shoulders, but will it stay there? We are close to ridding ourselves of that foolish king, his sycophants, and all those who lead him where they wish him to go. We cannae afford to have any suspicion turning our way."

"It willnae. The king's supporters will be so busy hunting Armstrongs they willnae have time left to look anywhere else." Walter stood up and stretched. "Come, let us go inside. The insects begin to feed upon me and we need to plan our next step most carefully. When next we meet with our compatriots, I want to be able to present a finely polished plan they will all be willing to follow."

David moved to follow him. "I was hoping for an early night and a warm wench."

"We will soon both enjoy those pleasures. I, too, wish to be weel rested so that I may watch those thieving Armstrongs rounded up and taken away in chains."

Ilsabeth remained still until she was certain both men were well inside the house before she began to crawl away to the safety of the wood separating her father's lands from Walter's. Once within the shelter of its deep shadows, she stood up, staggered over to a tree, and emptied her belly. The sickness tore through her until her stomach hurt and her throat was raw. She then stumbled over to the next tree, slumped against it, and fumbled with the small wineskin attached to her girdle. It took several hearty rinses as well as several deep drinks of the cool cider to clear the vile taste from her mouth, a bitter taste she knew was not wholly caused by her sickness.

"Bastard," she whispered when what she really wanted to do was scream the word to the heavens until her ears rang.

She had been such a fool. Beguiled by a handsome man, the thought of finally having a home of her own, and children. Walter had used her, had used her family who had welcomed him as one of their own.

Her family! Ilsabeth thought the fear that surged through her would have her retching in the bushes again, but she fought that weakness. She needed to have a clear head and to stay strong. She needed to warn her family.

With her skirts hiked up to her knees, Ilsabeth raced through the woods, desperate to reach her home. She did not know when the king's man had been killed, what the man had been doing here, or even where the body was, but instinct told her it would be found soon. From all that she had just heard, she knew it was meant to be found. Worse, she was certain Walter had left behind enough evidence with the body to point the finger of blame straight at her family.

"Wait! Two, wait!"

Ilsabeth stopped so abruptly at the familiar hailing that she nearly fell on her face. Steadying herself, she turned to see her cousin Humfrey racing toward her. As she struggled to catch her breath, her scattered thoughts latched on to that hated name *Two*. When her eldest sister Ilsabeth, the firstborn, had become Sister Beatrice, the family had asked her if she would take the name, as her mother loved it so. Since she had not really liked her own name of Clara much, she had been more than willing. But, instead of a nice new name, all her siblings and cousins had begun to call her Two, or Twa. When Humfrey reached her side, she punched him in the arm mostly out of habit. It was odd, she thought, how such mundane thoughts and actions had helped to still the rising panic inside.

"Ye cannae go home," he said, idly rubbing the place on his arm where she had struck him.

"I have to," she said. "I need to warn my family of the plot against them."

"Ye mean the one that has the king's soldiers at the gates yelling about murder and treason?"

Muttering curses that had the young Humfrey blushing faintly, Ilsabeth abruptly sat down. "I am too late. This is all Walter's doing."

Humfrey sat down facing her. "How do ye ken that?"

Ilsabeth told him all she had heard and smiled weakly when Humfrey patted her shoulder in an awkward gesture of comfort even as his handsome face grew hard with anger. "He wants our clan to take the blame, to be the lure the king's men chase about as he and his fellow plotters rid us of our king.

"I thought I had time to warn everyone, mayhap e'en stop it."

"Weel, there is still time to fix things."

"How so? Ye have just told me that the king's army is pounding on the gates."

"Aye, and your father is keeping those gates closed tight as everyone else flees. By the time those gates are forced open there will be no one left inside save for a few old men and women who have chosen to stay behind. Old and wee bit infirm, they cannae move quickly enough and refuse to be the ones to slow down all the others."

"They could be taken, killed, or tortured for information," she said, worried for those who would have to face the soldiers yet relieved that her family had fled.

"Nay, I doubt much attention will be paid to them."

"Ye have come to take me to the others then?"

"Nay. I have come to help ye flee elsewhere. Ye see, t'was your dagger in the heart of the dead mon."

Ilsabeth buried her face in her hands and fought the urge to weep. It was a weak thing to do and she needed to be strong now. "I had wondered where it had disappeared to," she said, and then looked at Humfrey. "Where am I to flee if nay with my family? I dinnae understand why I cannae just run and hide with them."

"Your father suspects 'tis Walter behind this for the bastard's name was mentioned as the one to lead the soldiers to proof of the Armstrongs' treachery. And now ye have told me that ye heard the mon say as much himself. Your father needs ye to seek help."

"From who? Our kinsmen the Murrays?"

"Nay." He handed Ilsabeth a piece of parchment. "Sir Simon Innes. Those are directions to where he is and a note to him from your father."

"Why does that name sound familiar?"

"Because the mon has saved two Murrays from hanging for murders they didnae commit. Your father says the mon will listen to ye and then hunt for the truth. And, ye can lead him to it, cannae ye."

Ilsabeth quickly glanced at it and then tucked the message from her father into a hidden pocket in her skirts. "I suspect neither of those Murrays was accused of treason."

"I cannae say, but right now all the soldiers have proof of is that the mon was murdered with your dagger."

"They dinnae need much proof of the other to make life for an Armstrong verra treacherous indeed."

"True, which is why we need to get yourself to this Innes mon as quickly as we can. He is a king's mon, too, and one who is widely trusted to find the truth."

Ilsabeth shook her head. "I am to go to a king's

mon to ask him to help me prove that I didnae kill another of the king's men? 'Tis madness. He willnae believe me."

"Mayhap nay at first, but he *will* look for the truth. 'Tis why he is so trusted. 'Tis said that he is near rabid about getting to the truth. And, Two, there is naught much else we can do to save ourselves. We are all going to be hunted now. E'en our kinsmen the Murrays will be watched closely. They probably have soldiers at their gates, too, though nay as we do, nay there to arrest them. None of us will be able to do anything to hunt down the truth. Save ye. Ye are thought to be inside the walls the soldiers are trying to kick down so they will all think that ye are now running and hiding with us."

"Maman?"

"She and a few other women are taking the youngest bairns to the nunnery and Sister Beatrice. One and her sisters will shield them."

"Maman willnae stay. She will go to be with Papa."

"Aye, most like, but ye cannae worry o'er all that."

Ilsabeth thought her heart would shatter. "This is all my fault, Humfrey. If I hadnae brought Walter so close to our family he wouldnae have had what he needed to use us to hide his own crimes."

"Nay, 'tisnae your fault. Your father ne'er suspected the mon of any truly ill intent." He stood up and held out his hand to her. "Come. Ye had best be on your way."

" 'Tis a long walk I will be taking," she said as she let him help her to her feet.

"Och, nay, ye will be riding. I have a wee sturdy

pony for ye and an old habit One left behind on her last visit home."

"Sister Beatrice," she muttered, unthinkingly correcting him in a way that had become almost a tradition. "I am to pretend to be a nun?"

"Only until ye reach this mon Innes. Ye can claim to any who ask that ye are on a pilgrimage."

Ilsabeth followed him to where a placid Highland pony awaited. While Humfrey turned his back, she changed into the nun's habit. She knew it was a good disguise. Most people saw the nun's attire and did not look closely at the woman wearing it. Rolling up her clothes, she moved to put them into one of the saddle packs and was a little surprised at all she found there.

"I have been verra weel supplied," she murmured.

"Ye ken weel that your father has always been prepared for nigh on anything and everything."

Recalling the many times her father had made them all practice fleeing some enemy, she nodded. "I had just ne'er thought there would ever be a real need for such practices."

"Nay. I ne'er did, either, but am sore glad right now that we did them."

"Do ye go to join my father now?"

"Nay." Humfrey grinned. "I go to take up my work in Walter's stables." He nodded at Ilsabeth's surprise. "A fortnight ago one of the Murray lasses sent word that she had seen a danger draw near to us, that she was certain there was a threat close at hand. Weel, your father then made certain he had one of his own get as close to all of his neighbors as he could. I have a cousin who is a Hepbourn and he got me work in Walter's stables. T'was too late though. I had only just begun to suspect something was amiss. Ne'er would have guessed it would be this."

"Nay, nor I."

Humfrey kissed her on the cheek. "Go. The soldiers will be busy at our gates for hours yet. Put as many miles as ye can between ye and them."

Ilsabeth mounted the pony and looked at her cousin. "Be careful, Humfrey. 'Tis clear to see that Walter doesnae care who he uses or kills to get what he wants."

"I will be careful. Ye, too. And do your best to see that the bastard pays for this."

"That I swear to ye, Humfrey."

Ilsabeth's mind was full of Walter's betrayal as she rode away. His betrayal and her own gullibility. She did not understand how she could have been so blinded to the evil in the man. Her mother had told her she had a gift for seeing into the heart of people. It had obviously failed miserably. The man she had thought to marry was a traitor, a killer, and saw her whole family as no more than lowborn thieves, vermin to be rid of. How could she not have seen that?

She also bemoaned the lack of information she had. For all she had overheard there were still more questions than answers. Just how did Walter, David, and whatever allies they had think to kill the king? Why did they even want to? Power? Money? She could not think of anything the king might have done to make Walter want him dead.

The more she thought on the matter the more

she realized she did not know Walter at all. The worst she had ever thought of him was that he was a little vain, but she had shrugged aside any concern over that fault. He had a fine, strong body, a handsome face, beautiful hazel green eyes, and thick hair the color of honey. One glance into any looking glass would tell the man he was lovely so she had told herself that a little vanity was to be expected. But vanity could not be enough to drive a man to plot against his liege lord, could it? Did Walter have the mad idea that he should be king?

As the evening darkened into night, she discovered one thing she did not think about was her own heartbreak. Her heart ached but it was for her family, her fear for them so great at times that she could barely catch her breath. It did not, however, ache for the loss of Walter, not even when she looked past the shock of his betrayal and the fury over what he had done to her family.

"I didnae love him," she said, and the pony twitched an ear as if to hear better. "All this, and I didnae even really love the bastard. *Jesu,* my family is running for their lives and for what? Because foolish Ilsabeth let herself be wooed into idiocy by a pair of beautiful eyes?"

The pony snorted.

"Aye, 'tis pathetic. All I feel is a pinch of regret o'er the loss of a dream. Nay a dream of that lying bastard, but of having my own home and some bairns to hold. I am one and twenty and I was hungry for that. Too hungry. The greed to fulfill that dream was my weakness, aye?"

With a flick of its tail, the pony slapped her leg.

"Best ye get used to my complaints and my blathering. We will be together for at least three days. Ye need a name, I am thinking, since 'tis clear that I will be babbling my troubles into your ears from time to time."

Ilsabeth considered the names from all the stories Sister Beatrice told so well. Although she preferred horses, good strong animals that could gallop over the moors and give her that heady sense of freedom, she had a lot of respect for the little Highland ponies. She wanted to give this one a good strong name.

"Goliath," she finally said, and was certain the pony lifted its head a little higher. "We will just make certain Walter's snake of a cousin, David, doesnae get near ye with a sling and a stone."

She looked around at the moonlit landscape and tears stung her eyes. Her family was spending the night running, finding places to hide, and keeping watch for soldiers. If any of them got caught they would face pain and humiliation, perhaps even death, before she could save them. It was so unfair. Her father had done his best to return honor to his branch of the Armstrong family tree and it did him no good. One whisper from Walter, one dead body, and everyone believed the worst of them.

Her father's insistence that everyone knew how to run and hide, speedily and silently, now made sense to her. All those well-supplied hiding places, all the intricate plans for scattering his small clan so far and wide it would take months to find any of them now revealed a foresight she had never seen or understood. Sir Cormac Armstrong had always known that the stain his parents had smeared the clan's name with and the many less than honest cousins he had could come back to haunt him no matter what he did.

"Oh, I shall make Walter pay dearly for this, Goliath. Verra dearly indeed."

Elspeth turned from staring out into the dark when Cormac stepped up beside her and wrapped an arm around her shoulders. "She is out there all alone," she whispered. "Alone and weighted with guilt for something that isnae her fault."

"She will be fine, love. Two is strong and stubborn," he said, and kissed her cheek. "She is also good with a knife and clever."

"She hates that name, ye ken."

"What? Two?"

"Aye. If ye werenae her beloved papa she would punch ye whene'er ye say it just as she does the others." Elspeth smiled faintly when he chuckled. "Tell me she will be safe, Cormac."

"Aye, loving, she will be."

"I want to believe that but she is my child, my Ilsabeth."

"Ye have two Ilsabeths."

"Nay, I have a Sister Beatrice and an Ilsabeth. Oh, my firstborn still loves us all and she will hide and protect those now in her care, but she is God's child now. Her heart and mind and soul belong to him. Ye could see it happen whilst she was still a child; the calling was so strong in her. But this Ilsabeth is all ours and carries a lot of both of us within her. Good and bad. She was still but a toddling bairn when I kenned I had given the name to the wrong lass. Ilsabeth was a name for a fighter, for a lass who grabbed life with both hands and lived it to the fullest."

"And all that is why our Ilsabeth who used to be Clara will succeed."

"Ye truly believe that, dinnae ye?"

"Aye, and so do many others. Did ye nay see that none scoffed when told of how we have sent her for aid? They ken the strength in the lass and the stubbornness that will keep her fighting for all of us until she wins."

"And this mon Innes will listen to her and help her?"

"Aye, I have no doubt of it. I have met the mon and he is one who cannae abide nay kenning the truth, cannae e'en think of letting a person suffer for a crime he, or she, didnae commit. Once she tells her tale, he will see at least the hint that there is something amiss and be on the trail like the best of hunting dogs. Believe me, from all I have heard, no guilty mon wants Simon Innes on his trail. And, aside from the fact that Innes is a mon who will be compelled to find the truth, how could he turn our lass away? Those big blue eyes of hers and all. I almost feel sorry for the mon."

"Why?"

"Because our Ilsabeth will turn his life inside out."

"And that is a good thing?"

"It was my salvation when ye did it to me, love. Mayhap it will be his."

Chapter 2

"Sister?"

Ilsabeth looked at the little boy who had just stepped out of the shadows cast by the thick trees at the edge of her small camp. She had known that he was there but had to admit it had been mostly luck that she had. He was obviously accustomed to, and skilled at, hiding from people. What he did not appear to be accustomed to was a full belly. He was all skin and bone covered in dirty rags. She suspected he had been orphaned or cast aside and sighed. She had stopped to prepare herself for the final steps of her journey, to decide just what she should say to Simon Innes when she rapped at his door, and not to have fate present her with yet another problem.

It could be a harsh world for children, especially those no one wanted or who had been left orphaned and alone. If she could, she would take them all in, but the lack of time to find them all and an empty purse made that an impossible dream.

Her family, both the Armstrong and the Murray sides, did their part to help such children and she had to be satisfied with that.

"Aye, laddie, what can I do for ye?" she asked, and immediately felt a stab of guilt for lying to a child, for allowing the boy to think her a nun.

"I was wondering if ye would share a wee bit of your food with me sister."

"Your sister? Nay ye?"

His fair skin blushed so red she could see it beneath the dirt smeared on his thin face. "Weel, I wouldnae say nay to a wee bite, if ye would be so kind. But, 'tis the bairn what needs it most."

Judging by the boy's height and the clarity with which he spoke, Ilsabeth wagered the lad was at least six, if not older. Lack of food could easily have halted his growth, however. That meant his sister probably was little more than a bairn.

She nearly cursed aloud. It was a poor time for her to stumble across a pair of foundlings. There was danger dogging her heels. Yet, she could not leave them starving at the edge of town as they had so obviously been doing. Sir Simon Innes was just going to have to understand that.

"Fetch the lass and come sit by the fire. I have enough for all of us," she said.

The boy ran back to the trees and tugged a tiny girl out from behind one. As the pair walked toward Ilsabeth's small fire, she studied them closely. It was clear to see where most of what little food the boy had found went. The little girl wore ragged clothes but there was only the faintest hint of hunger's sharpness in her angelic face. Thick red-gold curls and big brown eyes were enough to melt the hardest heart. Ilsabeth hoped Sir Simon did not prove her wrong about that for, unless the boy told her they both had kinsmen somewhere, these children were now hers.

"Your names?" she asked as she handed each of them some bread and cheese.

"I am Reid Burns and this is my sister Elen," the boy said as he helped the little girl eat her food, breaking it into pieces small enough for her to handle.

"And why is it that ye are wandering about here in the wood, and ye have near starved, Reid?"

"Our mither died and the mon she lived with tossed us out of the wee cottage he had given us. He said that he only let us stay there because my mither was warming his bed, but now that she was gone, he needed the cottage for his new lady."

There was a man who sorely needed a beating, Ilsabeth thought. "So neither of ye are his bairns?"

"Och, aye. Elen is his, but the mon has a wife and eight children so he didnae need Elen. I suspicion he didnae want his wife to learn that he was breeding with another woman." He blushed and cast her a nervous look. "Pardon, Sister."

Ilsabeth waved away his apology. "Ne'er apologize for the truth, nay matter how blunt and ugly it is. Who is this heartless swine who would toss aside his own bairn?"

"Donald Chisholm."

If she survived the trouble she was in, Ilsabeth swore that she would see to it that Donald Chisholm got a hard lesson in how a man should behave. She also decided the man was a complete fool to toss aside such children as she watched them both eat with a delicacy that belied their terrible hunger and revealed that their mother had not been some poor shepherd's daughter. The way Reid cared for his young sister brought tears so close to falling that her eyes stung and her nose filled so that she was forced to sniff a little.

"This was verra kind of ye, Sister," said Reid, watching Ilsabeth warily, his dark eyes holding the panicked look that men always got when they thought a woman was close to tears.

"Hold old are ye, Reid?" Ilsabeth bit back a smile at how relieved the boy looked when she spoke calmly, indicating that her urge to cry had vanished.

"Seven. Weel, nearly seven. Elen marked two years but yestereve."

"Greetings, Reid and Elen. I am Ilsabeth Armstrong." She waited patiently while he considered her words and was not surprised when he frowned.

" 'Tis an odd name for a nun." His eyes widened and he blushed. "But, ye ken, I havenae had much learning and all, so I wouldnae ken the way of it and all. I am certain 'tis a good, holy name and all. I just havenae heard it before."

Ilsabeth took a deep breath and decided the truth was the only path to follow now. "I am nay surprised for I am nay truly a nun. This is but a guise I wear to keep me safe as I travel to ask the aid of a mon. 'Tis also a disguise to keep me safe from my enemies. My dagger was found buried in the heart of a king's mon. I didnae put it there and I ken weel who did, but I was snared tight in his trap ere I even kenned it was set."

"Ye have no kin to help ye?"

"They are already being confronted by men demanding that they surrender me to them so that I can be brought before the king for punishment. One of my cousins caught me fleeing to my home ere I ran straight into the arms of those men. He gave me this nun's clothing, supplies, and this pony and told me to hie to Sir Simon Innes and ask for his aid in proving who really killed that mon. That is where I go now. In all truth, I am at the end of my journey and but sit here gathering the courage to go and rap upon the mon's door."

She could tell by the resigned look upon the boy's face that he had cherished the hope that she could aid him and his sister. Her tale had clearly killed that hope. The voice of good sense reminded Ilsabeth yet again that she was running and hiding for her life, that it was a very poor time to take two foundlings under her wing. She ignored it. She let her heart lead her. Nothing could change her decision to care for these children.

"I but tell ye this, Reid, so that ye ken weel what trouble ye will face if ye decide to stay with me," she said.

"Ye would take us with ye?"

"I cannae leave ye here, alone and struggling to find enough food to hold back starvation, now can I?" Ilsabeth bit back a smile when his child's face tightened with a very stern look and he straightened up, stung pride stiffening his backbone.

"I can care for us," he said in a surprisingly fierce voice.

"Aye, ye can, and ye have proven that, but would-nae ye like a roof o'er your head, clean warm clothing, a wee bed, and food when ye need it?"

"Ye think Sir Innes will allow us all into his home? 'Tis said that he is a mon with a cold heart, a mon who believes only in justice."

"Is that what is said of him? Ye came from this village then, did ye?"

"Aye. I wasnae sure where else to go once we were shut out, so I stayed close to the village."

Ilsabeth hoped part of the reason the boy lingered in the area was because there were some people kindhearted enough to give the children what scraps of food they could spare. "We shall go to Sir Simon's home. If he is too cold of heart to help me and take us all in, then we shall go and find another who will. My Armstrong kin may have had to flee and hide, but I have other kin. The Murrays havenae all taken to the hills. I didnae want to bring my trouble to their doors, but I will bring ye to them. They willnae turn ye away."

The boy stared at her for a moment and then smiled. Ilsabeth could see the beauty of the boy beneath the dirt and ravages of hunger. It was a smile she had to return and she vowed to herself that she would find these children a haven. If Simon Innes was too hard and callous to aid her, if only in helping the children, she would see them safely into the hands of her Murray kin.

A little voice warned her that she could be walking into danger if she tried to do that, but she silenced it. If Sir Simon refused to help her or even just the children, then she would have no other choice. Ilsabeth did not wish to face the danger seeking her out at home, however, so she silently prayed that Sir Simon Innes was not simply the cold seeker of justice that rumor named him. Unless, she thought with a faint smile, that included seeking a little justice on a certain swine named Donald Chisholm.

"Why are ye smiling?" asked Reid.

Noticing the way the boy eyed the bread and cheese she had left, Ilsabeth gave him some more to share with his sister. "I was just thinking what a surprise we shall all be for Sir Simon Innes."

"Och, aye. I dinnae think it will be a good one."

"We shall see."

"Why do your kin think he will help ye?"

"Because he has already helped two of my kinsmen who were accused of murders they had not committed."

Reid frowned. "Why do your kin keep getting into such trouble?"

Ilsabeth laughed and shook her head. "I dinnae ken, laddie. It does seem as if we are cursed sometimes."

"Aye, a wee bit. Or 'tis envy. My mither said envy can make people do mean things."

"Your mother was a verra wise woman."

"I miss her," he said softly, blushing faintly as he made the admission.

"Of course ye do. There is no shame in that. Now, I am thinking I have sat here long enough trying to gather up the courage to go to Sir Simon's house. If I dinnae have it now, I ne'er will. Best we clean up and finish the journey."

"Are ye afraid?" Reid immediately began to help Ilsabeth pack up her supplies.

"A wee bit," Ilsabeth answered as she dampened a cloth and gently wiped Elen's face and hands. "I want to put my faith in the mon my family has sent me to, but I have ne'er met him. 'Tis difficult to trust a stranger, especially when ye are dealing with matters of murder and treason. Aye, and he doesnae ken me, either, so why should he be believing a word I say?"

"But ye said he has helped your family before, aye?"

"Aye, he has helped the Murrays, cousins of mine. Dinnae ken them all that weel either so I cannae say I learned much of this Sir Simon from them. And, I am but half a Murray. The rest of me is Armstrong."

"Is that bad?"

" 'Tis nay a good thing in many eyes, laddie. My wee clan and my father the laird are all good, honest people, but the ones that came before them werenae. They put a verra dark stain upon the name and some of his kinsmen still arenae too honest." She winked. "There are a lot of reivers in the family, ye ken." She grinned when he giggled and then helped the children up onto Goliath. "I will try to nay be too insulted if he favors my Murray blood, at least in the beginning."

"If he doesnae help ye, then I will," said Reid.

"Ye are a good, brave lad." Ilsabeth grasped the reins and started to lead the pony into town. "Ye have your sister to watch o'er, however, so we must hope Sir Simon truly is the stalwart seeker of the truth all claim him to be."

Especially since she had come up with no other plan herself, Ilsabeth mused. She continued to try and think of one as she walked but facing the end of her journey inspired her no more than all the rest of the hours she had traveled to reach her destination. By the time she stood before the door to Sir Simon Innes's home, she gave up all hope of coming up with something clever and started fervently praying that the man would help her.

Simon Innes sprawled in a chair before the fire, a goblet of fine wine in his hand, and frowned down at the cat in his lap. It had been a mistake to give in to that spark of charity and feed the huge black and white tom. The animal had finished off the scraps he had given it and then moved in. He glanced down at his dog Bonegnasher, spread out gracelessly at his feet, a fresh set of scratch marks on his nose. Who would have thought his large, fierce dog would turn coward when slapped on the nose by a cat?

He sighed and lightly stroked the cat, causing it to rumble with a deep, raspy purr. It was, at least, a more pleasant noise than the animal's snoring. The beast also looked and smelled better since Old Bega had got her hands on it. The cat had endured her scrubbing, combing, and rubbing some oil on him to kill fleas with a quiet, injured dignity.

"Of course, for that small inconvenience, ye are now set in front of a warm fire, your belly full of chicken," he drawled, and then sipped at his wine. "I cannae believe I have let ye sit on me. Men dinnae keep cats, ye ken." The cat turned its head so that Simon could better scratch behind one of its tattered ears.

He was behaving like an old man, he thought crossly. Thirty years of living was just around the corner. Thirty was not old in his opinion, despite the fact that far too many people never reached that age. It was definitely too young to be spending nights sitting before the fire talking to his dog, or cat. Yet, it had been many months since he had done anything else. The only change in his new habit for far too long was the presence of an ugly cat. Simon winced. He was becoming a pathetic recluse.

It was time to get himself a wife, he mused, and fought to quell the curdling in his gut. Not every woman was faithless. Not every marriage was hell on earth. He had seen the good in such arrangements lately during his time helping the Murrays. The part of him that was still bitter and bruised from the past wanted to doubt, shuddered at the mere thought of marriage, but he told himself it was past time he overcame that dread. If Tormand Murray, a man who had seduced half the women in Scotland, could find a wife like Morainn, a loyal, loving woman with wit and spirit, Simon suspected there had to be one out there for him, too. Even James Drummond, a Murray foster son, a man accused of murdering his first wife, had found a good woman even as he fought to prove his innocence.

"So why am I sitting here stroking an ugly cat instead of a fulsome wife?" he muttered.

The cat briefly dug its claws into Simon's thighs as if to protest the unflattering adjective.

Simon winced but resisted the urge to shove the cat off his lap. He would never admit it aloud but he found the warmth, the soft fur, and the raspy purr of the animal oddly comforting. It was probably why some women favored the beasts despite all the superstitions swirling around the creatures.

Just as Simon was wondering if he should simply accept his fate and name the cat there was a rap at the door. He sighed in resignation as his man MacBean walked in immediately after the knock sounded. The man stubbornly refused to wait until he was told to enter. It had taken far too long just to get the man to knock at all.

"So, that cursed beastie is still about, I see," said MacBean, glaring at the cat. "Want me to toss it out?"

"I dinnae think it will stay out," Simon replied.

MacBean grunted. "The old woman shouldnae have wasted food and water on it. Beast is more tattered than my old aunt's blankets. Got more scars, too."

Simon gently bit his tongue to stifle the urge to ask MacBean about his old aunt's scars. Too much curiosity was one of his besetting sins. The craving he had for uncovering secrets and lies made it difficult to make and keep friends, although he could not fully regret that. He also admitted to himself that he had a few secrets of his own that he would prefer to keep buried deep in his past. Old Bega knew them for she had traveled with him from his boyhood home, but, despite how much she loved to talk, the woman held fast to them.

"What good is a cat when it's all fat and happy, I ask ye?" MacBean asked, obviously expecting no answer. "Only purpose the creatures have to be alive at all is to catch vermin. Beastie there isnae going to do that if the old lady keeps his belly full."

"MacBean," Simon said a little sharply to interrupt the man's tirade before it went any further, "did ye come in here only to speak of this cat?"

"Nay. Ye have a message from the king."

"I would think that something like that would take precedence over a discussion of this cat," Simon said as he took the message MacBean thrust toward him.

"King isnae trying to live here, is he? And he doesnae have fleas."

"I wouldnae be too sure of that and this beast has none since Bega tended to it."

"He will be getting them again."

Simon ignored the man as MacBean entered into a staring contest with the cat. The message held dire news, bad in so many ways that Simon swiftly finished off his wine and held the goblet out for MacBean to refill. A king's man had been murdered. Worse that man had been the king's own cousin, and one the king had been fond of. Young Ian Ogilvie had been following whispers of treasonous activities, of plots against his royal cousin and benefactor. The name of the clan held responsible was not familiar to Simon except for the fact that everyone knew of the Armstrongs, a border clan well known for its reiving ways. What chilled him to the bone was that this particular branch of the Armstrongs was connected through marriage to the Murrays. If the Murrays were not already in hiding, they might soon need to be.

"Bad news?" asked MacBean.

"Nay good. Murder, treason, accusations being flung about that have already cast a shadow on the Murrays." Simon drummed his fingers on the arm of his chair. "The Armstrongs involved are kin to the Murrays through marriage. A close enough bond to cause our king to wonder if they, too, now plot against him."

"The king and his advisors are forever seeing plots."

"True, but this one may nay be born of naught but suspicious minds. Sir Ian Ogilvie was certain there was a plot afoot and went in search of some answers. What he got was a dagger in the heart, an Armstrong dagger."

MacBean frowned and then shook his head, his thick, graying, brown hair shifting wildly with the movement. "Nay. Dinnae see that clan troubling itself much with treason and plots and all that. They dinnae follow many of the king's laws nay matter who sits on the throne so why bother plotting against the mon they dinnae listen to anyway? Now, if ye said they stole the king's cattle? Weel, I wouldnae doubt that. But treasonous plots? Nay."

"I feel the same. And, Sir Cormac Armstrong has appeared to be trying to rise above the reiving ways of so many of his kinsmen."

"Is the king asking ye to hunt down the killer?"

"Aye, that and to discover who else plots treason against him. I but wish he had asked that I prove who truly is the guilty one for the lack of that question makes me think he has decided the Armstrongs of Aigballa are guilty. That is worrisome."

Before MacBean could express his sour opinion about getting tangled up in uncovering plots for the king, there was a knock at the front door. He cursed and hurried away to see who was there. Simon smiled faintly over his man's ill temper and then frowned down at the message he still held.

He was going to have to answer the king's command, but he did not like it despite his recent craving for a puzzle to solve. This time he was not only trying to find the truth, he was going to have to try and protect his friends as he did so. Simon doubted Sir Cormac Armstrong's family had anything to do with treason, but that did not mean there was not one of his family who might play such a dangerous game. Pulling out that one rotten tooth could easily cost Simon some of the few friends he had.

MacBean's return drew him from his dark thoughts, and Simon looked at the man. "Weel, who was at the door? Was there another message?"

"Nay. There is a nun and two bairns," replied MacBean in a tone that would have better suited announcing death itself.

"A nun?"

"Aye, and she says she must speak with ye now. Have ye been breeding and nay told the old woman? That crone willnae be pleased with ye if ye have."

"Nay, I havenae been breeding and, if I had done so, Bega would already ken it for she would be helping me care for the child. Mayhap the nun wishes my help in finding the ones who should take responsibility for the children. Show her in, MacBean, and fetch us something to drink and eat."

The moment a grumbling MacBean left, Simon struggled to get the cat off his lap and stand up. He ignored the animal's growl of displeasure and tried to brush the cat hair from his clothes. MacBean clearing his throat caused him to look up and he slowly straightened. A slight wave of his hand sent the man off to get drink and food for his guests.

"Sir Simon Innes?" asked the nun.

"Aye," he replied, bowing to her. "How can I help ye, Sister?"

"I have need of your ability to find the truth."

The low, husky voice of the woman tickled to life feelings he should never have for a nun. To distract himself, he glanced at the two children who clutched at her skirts. They looked hungry and their clothes were mere rags, but he saw nothing of anyone he knew in their looks. "Ye seek the kin of these children?"

"Nay, for they have told me they have none. The only one they have who should be caring for them is the one who cast them aside, and some day, I will see that he repents that. Nay, I seek help for myself for I am in trouble as is my family."

"And who are ye?"

"My name is Ilsabeth Armstrong. I am the daughter of Sir Cormac Armstrong of Aigballa and Elspeth Murray."

Chapter 3

The first clear thought Simon had was that he was very glad that woman was not a nun. It made no sense since she was swathed in a nun's clothing so he shook that thought right out of his head. It was not as easy as it should have been to do so as he stared into her wide, bright blue eyes. There was innocence in those eyes, an innocence he was not sure he should put his trust in. There was also an odd mix of fear and determination to be read in her expression.

"I believe I was just reading about you," he said, and held up the message from the king, the royal seal easy to recognize.

For a moment he feared she would faint as all the color fled her heart-shaped face. Simon took a step toward her and then hesitated. Instead of swaying, she stiffened, her shoulders going back and her faintly pointed chin lifting. Some of the color began to seep back into her soft cheeks. There was a glint of anger in her beautiful eyes now. But, was the anger due to lies being told about her or the fact that he had already been told the truth? Simon wished he could trust his judgment when it came to women, trust it without indulging in a long time of subtle testing and spying. He had once and it had cost him dearly. Now it always took a lot more than a fine pair of eyes and full, tempting lips to win his trust.

"Your bairns?" he asked, and nodded at the two children, even as he decided she was far too young to be the boy's mother.

"Now," she replied. "Elen and Reid. Are ye willing to hear my tale or do ye take me straight to the king?"

He should, Simon thought. He should see her well secured in a prison while he searched for the truth. Good sense told him to hear her tale and then have her imprisoned while he verified all she told him. Instinct told him she was no more than a pawn caught up in someone else's deadly games. If she was a he, Simon knew he would trust his instinct. It was enough, however, to make him hesitate to hand her over to the king's soldiers, who would not treat her kindly. After so many betrayals, the king might not let her live long enough for Simon to find the truth and that would not only be a tragic waste but wrong.

"Sit," he said. "I will listen to what ye have to say and then decide."

Ilsabeth studied the man her family had sent her to. He was tall, six feet in length or more, and almost too lean, nearly lanky, but she did not doubt the strength in those slender limbs. His face was not one to make anyone expect any mercy from the man. It was all sharp lines from the high cheekbones to the firm jaw. Even his nose was a sharp angle and nearly too big for his face. Thick black hair was tied back and she suspected it was longer than many men wore their hair. Straight black brows and long dark lashes did nothing to soften the hard cold steel color of his eyes. The only softness she could see on his face was in the touch of fullness in his bottom lip. There was certainly no hint of it in his deep, cold voice.

So why was she thinking of nipping at that lip? she asked herself. Something about the man had her blood singing in her veins. Ilsabeth began to fear that her mother and cousins had not been simply fanciful when they had spoken of meeting the man meant just for them, of pounding hearts and heated blood. A part of her mind was almost purring in delight as she stared at this cold man who held her life in his elegant, long-fingered hands.

Shaking free of her bemusement, she ushered the children toward a settee near the fire. She sat down and the children huddled close to her on the seat. Ilsabeth watched Simon turn his seat to face her squarely and found herself fascinated by the graceful way he moved. She inwardly cursed herself for that. Now was a very poor time to go all dewy-eyed over a man, especially since she had been so horribly betrayed by one only days before. It did, however, prove that she had not been in love with Walter and she found a small comfort in that.

"Ah, your confession will have to wait a moment," Simon said when MacBean and Old Bega entered the room with trays of food and drink.

Ilsabeth glared at him, annoyed by the word *confession*, but her attention was quickly taken up with the woman Sir Simon introduced as Old Bega. Plump, gray-haired, and plainly not intimidated by her stern master, the woman fussed over the children. The bone-thin man named MacBean just scowled at them.

"Och, look at these wee beauties," said Old Bega, almost cooing at the children. "They need washing and some clean clothes. Aye, they do." She grasped Elen, picking the little girl up in her arms, and took Reid by the hand. "You two just come with me and I will see to that right now. Then ye can come back and join in this feast."

"But—" began Ilsabeth, not sure she wanted to be left alone with Sir Simon.

"Wheesht, dinnae fret," Old Bega said as she began to walk away. "I will bring them back to ye as soon as they are clean and out of these rags. Come, MacBean."

"Come, MacBean," grumbled that man, but he followed her. "Fetch this, do that. Wheesht, ye do ken that I dinnae work for ye, old woman."

The door shut firmly behind them and Ilsabeth stared at it, fighting the strong urge to follow the group. She then looked at Sir Simon with suspicion. It was difficult to see how he could have planned such a thing, yet the removal of the children from the room was very convenient for him.

"I had naught to do with that," he said. "Bega cannae abide dirt and loves bairns. 'Tis all that was. It is, however, verra convenient and I willnae deny I would have done it if I had had time to think of it. 'Tis best if we discuss this matter without the bairns here."

"Mayhap." Ilsabeth helped herself to a drink of

cider and a honey-sweetened oatcake. "So, ye wish me to begin my *confession* right now, do ye?"

"That stung, did it?" He pushed aside the strong urge to kiss away the scowl that twisted her soft, full lips.

She rolled her eyes and then asked, "Do ye want me to start from the moment I began to sink into this mire? Or, do ye wish to just ask me questions?"

"Just start at the beginning and ye can take that thing off your head first. Ye dinnae need to play the nun any longer."

The moment she took off the wimple, Simon wished he had not told her to do so. In taking it off, she had loosened whatever had kept her hair pinned up beneath it. Thick waves of hair so black the fire's light bounced off hints of blue in its depths fell to her waist. His hand tightened on his goblet of wine as he fought the urge to touch it. When she idly ran her fingers through her hair, obviously relieved to be rid of the headdress, his body tightened with a rush of lust so strong he almost groaned aloud. He was relieved when she began to speak despite the allure of her husky voice for it gave him something to concentrate on, something aside from his need to feel all that glorious hair brushing against his naked skin.

"I now see that it all began when Sir Walter Hepbourn began to court me." She scowled. "I should have been more wary, looked more closely, for no one of his ilk had ever done so before, but I am one and twenty and didnae wish to miss my chance to have my own household and some bairns."

Simon wondered how such a tempting armful of woman could ever fear becoming a spinster. She was small and the nun's attire hid a lot but not enough. He could see that she had softness enough to please a man.

"So, we soon became betrothed. Then, as the time to marry drew nearer, I sensed a change in the mon. I thought he might have gotten himself a mistress." She blushed. "He is a virile mon and, weel—"

"Wasnae being verra virile with you?"

"Nay, he wasnae. He tried once and I pushed him away. After that he ne'er tried again. 'Tis why I began to think he had a mistress. So, after I visited his home for a wee while, I said my fareweels, walked away, and then, after hiding away for an hour, mayhap longer, I crept back. Instead of a mistress, I heard him talking to his cousin David. David was praising Walter for his great sacrifice." She knew bitterness and anger were seeping into her voice but could not help it. "Walter declared that his sacrifice would be short-lived. What David said next told me what had happened."

"And that was?" he asked when she fell silent.

"David wondered how Walter could claim he was making no sacrifice when anyone accused of murdering a king's mon didnae live long. I thought it was Walter who would be sacrificing himself but soon realized that I was a fool to think that. He planned to use me as his sacrificial lamb. He also said he planned to rescue me, that I would certainly have to flee Scotland then, and he had a wee house in France where he planned to keep me."

Simon could see that it pained her to tell him that and he wondered just how much she had cared for Hepbourn.

Ilsabeth took a deep breath in an attempt to

push aside her growing anger. "David was appalled because he thought Walter still intended to marry me. Walter made it verra clear that he had ne'er intended to marry me, that I was beneath him, and that he would ne'er sully his fine bloodline with an Armstrong. He just didnae wish for me to die until he had me and was weary of me.

"The whole betrothal was naught but part of his plan. He wanted to get close to my family so that he could learn enough about them to ken how he could place blame and all suspicion on them. The mon wants rid of my whole clan. He e'en thinks that he may be able to get some of our land if he steps right and gets close to the king. Or mayhap once the king is gone, he feels the new men in power will reward him with it." She frowned. "I think he kenned we wouldnae just cry innocent and be taken for he saw the chance that the king's men would be verra busy trying to gather us all up. That would allow him to do as he plans for they wouldnae have the time to look anywhere else."

"Did he say exactly what his plan was?"

"Nay. David spoke of ridding themselves of that foolish king, his sycophants, and all those who led him where they wished him to go. Neither mon wants any suspicion turning their way. I can only think that Walter wants my kin hunted down and hanged ere he does whate'er he now plots to do, thus giving him the chance to grab our lands. Although he did think that the new king might weel gift him with them. They went inside after that."

"And ye ne'er tried to find out more?"

"I didnae have the time. Walter spoke of needing to plan his next step most carefully and of wanting to be weel rested so that he could have the pleasure of watching my family rounded up and taken away in chains. I ran for home, thinking to warn them of his plots, but my cousin Humfrey caught up with me. He told me it was already too late, that my own dagger had been in the heart of a king's mon, and that soldiers were already pounding at the gates of Aigballa. My family gave him what I needed to travel and sent him after me to tell me to come here." She shook her head. "And to think I thought Walter's only real fault was that he was vain."

"Ye betrothed yourself to a mon ye thought was vain?"

"He had some cause to be so and his mother spoiled him." She pulled the letter from her father out of her pocket where she had hidden it and handed it to him. "It doesnae say much save that my father suspects Walter and that I am to come to you and seek help. So, are ye going to help me? Or, do ye send me to the king?"

Simon did not answer her for a moment, taking the time to read the short message from her father instead. There was little to be found in the words Sir Cormac had written to help Simon make any judgment. The man simply thought to aid his daughter. The only thing that weighed in the favor of the Armstrongs was that they knew his reputation, therefore, sending Ilsabeth to him implied that they believed the truth would free them and reveal their innocence. The cynical part of Simon wondered if they hoped he would think exactly that and thus believe them cruelly wronged.

"Nay, I willnae send ye to the king now," Simon said as he handed her back her father's message.

"Howbeit, ye will be closely watched and ye had best nay leave this house."

Ilsabeth swallowed the angry words she ached to spit out at him. She told herself that he did not know her and he had every right to need proof of her innocence before he believed in her. She was marked a traitor and a murderer. Such crimes put anyone who helped her in danger. It had been foolish to think that her word on all that had happened would be enough. Ilsabeth welcomed the return of the children for it kept her from saying something that could push away the only man who could keep her from the brutal death handed out to traitors.

Bega worked fast and efficiently, she thought, as Elen and Reid hurried to her side. They were both clean and dressed in simple, well-made clothes. Even though Reid's hair was still wet, Ilsabeth could now see that he had dark red hair. She served them both some of the food and drink and decided they were handsome children. All she could do was care for them as long as she was able and pray that Simon would see them into the care of her family if she did not get free of Walter's plots. Ilsabeth refused to even think of the possibility that her whole family might well be caught in Walter's trap.

A tap on her shoulder drew her attention away from the children. Ilsabeth looked up at Sir Simon, who now stood at her side. A quick glance around revealed that the two servants had left. He nodded toward the window and then walked toward it. After seeing that the children were well occupied with the food, she went to join the man.

"Whose children are they?" Simon asked.

"Mine," she replied, knowing that some of her

stubborn determination to keep Elen and Reid could
be heard in her voice.

Simon almost smiled. Ilsabeth looked stubborn
enough to fight him for the right to keep the two
children. The fact that she was caring for and protecting two foundlings did a lot to make him favor
her tale of betrayal, but he did not say so. He just
quirked one brow at her, silently demanding her to
tell him the truth.

Ilsabeth sighed, recognizing that look on his
face. She had seen it on the men in her family too
often. The man would stand there like a rock until
she told him the truth. As quickly and quietly as she
could, she told Simon all Reid had told her. The
flash of anger in his eyes left her thinking that he
might not be quite as cold as rumor said he was. He
did not care for how the children had been treated.

" 'Tis a poor time for ye to indulge in such charity," he said.

"That may be, but it willnae stop me."

"And what if ye arenae able to free yourself and
prove your innocence?"

It was not easy to shrug aside the part of her that
was angered by the implication that she might actually be guilty of the crime she was accused of, but
Ilsabeth did it. He had said he would search out the
truth and that was all they had asked of him. She
had to believe that he would be able to prove her
innocent and save her and her family. Then she
would be able to save Elen and Reid.

"I am nay such a fool that I think this will all be
untangled and in my favor quickly or easily. That is
nay a good reason to leave two bairns to starve,
however. If I am unable to keep them and care for

them, I have a verra large family that will fulfill my promise to them. All I will ask of ye is, if I am unable to get them to my family, ye will do so for me."

He nodded as he led her back to the children. "Ye will stay here and I will go to court on the morrow to see what news there is. Dinnae think ye can slip away. MacBean may look and sound like a bad-tempered fool, but he will prove to be a verra efficient guard if ye try to test him."

"I will stay here, Sir Innes. This is where my father sent me because he believed ye could help me. Nay, just me, either, but my whole family. I willnae do anything to make their suffering continue any longer than it must to catch the ones who use us to hide their own crimes. Now, will ye swear to take the bairns to my family if I am unable to do so?"

"Aye."

Ilsabeth nodded and turned her attention to the children. She could feel Simon watching her. Even the huge dog he had and a rather ugly cat sprawled before the fire watched her and the children closely. By the time Old Bega returned, Ilsabeth was more than ready to seek a bed just to get away from that scrutiny.

The way Old Bega cooed and fussed over the children eased some of Ilsabeth's fear for them. She might not be all that certain of what Sir Simon would do if she was taken away, despite the vow he had just made, but the woman would never let any harm come to Elen and Reid. The moment the children were settled in two small beds, Old Bega led Ilsabeth to the bedchamber right next to them. It soothed Ilsabeth to know that they would be close to her in the night.

"Ye dinnae need to fret o'er the bairns," said Old Bega as she readied the bed for Ilsabeth, turning down the heavy blankets to reveal some very fine linen sheets. "I dinnae ken what trouble ye are in, but ye can shake aside any fear for them. Ye are nay a nun so where did ye get the clothes? Ye didnae rob a nunnery, did ye?"

"Nay, my sister is a nun and we got them from her," replied Ilsabeth, as, with Old Bega's help, she unpacked the few belongings she had. "Has Goliath been seen to?"

"Goliath? The wee pony?" Old Bega laughed when Ilsabeth nodded. "Aye, tucked up warm in the stable."

"Good. He served me weel."

"Ye rest, lass. Sir Simon will solve this trouble for ye."

Ilsabeth just smiled and then, as soon as the woman left, began to shed her clothes and wash up before getting into the bed her body ached for. The moment she curled up under the covers, she sighed with relief and closed her eyes. Her mind was full of worry and fear for the fate of her family, but she forced those concerns away. Sleep was needed for a sharp mind and a strong body. She would be in need of both in the days to come.

Sir Simon Innes's face appeared behind her eyelids and she nearly cursed. He drew her to him despite his distrust and his apparent coldness. If anyone had ever asked her what she sought in a man, nothing she would have replied would have matched that man. Yet, despite all that was wrong with him, her heart and her body kept saying they wanted him for their own. That was something she would have to fight. The man might free her of the nightmare she was caught up in, but he could also lead her to the gallows. It would be a mistake of the greatest kind to allow the man to get into her heart or her blood. Matters were bad enough as it was without becoming attached to a man who just might be the one putting a rope around her neck.

"Ye cannae think that lass is a traitor and a killer," said MacBean after Simon told him why the woman now sleeping upstairs had come to him.

"Dinnae tell me ye think women incapable of such things," drawled Simon, and sighed when the cat leapt up on his lap the moment he sat down before the fire.

"Nay, they can be as vicious and devious as any mon. But that wee lass? Nay, I cannae believe it."

"Why? Because she has sweet innocence on her face? Or big blue eyes?"

"Nay. Because she has taken in two bairns nay her own despite running for her life. And that is what she is doing, isnae it? Running for her life?"

"Aye. As is her whole family, the Armstrongs of Aigballa. Soon many of the Murrays may have to do the same."

"Ah." MacBean crossed his arms over his thin chest and nodded.

"What do ye mean—ah?"

"Ye will sort this out for the Murrays, aye? Nay matter what ye think of that wee lass, ye will work hard to make sure she is innocent or, at least, that the Murrays dinnae suffer for her crimes. Still dinnae think she did what they say she did."

"Her dagger in Sir Ian Ogilvie's heart says different."

"And ye ken as weel as I that it doesnae mean she put it there."

Simon rested his head against the back of the chair and sighed. "I do ken that. I also ken that I have naught but her word on who is responsible. 'Tis nay my way to accept nay more than a person's word on their innocence."

"It isnae? Thought ye did just that with both them Murray lads. Ye willnae do it for her because she is a bonnie lass and dinnae try to tell me otherwise. It has been ten years, lad. Bury the past."

Simon watched MacBean walk out of the room and softly cursed. The trouble with servants who had been with a man for most of his life was that they knew most of his secrets. The man's insight was also irritating. Simon would rather cut out his own tongue with a dull blade than admit it, but MacBean was right. One reason he hesitated to take Ilsabeth Murray Armstrong at her word was because she was a bonnie lass.

Memories swarmed into his mind and sweat dotted his brow as he fought them. He had been a fool at eighteen, a fool who had thought himself a grown man and one who knew all about women just because he had bedded a few. Sweet-faced Mary with her tempting body and tears had led him along by the nose. His brutal brother's third wife, she had been only a few years older than Simon, but she had been many years older in guile and experience. She had even been able to draw him close to the home he had left at the age of ten swearing he would never go back.

Guilt over what he had done could still bring a sour taste into his mouth even though he knew he had not hurt his harsh brother's feelings. His pride, surely, but Henry Innes had not loved Mary any more than he had loved his other two wives. What troubled Simon was that he had not seen the lies, the manipulation, the betrayal. Neither Mary's nor Henry's. He had not seen the truth. He knew that was why he sought it so avidly now.

Seeking the truth back then had only added to his pain, but that had not turned him away from it. Simon stared into his goblet at the dregs of his wine and sighed. He had accepted the beating and the scars it left as his due for breaking one of God's laws. What he could never accept was that he had given his heart and sympathy to a woman who had deserved neither, and worried, for a brief naïve time, about a brother who had no love or respect for him. No brother should have used his kin as Henry had used him.

He shook away the memory of that time and turned his thoughts to Ilsabeth Murray Armstrong. It annoyed him that his body hardened when her image appeared in his mind. He was going to have to be very careful about that. Simon wanted to blame the sudden, fierce attraction he felt for her on the fact that he had not had a woman for a long time, but he knew that was a lie. It was something about her, the way she stood firm before his stare, a stare that had made even grown men quiver with fear. Her glorious hair and her beautiful eyes drew him like a wasp to honey. She was dangerous.

Then again, could he resist if she tried to seduce him to influence his decision on her innocence or guilt? Probably not, he decided, but he would still seek the truth. He would just find a little enjoyment and pleasure as he did so. Simon felt certain that, although his body might succumb, nothing she could do would change him from his course. It could be that giving in to his lust for her could clear his mind enough so that she could no longer cloud it with her scent and her husky voice. It was something to consider.

Simon nudged the cat off his lap, stood up and stretched. He would be spending a lot of time in court over the next few days and it was best if he got some sleep. A man needed a sharp mind to weave his way safely through all the intrigues, lies, and betrayals that went on in the king's court. It was good to have another puzzle to solve, he mused as he strode off to his bedchamber, Bonegnasher and the cat at his heels.

It was not until he was settled into his bed that he realized there was another more subtle reason that he was eager to get started ferreting out the truth. A part of him wanted to prove that Ilsabeth Murray Armstrong was innocent. Worse, to his way of thinking, it was not simply his thirst for justice that made him eager. It was a pair of bright blue eyes and a soft, husky voice that acted like a caress on his skin every time she spoke. Simon cursed. Ilsabeth was definitely trouble and not just because she was caught up in plots, murder, and treason.

Chapter 4

Sir Walter Hepbourn was the type of man most women found very pleasing. Shining fair hair, a flirtatious smile revealing good teeth, and a well-muscled form dressed in the finest court clothing. Simon wondered why all of that irritated him so much. If what Ilsabeth told him was true, it was very daring of the man to come to court so soon after committing the murder of the king's cousin and throwing around false accusations. He must have left not long after Ilsabeth had. It would have been wiser to stay close to his home until the suspicions against the Armstrongs had hardened.

Simon nearly grimaced in disgust over the way the man played the stunned, embarrassed, and heart-bruised betrothed who had been betrayed and used by his love. It was all an act. Simon was certain of it. Unfortunately, his certainty did not mean the man was guilty of all Ilsabeth said he was. It just meant that Sir Walter knew how to play with the sympathies of the courtiers who clung to the king's court in the hope of some favor.

One other thing that Simon was now certain of was that Sir Walter Hepbourn thought himself far and above any Armstrong. The man's distaste for that clan wove around and through every word he spoke. After two days of watching the man, however, that was the only suspicious thing Simon had discovered. Why, if Hepbourn so utterly despised the Armstrongs, had the man betrothed himself to one of the clan's daughters? Ilsabeth's explanation was the only one that made sense, but he would not accept that as fact just yet.

It was another puzzle, however. The more Simon sought out the truth, one he now confessed to himself he was eager to find so that his attraction to Ilsabeth was no longer a danger to himself, the more puzzles he came across. He did not find it all that difficult to believe that Hepbourn would do all Ilsabeth said he had and Simon knew that was one small step toward uncovering the truth needed to prove she was innocent.

"Psst! Simon! O'er here."

As covertly as he was able, Simon moved toward the shadowed alcove that sibilant command had come from. He had the strong feeling that not all the Murrays had disappeared from court. Either that or they had sent a friend and ally few in the court would associate with their clan or the Armstrongs. Yet the man had called him Simon, an informality that implied a close relationship. Once within the alcove, Simon studied the man who had called to him. Even in the deep shadows he could see enough to know who faced him now.

"I dinnae think it is wise for ye to be here now, Tormand," Simon said, shifting so that he could keep a close eye upon all the other people in the hall.

"How did ye ken it was me?" Tormand asked, his annoyance over the easy recognition clear to hear in his voice. "I thought myself weel disguised."

"Smearing something white in your beard and hair and wearing ugly clothing isnae a verra good disguise, leastwise nay to one who kens ye as weel as I do. Nor, I suspect, to the many women here who kenned ye verra weel indeed ere ye got married. And how is dear Morainn?"

Tormand cursed softly. "Fine. Healthy. The bairns are healthy. Is Ilsabeth safe?"

"Safe enough. She is secure within my home."

"Secure as in safe? Or secure as in imprisoned?"

The thread of anger in Tormand's voice told Simon he was right to think that trying to prove Ilsabeth innocent could become very complicated. He had several close friends amongst the Murrays and they were a very closely bound family, their loyalty and affection stretching out to even the most distant cousin. If he could not save Ilsabeth, or he decided she was guilty, Simon knew he could destroy friendships, even make a few enemies.

"Ye would rather I had sent her to the king?"

"Curse it, Simon, that lass didnae kill that mon nor would Cormac have anything to do with treason."

"Ye ken Ilsabeth weel, do ye?"

"Nay weel, but I do ken her. I also ken Cormac. He has spent his life trying to scrub away the stain his parents left on their name. He wouldnae toss aside a life's work or endanger his own child."

Simon did not think so either, but men had done stranger things. Fathers did not always have full control over or knowledge of what their children were doing. The fact that it made no sense for Sir Cormac to plot treason or Ilsabeth to kill a man she did not even know was not enough to declare them innocent, mere victims of someone else's plots.

"Ye ken weel that I always seek the truth," Simon said. "Always. My way worked for ye and for your cousin James. If Ilsabeth is innocent, I will prove it and find the guilty one, but allow me to say *if* until I get that proof."

Tormand sighed. "As ye wish. Did she tell ye what happened? Did she e'en ken anything at all?"

After a moment's hesitation, Simon told Tormand all Ilsabeth had told him. "It sounds as if it is the truth." He caught sight of Hepbourn. "And that man is vain and foolish enough to be a traitor. But I need more than her word and the word of her kin. Proof, nay just my word or belief in her innocence, is what will get her free of this deadly tangle. 'Tis why her father sent her to me. He trusts me to find that proof."

"I ken it. I do," muttered Tormand. " 'Tis just that I want this shadow o'er us all to go away. I want an enemy I can get my hands on instead of naught but accusations, lies, and whispers. I want Cormac and his clan to be able to cease running and hiding. God's tears, if this continues for much longer there could weel be a lot of my clan running right alongside them."

Simon understood his friend's frustration. He

shared it. Patience was something he had taught himself, learning that finding the truth required slow, tedious work at times. He was finding that patience difficult to cling to now. Simon tried to tell himself that was because the king was in danger, but he knew that was a lie. He wanted to grasp some hard fact, even some hint, of what plot was afoot and who was behind it for one reason only. He did not want to see that flare of hope in a pair of beautiful blue eyes die again, as it did each time he returned home with no news, no answers.

"We need to find David," he said.

"David? Who is David?"

"Sir Hepbourn's cousin. If what Ilsabeth tells me is true," he ignored Tormand's whispered curse— "this David is part of the plot. He follows Hepbourn, and a follower can often be a weak spot in any plan, easily broken." Simon could see that some people were beginning to take too much notice of how he remained in the shadows. "Ye cannae be seen here nor can ye be seen to be helping me, but mayhap ye can move about enough to aid me in finding this David. Mayhap Morainn can help, too. I dinnae suppose she has had a vision about all of this."

"Nay. Not one about what is happening now. She did have one in time to make certain that Cormac was ready when the danger came. By the time the soldiers entered Aigballa the only ones left inside were the old and the lame. The soldiers soon decided they were of no use but I fear a few died ere the soldiers gave up trying to get them to help take down their laird. Now the soldiers camp within the walls of Aigballa and word is that, if they arenae driven away soon, t'will be years before Cormac can clean up the mess they will leave behind."

"I will see that he is recompensed for this. Nothing can bring back the dead, but some payment will help ease the burden of the damages done and make certain no more die as they try to restock their stores. One thing ere ye leave—"

"I am leaving, am I?"

"Aye. Too many grow curious about the shadow I speak to. Ilsabeth has two children."

"Nay, she doesnae. She is a maid."

"Foundlings, ye fool."

"Bad time for her to take them in, but I cannae fault her for that."

"Nay, and I dinnae. Howbeit, she has made me swear that, if she cannae care for them, I will see them safely to your family."

"Agreed."

"Good. That is if Old Bega will let them go."

"Ye would let them stay with you?"

"Dinnae sound so surprised. I like children. I particularly like these children. And Old Bega has already clasped them close to her heart. I just wanted to be certain there was a place for them nay matter what happens. Now, go, because a few people have grown brave enough to draw nearer and your disguise wouldnae fool anyone."

A moment later, Simon knew he was alone. He walked out of the shadows and made his way toward Sir Hepbourn. It was past time to have a talk with the man. If luck was with him, he might just get the fool to say something that would help show Simon which way to look next for the truth he sought. The way people around Hepbourn slowly stepped back as Simon approached was a little amusing. His reputation as the king's man, or the king's hound as some called him, made many people nervous.

"So, Sir Simon, the king has set ye on the trail of the traitors, has he?" asked Sir Hepbourn.

"He has," Simon replied, thinking that the man was cleverly bold to bring the matter up so quickly, or innocent. Simon's instinct told him it was the former. "I but wondered if ye had an opinion on where your lady might have fled. As the mon who was to be her husband, I thought ye may ken a secret or two that would help us find her."

"Ah, weel, I assumed she was hiding with the rest of her clan."

"Did ye. One shouldnae assume anything about a lass who would stab a mon in the heart and plot against the king." The flare of anger in Hepbourn's eyes pleased Simon. "Ye must have spent some time at Aigballa."

"I did indeed." Sending a brief, sad smile to the people nearest them, Hepbourn sighed. "A secretive lot they are. I thought that their reluctance to fully embrace me as a new member of their clan, as the mon who would soon claim the laird's own daughter as his wife, was odd. Now I ken that they didnae wish to risk the chance that I might uncover their plots or any of their bolt-holes."

"Mayhap such confidences would have come later, once ye were truly the lass's husband."

"Mayhap. Yet, Ilsabeth is one and twenty, far past marrying age. Ye would think her father would have welcomed a husband for her with open arms, especially one of my standing. But, I often got the feeling Sir Cormac watched me as if he feared I was about to rob him blind." He laughed and shook his head.

And mayhap Sir Cormac sensed that ye were a threat to not only his daughter but his whole clan, Simon thought. "Did ye ken that the king's own cousin was in the area, a lad he was verra fond of?"

"Nay. He ne'er approached me, nay e'en for a bed to sleep in for the night. I assumed that he was there to watch the Armstrongs, that he had some idea that they were a threat to our king, and that is why the poor mon was murdered and left in a field of thistles to rot."

"Assumptions again. Dangerous things, assumptions."

Simon asked a few more questions and then walked away, ignoring the sudden flurry of whispers that erupted behind him. He needed to leave the court and think hard on his conversation with Hepbourn. Every word the man had uttered had carried the taint of falsehood. Hepbourn was clever, however, never saying anything that could draw suspicion to him yet constantly strengthening the suspicions that had sent the Armstrongs into hiding.

What kept Simon's interest in the man keen, however, was the utter lack of doubt the man showed about Ilsabeth's guilt. The man had courted her for months, become betrothed to her, yet he had never once expressed disbelief that the woman he had meant to wed would kill a man and plot to kill the king. Nor did Hepbourn make even the slightest attempt to seek the truth himself, if only to ease his own humiliation or to gain some revenge for being made to look the fool. The way Hepbourn was acting was wrong and it made Simon more certain, with every word the fool spoke, that Hepbourn was a very guilty man. It would take time, and luck, to prove exactly what the man was guilty of.

Children's laughter greeted Simon as he entered his home and the sound caused a strange pang in his heart. The laughter belonged, he thought as a somewhat tousled MacBean arrived to take his cloak and gloves. Simon stepped into his hall to find Ilsabeth and the children wrestling together on the floor, Bonegnasher occasionally hurling its furry body into the melee. The cat was curled up in a chair safely out of the way.

"Si—mon!" called Elen when she saw him, and immediately ran to him.

Simon caught the child up in his arms. She put her small arms around his neck and hugged him. It felt good, he thought. It was a welcome home any man would enjoy. He realized he had quickly come to like arriving home to his three guests and that worried him. Simon knew that he was seeing what his life could be like with a family of his own and the lack of it would hit him hard when Ilsabeth and the children were gone. He was going to have to try harder to hold himself away from them, to continue to simply seek the truth and not fall into some impossible dream of hearth and home.

Ilsabeth stood up and smoothed out her skirts all the while keeping a close watch on Simon. When Elen had rushed to greet him, Ilsabeth had seen those cold gray eyes soften. Something very like a smile had touched Simon's mouth. Then his expression had hardened again, as if he had suddenly realized what he was doing and retreated into the cold tool of justice he so tried to be.

She knew there was more to him, however. He might keep his distance but he was good to the children. He had not sent her to the king to sit in a damp, filthy dungeon while he searched for the truth and the real traitors. It was that part of him that he tried so hard to keep hidden that she wanted; it was that man who had her feeling things she had never felt before, wanting things she had never really wanted before. Ilsabeth was determined to get Simon to stop burying that man under the ice.

"We need to speak privately," he said as he set Elen down only to have the child hug his leg.

"After the evening meal and the children are put to bed then," said Ilsabeth.

"Agreed."

After gently removing Elen from his leg, Simon left. Ilsabeth suspected he was headed to the little room that held all his papers, the room where he wrote down all he had learned and needed to learn to find the answers he sought. She had sneaked a look into that room. It was small, dark, and eerily tidy. Simon probably thought it was a perfect reflection of the man he was but, in her heart, she knew different. The problem was that she was the one he was seeking the truth about this time, and that fact gave him the strength to keep her at a distance.

As she began to ready the children for the evening meal, she wondered if Simon would soften a little when he found out that she was no more than a pawn in Walter's game, the innocent fool who had put herself in a position to be used. She hoped so for, the moment she found a chink in Sir Simon Innes's armor, she was going to chip away at it until she found the heart of the man. If luck was with her, he would then give her the chance to win it for her own.

The soft rap at the door of his ledger room drew Simon from his dark thoughts. He knew it was Ilsabeth and he almost resented the way his heart skipped a beat in anticipation of seeing her. She was inching her way beneath his skin, he thought crossly, and he could not seem to stop it. The best thing he could do was solve the puzzle and get her out of his home as fast as possible. While it was true that he had lately been thinking of having a wife, he did not want one who could so easily unsettle him with just a smile.

"Come in," he called as he did his best to shore up his defenses against her.

Ilsabeth entered the room and his defenses cracked as he politely stood up. Simon inwardly cursed but did his best to hide his irritation. It was not Ilsabeth's fault that he was discovering a weakness for big blue eyes and long black hair.

"Ye said we needed to talk privately," she said as she took the chair facing his worktable and he sat down. "Have ye discovered something that will help me?"

Simon sat down and studied her for a moment. He saw no harm in allowing himself to enjoy how pretty she looked in her dark blue gown, her thick hair tumbling wildly around her shoulders. He was just a man after all. This gown revealed her womanly curves as well. Full, high breasts, a small waist, and hips any man thinking of children would approve of. His palms itched with the need to touch all that softness. Simon struggled to rein in the lust that was getting harder and harder to control.

"I havenae found anything to proclaim your innocence to the world and set ye and your family free. Nay yet." He fought the need to reassure her when the hope in her eyes abruptly dimmed into grim acceptance. "What I have discovered is that Hepbourn is no innocent fool tricked by a wicked woman." He nodded when she made a scoffing noise. "Near every word out of his mouth is a lie. Tell me, when he asked for your hand, did he declare an undying love or something of that ilk?"

Ilsabeth thought Simon sounded far too cynical about such declarations of love and devotion. There was nothing to mock in such heartfelt emotions. Some men and women actually meant them. Ilsabeth wondered who had said them to him and then proven her words a lie.

"He did," she replied. "I wasnae so certain I believed him. I had the thought that he was just saying what he felt was right when asking a woman to be his wife. Fool that I was, I still thought he would make a good husband. But why is what he said then of any importance?"

"I just wondered, for he is already at court and has never once spoken of how ye couldnae have done what they said ye did. He has given ye nary a word of defense. He hasnae e'en acted confused, uncertain, about what is said of ye. That isnae right."

"What does he say?"

"A great deal about how he was a fool nay to see what ye had planned. He also makes certain to remind anyone who will listen to him that the Armstrongs are traitors and ye are nay only a traitor but a killer. 'Tis a verra odd thing for a mon who was betrothed to you to do."

"He is trying to protect himself and his family."

"That could have been done by staying at home. Instead, he has come to court and makes certain that no one forgets what ye and your clan have been accused of."

Ilsabeth was so angry she wanted to hit something. Going to the court and punching Walter in his elegant nose was a tempting thought. Only the sure knowledge that she would be immediately taken up by the king's soldiers kept her from doing so. She would rather her innocence was proven before she was executed.

" 'Tis difficult to ken how I didnae see what kind of mon he truly was," she murmured, and shook her head at her own idiocy.

"He is verra good at hiding his true intentions."

"Ye saw them."

"I wasnae looking for a husband," he drawled. "Most of the ones he is wooing at the court dinnae ken that he is lying to them. Hepbourn uses his fine looks and smile to the best advantage. Your father ne'er liked him, did he?"

"Nay, not verra much." Ilsabeth smiled. "He said he thought the mon was too good at saying what others wanted to hear, but my father's greatest worry was the mon's mother. He didnae think I would be allowed to take my rightful place in Walter's household. My mother convinced him that I would."

"Do ye think his mother is part of all this?"

"I am nay sure. She does see herself as being of far more importance than she is and she does rule Walter in many ways. I cannae believe she has no idea of what he is plotting and yet I cannae think she would easily ignore something she didnae agree with. What I can see is that, if power and riches were promised, she would believe she and Walter deserve them."

Simon nodded, thinking it might be time to have someone speak with Walter's mother. "I also saw your cousin Tormand."

"Is he weel?" She frowned. "And shouldnae he be staying away from the king and all his people for a while?"

"He should stay far away but he willnae. I have set him to finding David. Do ye happen to ken what David's last name is and where he lives?"

" 'Tis Hepbourn and he mostly lives with Walter. I had the feeling he has done so for a verra long time."

"Good." It would be the first place Tormand looked, Simon thought. "Tormand also said that your family is still safely hidden away. The soldiers hold Aigballa and I fear a few of those who stayed behind were killed when the soldiers came through the gates."

Ilsabeth fought back an urge to cry. She would save that for when she was private. The ones who had stayed behind at Aigballa had chosen to do so knowing the risks. They had undoubtedly bought her family a little more time to get away and for that they would be forever honored. She just prayed that she would have a chance to make Walter pay dearly for their lives.

"I want him dead," she whispered, shocked at her own words.

"Of course ye do. He is doing his best to destroy your entire family whilst seeking to enrich his own."

She stood up and began to pace the room. It was difficult to do so, but she finally stopped before a heavy tapestry that depicted the Garden of Eden complete with a particularly horrific-looking snake. That was Walter, she thought. The man had promised her a home and a family, things she had craved, and yet he had delivered only destruction. She tensed when she felt Simon step up behind her.

The fact that he could not abide Ilsabeth's sorrow, that he had actually stepped up to try and soothe her, told Simon that he no longer thought her guilty of anything more than choosing the wrong man while attempting to find herself a good husband and have her own family. "We will find the truth," he said, and inwardly grimaced, wishing he had a more gifted tongue.

Ilsabeth turned to face him and found herself nearly in his arms. It was tempting to hurl herself against his chest, using his strength to calm her fears and ease her grief. Tentatively, she placed a hand on his arm, needing to touch him, and felt his muscles tense beneath her palm.

"I am afraid," she said, and even she could hear the truth of that in her voice.

"I willnae tell ye not to be," he said, and gave in to the temptation to touch her hair by brushing back a thick lock that had slipped forward over her slim shoulder. "There is reason to be afraid and the fear will make ye take care. But ye were right when ye said Walter was a vain mon. He is verra vain and that can be a weakness. He also believes himself safe. Another weakness. Dinnae think that we willnae solve this puzzle, for we will. 'Tis just that sometimes it takes more work and time than one would like."

She rested her forehead against his chest, idly wondering if he realized he was still toying with her hair. "There is only one thing that truly puzzles me about all this. I would have ne'er thought Walter was brave enough or clever enough to plot against the king. The mon can barely plan weel for a journey to the next village. He expects it to just be done. He says he is going and then waits for the horse, and all else that is needed, to be brought to him. So how could such a mon plot out a way to bring down a king?" She felt Simon tense against her, his fingers tightening in her hair, and she leaned back a little to look up at his face. "What is it? Have ye thought of something?"

"Nay, ye have. There is someone behind Walter."

"Someone who is the true chess player in this game?"

"Exactly."

"Weel, he did speak of his compatriots but he also spoke of the new king and didnae imply it would be him. Oh, and how he needed to complete his plans and make sure they would be acceptable to his compatriots. That must have been his vanity speaking because I truly dinnae believe the mon can plan anything."

Simon had suspected that Walter might not be the leader, but Ilsabeth's insight into how the man behaved made him certain of it. That meant that Walter was also a follower and, from what Simon had seen of the man, he would be one who would be easy to break. The only problem was that, by appearing at court, Walter had made it difficult to just grab him and take him somewhere to be thoroughly questioned.

His mind still busy trying to figure out how he might yet accomplish capturing Walter, Simon looked down into Ilsabeth's upturned face. He suddenly realized that she was almost in his arms. Everything within him ached to pull her close and he tried to fight the temptation. Then she smiled at him.

Ilsabeth had a quick look at how Simon's eyes darkened nearly to black and then his mouth was on hers. She was not sure what had prompted the sudden kiss but she was determined not to do anything to make him stop. His mouth was soft and warm as it moved over hers. She wrapped her arms around his neck to steady herself and allowed the heat and desire stirred to life by his kiss to sweep over her. When he nudged at her lips with his tongue, she readily parted them. The kiss deepened and Ilsabeth shivered with delight. He tasted so good. With each stroke of his tongue within her mouth she pressed even closer to his hard body. And then, so abruptly she nearly fell, she was released and pushed away from him.

"Nay," said Simon, shaking his head to clear away the haze of passion. "Nay."

Before she could say a word, he fled the room. Ilsabeth placed her hand on her bosom, not surprised to find that she was panting softly and her heart was racing. Walter's kisses had never made her feel this way.

Frowning at the door for a moment, she then looked around. Simon had fled his little dark room.

She smiled. Her brief fear that she had kissed so badly or tasted so vile he had been repulsed melted away. Simon had run away from her as if she were a demon about to tempt him into selling his soul. He did not hate kissing her; he liked it far too much.

Straightening herself, she smoothed down her skirts and headed out of the room. A man did not run away like that unless he liked the kiss so much, he feared it. Ilsabeth was determined to make sure that Simon kissed her again. And again. Until his fear of it faded.

Simon watched Ilsabeth leave his ledger room and then slipped back inside. He could still taste her on his mouth, still feel her lithe soft body pressed against his. His body was as hard as a rock and aching in protest of his pushing Ilsabeth away. Never had a kiss affected him so.

Ilsabeth was a dangerous woman, he thought as he filled a goblet with wine. A hearty drink did little to ease the taste of her from his tongue but it did help to ease the desire knotting his body. He was going to have to be more careful, he thought. If nothing else, Ilsabeth had been put under his protection by her own family and all of her family was looking to him to save her. It would be dishonorable, and a breach of that trust, to seduce her. Simon just prayed that she did not try to seduce him. He did not think he had the strength of will to resist that.

Chapter 5

Ilsabeth tried to keep her gaze fixed upon her sewing, fighting the urge to look at Simon as they sat together in his hall. It was late, the children were asleep, and she could not help but wonder if Simon would take advantage of their solitude to kiss her again. She had quickly recovered from her sense of insult over how hastily he had fled from her yestereve, but that did not mean she would accept him ignoring her as he was attempting to do. She was still sure that a man only fled a woman's kiss because he was afraid of where it would lead, to far more than a playful romp in the bed. It was also a comfort to know that at least a few of the overwhelming emotions he stirred within her were shared.

Daring a glance at him from beneath her lashes, she caught him staring into the fire with his still unnamed cat sprawled in his lap. Ilsabeth decided that he did not name the cat because he was pretending that he did not want it. It was similar to how he acted with her. She could understand some of Simon's reluctance to go beyond one stolen kiss for she was still accused of murder and treason. Even if he now believed in her innocence, he was a king's man and could not entangle himself with such a woman. If nothing else, it could cause others to question his honesty and she knew Simon would suffer greatly if that happened.

There was a wild spirit within her that was pressing her to try and seduce the man, but Ilsabeth fought to ignore it. What did she know of seduction? Ilsabeth believed that seduction was wrong, too, unless it was a game played out between two lovers. Seduction was one person using guile to make another do something she did not truly wish to do, no matter what her body begged for. She could never do that to Simon.

For all Simon's refusal to openly declare her innocent until he had more proof than her word, she still wanted Simon in ways she had never wanted Walter. Walter had never made her heart pound so hard she could hear the echo of its beats in her ears. Nor had he ever made her want to tear off his clothes so that she could admire his body, touch his skin, taste it. Sir Simon Innes was the man meant to be hers, the man every part of her cried out for, but she would win him honestly or not at all. Seduction only served to stir a man's desire and, from what she knew of men, that was no great feat. She wanted to stir Simon's heart.

Ilsabeth inwardly grimaced. That could prove a task far beyond her ability. She had not reached the age of one and twenty unwed because she was too particular in her taste. There had been few men interested in her as a woman, a wife, and the possible mother of their children. The only man who had really courted her and asked her to marry him was Walter and he had done so just to use her to hide his crimes and destroy her whole family. She now understood that what she had seen as an honorable resistance to despoiling his bride before they were wed was actually Walter's utter distaste for her. Perhaps she should not be so confident of the reasons she thought Simon had run away from the kiss they had shared.

"Sir, there is a rogue at the door to the kitchens," announced MacBean.

Startled by the man's silent entry, but very glad to have her increasingly morbid thoughts disrupted, Ilsabeth smiled at MacBean. As always he looked as if he had just swallowed something bitter. "A rogue?" She glanced at Simon. "Ye ken many rogues, sir?"

"Aside from ones who neglect to knock at a door before they enter a room?" drawled Simon, scowling at MacBean, who ignored him. "Nay. Who is this rogue, MacBean?"

"I am nay a rogue," came a voice from just outside the door to the hall. "I am a married man."

Simon sighed. "Let him in, MacBean."

"Tormand!" cried Ilsabeth when the man slipped around MacBean and grinned at them. She tossed aside her sewing and ran over to hug her cousin.

"Ye are looking verra weel, lass," said Tormand after kissing her on the cheek.

"Thank ye. So are ye. Any new news of my family?"

"Some, and I will tell ye as soon as I have some wine."

A muttering MacBean soon served them all some wine and then left. Ilsabeth sipped hers as Simon and Tormand drank their wine, idly exchanging pleasantries she had no real interest in. Her concern for her family made her impatient, however. She did not press them but she did begin to tap her foot, unable to quell that outside sign of her growing impatience.

"Easy, lass," Tormand said, and grinned at her again from where he sat beside her on the settee. "Matters have changed little. Your family still evades capture. 'Tis said that the king's soldiers have already ceased to avidly hunt them, waiting for some traitor to tell them where to look. I am here for two reasons. I was asked to see for myself that ye are weel, Two, and to pass on some information from Humfrey. Both requests arrived after I saw Simon yestereve."

"Two?" Simon frowned. "Why did ye just call her Two? Are ye a twin, Ilsabeth?"

"Nay." She glared at Tormand, who just laughed, as unaffected by her anger as her brothers always were.

"She used to be named Clara," Tormand explained. "Cormac's firstborn was called Ilsabeth but she had the calling and became Sister Beatrice. Elspeth loved the name Ilsabeth so much, however, that she asked the lass here if she would mind taking it on. Afraid we all began to call her Two after that."

Ilsabeth sighed. "E'en Two is better than Clara." She could see that Simon was fighting a grin and she glared at him. When that expression of her displeasure had as little effect upon him as it had upon Tormand, she looked back at her cousin. "What did Humfrey have to say?"

"Aside from complaining that Hepbourn left as soon as he realized ye hadnae been caught and that the mon's mother is a verra harsh taskmaster, he told me that David is on his way to join up with Hepbourn," replied Tormand.

"Good," said Simon. "The mon is most kind to save us all the trouble of hunting him down."

"We must be sure to thank him for that kindness when we get our hands on him."

"Ye think David could be useful?" asked Ilsabeth, frowning at the thought of the pale, chinless David being good for much of anything aside from stroking Walter's vanity. "He isnae a plotter. He but follows Walter about like a faithful wee pup."

"Exactly," said Simon, satisfaction heavy in his tone. "He is a follower. Followers can be a weakness one can use against the leader."

"I am nay sure Walter cares enough for David, or anyone, to risk himself to save the mon."

"So I think and soon David will be made to see that, too."

Ilsabeth rubbed her forehead as the pinch of a headache lodged itself there. "I fear I cannae make sense of that. How does that help us?"

Simon suddenly felt like laughing he was so pleased by her utter confusion. Ilsabeth was no plotter. He had begun to see that more clearly with every passing hour in her presence, but the way she acted now only confirmed his opinion. She had a keen wit but not a devious one. He had suspected it when he realized she had barely escaped the trap set for her and might not have done so if her father had not planned for the need of one. Ilsabeth was a complete stranger to deception.

"He *follows,* Two." He grinned when she glared at him for the use of that name. "Followers are near always weaker than their leader. They often, quite foolishly, believe their leader will help them, keep them safe, and all of that. When they discover their leader is more than ready to cast them to the wolves, their loyalty shatters."

Shaking free of her bemusement over how handsome Simon looked when he smiled, Ilsabeth said, "Oh. And then they spill out all of their secrets, suddenly verra willing to take their leader down with them."

"Aye. Or so we hope. At times a follower is so afraid of his leader that, despite the leader showing him that that man cares nothing for his men, nothing will bring the follower to tell me what he knows. This will all depend upon how committed David is to the cause of bringing down the king. I but wonder who they think to replace the king with."

"I wouldnae be surprised if Walter thought he should be set upon the throne e'en if he isnae the one planning all of this. He ne'er fails to let people ken that he has the blood of the Bruce in his veins."

"So claims half of Scotland," muttered Tormand as he poured himself another drink of wine.

Ilsabeth laughed. "True, but I think Walter may actually have a rightful claim although 'tis but a few wee drops, weel watered down and weak. However, as I told ye, Walter spoke as if another mon was to take the throne."

"He may just nay wish the burden of it, only the benefits of helping another mon take it. And, since it isnae Walter, then it is someone Walter believes will lift him higher in importance and power, enriching him," said Simon. "Curse it, I need names. Names will give me the power to proclaim your innocence and get the soldiers away from ye and your family. If we can get our hands on David I just might get some."

"How do ye plan to get him? It willnae be easy to catch someone at court and spirit him away. If it was, I think ye would already have Walter in your hands, wouldnae ye?"

"Hepbourn is making himself far too noticeable. I dinnae think David will."

"Ah, nay, he willnae. Nor would Walter allow it."

Ilsabeth listened as the men talked over ideas for getting their hands on David. She did not wish to know how they would get the information they hoped to get from the man. All she wanted to accomplish was to lift the cloud of suspicion off her and her family. David was part of the plot that had sent her and her family into hiding, and he was one of the ones plotting against the king, so he deserved whatever he had to suffer.

"Weel, I think that gives us enough ideas to mull over," said Tormand as he stood up. "I must needs get back to my wife. She doesnae like me coming so close to the court although she kens it is necessary." He kissed Ilsabeth on the forehead. "Dinnae worry so hard, lass. Your father will keep your family safe and Simon will keep ye safe. We will soon drag the real traitors before the king. Next time I come, I will try to be in time to meet these children ye have taken in."

The moment Tormand was gone Ilsabeth picked

up her sewing and stared at it blindly. She wanted to believe Tormand's assurances, but her fear for her family would not allow her to do so. There was so much that could still go wrong. She should not even be here, but with her family. She ached to be with them as they fought this battle.

A battle they faced because she had been blind to the man she had chosen to be her husband. Ilsabeth took a deep breath as she fought the strong urge to cry. She suffered no pain at the loss of her betrothed but she did hurt over the loss of her dream of a home of her own and children. She also grieved over what that dream was now costing her loved ones.

"Ilsabeth?"

She could not look at Simon, knowing that her eyes would show her sorrow. "Nay, I shall be fine."

There was no mistaking that waver in her soft, husky voice and Simon would swear that he could feel her sorrow. He moved to sit beside her and put his arm around her. It was a dangerous thing to do but he could not smother his need to offer her comfort. When she leaned into him, her soft body pressing against him, everything inside him tightened with need. The clothing they wore was suddenly a painful, unwanted barrier between them. Even the scent of her had him aching to taste her skin. Sympathy, he sternly told himself. Only sympathy. A particularly insistent part of his body paid no attention.

" 'Tis all my fault," she murmured, resting her cheek against his chest.

"Nay, the fault lies with Hepbourn," said Simon. "He is the one who plots against the king, used ye, and now uses and defames your family to protect himself."

"Ah, so now ye believe me?"

He sighed and gave in to the temptation to rest his cheek against her soft hair. "Aye. I still need proof, however, and that shall nay be easy to get. Traitors ken what fate awaits them and 'tis nay a simple hanging."

"I dinnae think a hanging is so verra simple but I ken what ye mean. Compared to the horrific punishments dealt out to traitors, a hanging would seem preferable. That makes them verra cautious.

"I should be with my family," she abruptly said in a quiet voice. "I should be standing with them at such a time."

"Nay. They sent ye here. This is where they wish ye to be. Dinnae forget what Tormand said. The soldiers arenae even hunting them much any longer. They willnae, either, unless the king sends someone to push them to it. That gives us time."

Ilsabeth wondered if he was aware that he was rubbing his cheek against her hair and caressing her arm with his hand. She was no longer on the verge of tears but decided to stay right where she was. Being held close to Simon not only made her blood run hot, it made her feel safe. She could sense the strength in him and it was as if it shielded her.

A quick glance down was enough to tell her that he also desired her. It was heady knowledge but she was not sure how to act upon it. In the short time she had known him, she had learned that Simon was an intensely honorable man. Whatever else might hold him back from satisfying the desire he felt for her, the fact that she had been put under his protection would be a strong part of that. Ilsabeth did not know whether she could or even should try to surmount that particular wall.

But how she wanted to, she thought, and sighed. The idea of giving her chastity over to a man she was not married to did not bother her. She was a Murray woman, after all, and when a Murray woman found the man she wanted, she gave him everything. What troubled her was how badly it would hurt her if all he felt for her was desire. If, when this all ended and she was free, he sent her home with no word of love or promise of a future, Ilsabeth feared she would know a pain that time would never heal. It would be a big risk to give him everything she had to give with nothing but the hope that he would return her feelings and Ilsabeth was not sure she was brave enough to do that.

"Hey, lass, have ye gone to sleep?"

The hint of amusement in his voice caused her to lift her head and smile at him. Ilsabeth saw the way his eyes abruptly darkened. Her body responded to that look with a heat that nearly made her gasp. Suddenly she understood why some of her married kinswomen would blush when their men looked at them. They were seeing that look in their men's eyes.

Simon softly cursed even as he pulled her face closer to his, unable to resist the urge to kiss her, to taste that lush mouth that tempted him every time he looked at it. When Ilsabeth smiled at him, her eyes all soft and warm, his will crumbled. All he could think of was how much he wanted her to keep looking at him like that. It was madness.

She was his weakness, he thought with a touch of alarm. He had spent years hardening himself in heart, body, and mind, yet this small woman with big blue eyes easily cut through his armor with a smile. Simon knew he ought to run far and fast but then his lips touched hers, and all his fears were burned away by the heat that flooded his body.

Ilsabeth wrapped her arms around his neck and held on tight. She parted her lips with no urging from him, eager to taste him. When she tentatively parried the strokes of his tongue with her own, he groaned and the sound made the fire inside her burn even hotter. She could stir his passion and, at the moment, that was enough.

He pushed her down onto the settee and Ilsabeth welcomed the weight of his body as he covered her. She was surrounded by the heat and scent of him and it made her desire rise so quickly and fiercely that she had no thought but of him, of his taste, of his touch. She wanted his clothes gone; hers as well. She needed to feel his skin beneath her hands. When he began to kiss his way down her throat she realized he had tugged her gown down to free her breasts. Ilsabeth knew she was blushing but she did not stop him. Her breasts ached for his touch.

When he kissed her there, she shivered, despite the fire the caress ignited inside her. A small part of her gasped in shock that she was allowing a man who was not her husband, not even her betrothed, to touch her and kiss her so intimately, but need smothered that spark of embarrassment. She threaded her fingers through his thick hair and held him close, silently urging him to continue, and reveled in the way his hands and mouth worked such magic upon her skin.

A little voice in Simon's mind whispered that he had gone too far, but the sight of Ilsabeth's full breasts, her nipples taut and begging for his kiss, made it easy to ignore the warning. He filled his hand with the soft weight of one as he feasted on the other. The soft cries escaping her and the way her lithe body arched against his completely silenced that warning. The only thought remaining in his head was that he had to be inside her soon.

"Mama?"

At the sound of a child's voice, Simon tensed so quickly it hurt. Elen was in the room. Simon stared down at the woman sprawled beneath him and slowly came to his senses. Her breasts were bare, the hard tips wet and glistening from his greedy attentions. He could even see a touch of redness from his emerging beard. His hand was under her skirts. Simon knew he had been within a heartbeat of taking her on the settee. He met her gaze and the warmth there, still visible despite her blushes, told him that she would have let him.

Shielding her with his body as best he could, he eased up from her enough so that she could quickly fix her bodice. The moment she was decent again, he leapt off her as if she were on fire. There was no hiding the way his body still ached for her, but, fortunately, Elen was too young to recognize what ailed him.

"Best ye see what the child needs," he said, and strode out of the room certain he heard her whisper *coward*.

She was probably right, he thought as he shut

himself in his ledger room and poured himself some wine. The first drink went down fast and he poured another before he collapsed in his chair. Simon winced at the word *coward* but it suited him and that was humiliating. Ilsabeth was a tiny woman yet he kept running from her as if she were some demon out to steal his soul. Nay, he thought, he did not run from her, but from all she made him feel.

He should leave, go to the tavern, and spend himself on a woman there, pounding into some strange wench until he was too weak to walk and Ilsabeth's taste no longer lingered on his tongue. It was difficult to deny Ilsabeth's allure because he had been months without a woman. His bout of celibacy had gone on for too long and that was why his control was so ragged and weak. A wild, exhausting night in the arms of some skilled whore was just what he needed.

The moment the thought entered his head, he knew he would not do that. He did not want some tavern wench. Even if he could stir up enough interest to take one, the moment the raw need passed, he would be aching for Ilsabeth again. Simon knew he was trapped. He could not rut her out of his mind and he could not send her anywhere far away from him.

"And I obviously cannae control myself if I get close to her," he grumbled.

He closed his eyes and took several slow, deep breaths to tamp down the fire still raging through his body. If he did not find the real traitors soon, he would have to explain to the Armstrongs and the Murrays why he had despoiled the woman they had entrusted to his care. That was not a confrontation he wanted to endure.

Then again, he mused, he could always marry her. A heartbeat later, he cursed. A large part of him was delighted by the thought, easily imagining her tucked up in his bed every night, but another part cringed. Ilsabeth Murray Armstrong would not be the placid, undemanding wife he had often envisioned. She would expect him to give her some part of himself, might even demand love or something closely resembling it. From all he had heard, Murray women were notorious for that.

"God give me strength," he muttered, finishing off his second drink and contemplating a third. Getting roaring drunk was beginning to look like a good idea.

Ilsabeth tucked Elen back in her bed. "There ye go, lass. Now go back to sleep like a good lass. Ye have Reid here, aye? He will keep ye safe."

"Aye," the child said, and looked at her brother. "He big."

"He is. Big, and strong, and verra brave."

It took a little more convincing before Elen let her leave, the fears that had caused the child to come looking for her finally eased. Ilsabeth headed straight for her bedchamber, eager for some time alone with her thoughts. She doubted she would see Simon again for quite a while. It would not surprise her if he stayed away for days this time. The children would miss him and that would make her feel guilty for driving the man away and furious at him for running away.

He did not need to run. She was shamefully willing to give him what he wanted. Unfortunately, his wanting seemed to flare and wane with an annoying regularity.

"I wonder if the other women in my family had this much trouble with their men," she wondered aloud as she began to shed her clothing.

A glance at her breasts revealed a few reddish marks made by Simon's beard-roughened skin. The sight made her shiver with a blaze of renewed desire. Ilsabeth knew she would never forget how it felt to have his mouth there. Even the roughness of his cheeks against her skin had felt good, although she suspected his freshly shaved face would feel just as delightful.

"How odd. I have gone from wondering why people seemed so enamored of lovemaking to a complete wanton."

For a moment she wondered what her father would say if she reached out and took what she wanted from Simon yet returned home without the man as her husband. He would be angry but Ilsabeth doubted it would be because she had handed her virginity to a man who could not love her. No, her father would be angry because he would fear that her heart was broken. Ilsabeth suspected it would be, even though she was not ready to put the name of love to what she felt for Simon.

Simon who was hiding in his little room, she thought crossly as she dressed for bed. She wondered what had happened to him to make him try to remain so cold and distant from everyone. Ilsabeth suspected he would not thank her if she pointed out to him that he failed in that. The way he treated his dog and that ugly cat, as well as how he treated the children, MacBean, and Old Bega, told her that he was no cold, heartless man. He just wanted to be and that was what she did not understand. Even his relentless search for the truth and for justice revealed the man beneath the shell. A man had to have a heart to be so determined that no innocent paid for the crime of another.

She wished her mother or one of her married cousins was near. Ilsabeth wanted someone to talk to, someone who had suffered some of the same problems with her chosen man. Any advice would be welcome for she had little idea of what to do next.

Ilsabeth softly cursed as she crawled into bed. She knew what she *wanted* to do, what she *needed*. The women in her family did not believe young maids should be kept utterly ignorant until the moment they found themselves in bed with a husband. When Simon had pushed her down on the settee, she had known exactly what would happen and had been eager for it. Her problem was trying to understand why he kept stopping and how she might get him to cease fleeing her arms. That required the wisdom of women who had dealt with men more intimately and longer than she had.

"I am naught but a bairn when it comes to men," she grumbled.

Knowing there was no sense in losing sleep over the matter, she closed her eyes. Each time Simon drew near her, his passion ruled him a little longer than it had before. There was hope that she would soon learn the great mystery between men and women. Ilsabeth just hoped she did not have to wait too long. Her last clear thought was a mean one. She hoped Simon was as achingly unsatisfied as she was.

Chapter 6

Simon studied the small, stone cottage where Sir Donald Chisholm was hiding his newest mistress. The man was married with eight children. Simon had to wonder why Donald had any need for a mistress unless the man's poor, beleaguered wife was so worn out she could not accommodate the man any longer. Not that he considered that a good excuse for adultery. It also disgusted Simon to think of the money the man spent on this fleshly indulgence, money that would be better spent on his wife and children.

He rapped on the door. "Open in the king's name!" he ordered, and nearly grinned at the image of the faithless Donald scrambling into his clothes as he tried to think of a reason why a king's man was looking for him. Even the innocent felt a twinge of alarm when a king's man came hunting for them.

The disheveled, half-dressed man who appeared in the doorway a few minutes later was so plain, so

intensely ordinary, Simon was surprised the man
could breed a child as lovely as Elen. He almost felt
sorry for the women in Donald's life. Simon
doubted the man made up for his lack of looks with
skill in the bedchamber. A man who would toss
away his own child and be unfaithful to a wife who
gave him eight children would not be the sort who
would care for his woman's pleasure. He was probably one of those fools who believed a woman felt
none or could be happy just because the man in
her bed found his.

"Shall we step inside, Sir Donald?" Simon asked,
aware that the man recognized him by the way Donald grew a little pale. For once Simon felt no twinge
of regret over that reaction to his presence.

Donald stumbled back a few steps as he nodded,
staring at Simon in fear and horror. His small eyes
were so wide, Simon was sure they had to sting. He
looked around the cottage as he walked inside. Sir
Donald Chisholm obviously spent enough to keep
his mistress comfortable but there was nothing lav-
ish, unless one counted the wooden floors and the
glass in the windows as extravagant. Simon idly
wondered if the man's wife was allowed such things
or if Sir Donald spent most of his funds on this little
cottage for he knew the man was not particularly
rich.

"How may I be of service, Sir Simon?" Donald
asked as he shut the door and then slumped
against it.

Yet again, Simon did not find it irritating to be
looked at as if he were the devil himself come to
steal the man's soul. He decided there was obviously some good use to be made of his reputation.

"Do ye happen to ken a child named Reid Burns and another named Elen Burns?"

"I am . . . I did . . ."

"A simple aye or nay will be enough of an answer."

"Aye. Weel, nay. I mean I ken them but have naught to do with them."

"That was quite plain to see when I found them. The boy was naught but skin and bone. If he found any food after ye cast him and his sister into the street, he gave most of it to wee Elen. Both of them had not but rags to wear and nay even a thin blanket to sleep upon. And ye do ken who Elen is, dinnae ye? Your own wee daughter?"

"Who says she is my daughter? I ne'er claimed the brat and her mother was no sainted virgin, now was she." The courage Donald had gained from his sense of outrage faded rapidly beneath Simon's cold stare. "For sweet Mary's sake, they are but two wee bastards. How is their fate any of the king's business?"

" 'Tis nay the king's business. 'Tis mine. I have taken the two children into my home."

"Ah, weel, good. Aye, verra good of ye. They will work hard for ye and nay be much trouble at all."

The man deserved to be beaten into a stain upon the floor, Simon thought, but he slowly unclenched his fists. "Ye, sir, are a swine. Ye toss out two bairns ere their mother is cold in the ground, caring naught for their grief or innocence. Ye ken weel all the horror a child alone can face. And why do ye do so? To have room for the woman who will replace their mother in your adulterous bed." Simon idly wondered if that sounded a little too pious and then decided he did not care. "Did ye e'en take the time to have the bed linen freshened ere ye put a new woman in the bed? Reid may nay be of your blood, and I can only think that a blessing for him, but ye became responsible for him when ye took his mother into your bed. And Elen is of your own blood thus ye are most certainly responsible for her and ye ken it."

"Do ye want me to take them back? Is that what this is about?"

"Nay, I wouldnae put them in your care again. I ken that the moment I wasnae looking ye would just toss them back out again. Nay, what I want from ye is money, a nice sum that can be set aside as Elen's dowry and more for Reid so that he has some choice as to what he will become when he is grown."

"That lad is no blood of mine! I shouldnae have to pay anything for his comfort. He is naught but his mother's get and, e'en though she said she was a widow, he was probably just a bastard."

"When ye took his mother as your mistress ye accepted responsibility for her child. She also bore ye a child who is Reid's sister, and that, too, makes ye responsible." When Donald began to stutter out another protest, Simon grasped the man by the shoulder hard enough to make the man gasp and go pale. "And *I* have decided that ye are responsible. Do ye wish to object to my decision in this?"

Donald was as great a coward as Simon had thought he would be and quickly agreed to all Simon demanded of him. It disappointed Simon a little that he would have no opportunity to beat the money out of the man. Any man who could toss two small children out into the dangerous streets, one of them his own child, deserved to be soundly beaten, but Simon knew it was best if he restrained the urge. It would not do for him to get a reputation as a brute. People might be afraid of him but they did not yet fear him because he would cause them physical pain in any way and he preferred to keep that so. As Simon waited for the man to gather up what money he could, he decided he could not allow the man to get away with such callous treatment of children without suffering some retribution, however.

The moment Donald handed him the money he had found, nervously swearing to get the rest as soon as he could, Simon punched him in the face. Donald stumbled back against the wall and slid down it until he was sitting on the floor. Holding his bleeding nose, Donald stared up at Simon in stunned fear.

Simon crouched down to stare at the man, making no attempt to hide his anger and contempt. "Ye deserve to be beaten within an inch of your miserable life for what ye did to those children and the way ye dishonor your wife, but I have lost the taste for it. There is no satisfaction to be found in beating on a coward. And, heed me weel, dinnae try to cheat those bairns of the last of the money ye just promised to give them. If ye do, I will swallow my distaste for beating such a whining, wee bastard, and leave ye unable to breed any more bairns. I suspicion your wife would thank me for it, too."

Pleased with the terror he could see in Donald's eyes, Simon left. Elen would have a dowry and Reid would have choices in life, he thought as he walked toward his home, and he was satisfied. He knew the Armstrongs and the Murrays would care for the children, as would he if the need arose, but the money would help no matter where the children lived or with whom.

"Ah, weel met, Sir Simon. Might I speak with ye for a moment?"

The sight of a smiling Sir Walter Hepbourn stepping up to him soured Simon's mood, but he stopped and bowed faintly in greeting. "How can I be of service to ye, sir?"

"I but wondered if ye have had any word on the whereabouts of Ilsabeth?" Walter asked.

"If I had it would be the king's business, Sir Walter."

" 'Tis mine as weel, is it not? I was the mon who was to wed her and the one made a fool of by her treachery. Her actions could have blackened the good name of Hepbourn. And, from all I have heard, the king's soldiers havenae gathered up a single one of those traitorous Armstrongs. I humbly beg your pardon if ye feel I am intruding on such matters, but I begin to grow, weel, uncertain."

The tone behind that apology held no humility at all, but Simon's attention was caught by Hepbourn's last words. You begin to grow afraid, thought Simon. Things were not going as planned for the man and fear was beginning to trickle through Hepbourn's veins. Simon wondered if the one at the head of this plot was making his displeasure known. He hoped that leader did not punish failure with a knife across the throat as Hepbourn could yet be of use. It would also be too quick a death for the man who had used Ilsabeth and put her life in danger, he decided.

"There is no need to worry, Sir Walter," Simon said. "We will soon find the traitors. I work diligently to do so as do my men. Now, if ye will be so kind as to pardon me, I must be on my way. Good eve to ye, sir."

Simon caught a brief glimpse of fury on Sir Walter's face before the man bobbed a swift and shallow bow and walked away. Did Hepbourn truly think it would be so easy to get information from him? The man's arrogance was astonishing. Simon did not understand how a woman like Ilsabeth could have even considered marrying the fool.

As soon as Simon began to make his way home again, he wondered if Hepbourn had yet noticed that he was being closely watched. That would certainly be enough to make the man nervous and Hepbourn had definitely been uneasy. A moment later he shook his head, denying that possibility. He and the men he used were good at what they did. If Hepbourn had seen anything, it could have been no more than a fleeting shadow, something to frown over for a moment and then forget. Hepbourn was simply worried that the plot against the king was faltering and, if it failed, so did Hepbourn's chances at any fortune he had planned to gain from it all. With the Armstrongs still free and Ilsabeth not yet caught and condemned, the shields Hepbourn had put between himself and any hint of wrongdoing were weakening.

The man behind this plot was the one he needed to find but he knew that was not going to be easy. It was clear that the leader of the ones plotting against the king stayed deep in the shadows. Simon had told his men to keep a close watch for Hepbourn or his cousin meeting with another man and there had been no word of that happening yet. He could only hope that they got their hands on David soon. Every instinct Simon had told him that that man would break easily and give them most, if not all, the information they needed to put an end to the game.

Once inside his home, Simon slipped into his ledger room. It was a cowardly thing to do, but he could not face Ilsabeth just yet. He needed to carefully plan what he would say to her so that he could say it quick and then put some distance between them. It was what he had been doing since the moment he had risen from her arms two days ago and fled to this room. Although it did little to cure him of his aching need for her, it did stop him from acting on it.

A soft rap came at the door and he tensed. Realizing he was actually afraid that it was Ilsabeth, Simon forced himself to relax. When Reid stepped inside in answer to his invite to enter, the disappointment that stung his heart irritated Simon. It was almost humiliating to know how little success he was having in keeping Ilsabeth at a distance.

Forcing himself to smile at the boy as Reid approached his desk, Simon asked, "What can I do for ye, laddie?"

Reid clasped his small hands in front of him, looking far too intense and serious for such a young boy. "I but wondered if ye can tell me if Ilsabeth is safe yet."

"Nay yet, laddie, but I intend to see that she is verra soon."

"Oh." Reid sighed and his small shoulders slumped a little. "I dinnae like how sad she grows sometimes. I dinnae like to think me and Elen might lose her."

"I dinnae plan to lose Ilsabeth to the plots of others, lad. But, if it will calm your fears, ye need nay worry that ye and Elen will be cast out into the street again. I have sworn that, if aught happens to Ilsabeth, ye and your sister will be taken to her family, either the Armstrongs or the Murrays." He smiled again. "That is if Old Bega will let ye go anywhere."

"Ilsabeth told me that she has made sure we will be cared for, but I would prefer to stay with her. She is teaching me a lot of things that will help me be a mon who can earn some money, more than a wee coin tossed to me here and there. I am nay yet sure what that could be, but I do ken that what she is teaching me will help and then I will be able to take proper care of Elen."

"Reid, I willnae lie to ye and say this will be easy or that the road to getting her free of this tangle will be a smooth one, but I am doing all I can to find the ones who really plot against the king. I dinnae want her or her family to have to run and hide any more than ye do."

"I ken it, sir. I but thought I would ask and so came here as we dinnae see ye much anymore."

That stung and Simon had to force himself not to grimace. He had not given much thought to the children, to how they might see his absences. He thought of how pretty little Elen always ran to him with a sweet smile, asking for a hug and kiss when she saw him, and inwardly cursed.

" 'Tis difficult, lad. Hunting down a truth that many wish to keep weel hidden can take a lot of a mon's time." He stood up. "But, I have some time now and isnae it time for Old Bega to try and kill us with more of her food?" He grinned when Reid laughed. "Come along then. We shall all dine together this eve."

The boy fairly glowed with his pleasure as Simon took him by the hand and led him out of the room. That only added to Simon's guilt. When had he become so concerned about his own fears and emotions that he could have missed the need the children had for his company, for something that faintly resembled a true family? It was not going to be easy but he was going to have to find a way to be near Ilsabeth more often and yet keep his lecherous hands off her.

Ilsabeth was so stunned when Simon joined her and the children for the evening meal that she almost gaped. She avoided that embarrassment but it was difficult to hide how his presence unsettled her. It also puzzled her for she had been so certain that he would avoid her as if she had the plague for a few days more. Yet here he was, seated at the table, talking to her and the children as if he had not spent the last two days gone or hiding in his ledger room. Ilsabeth did not think Simon had had a sudden change of heart or mind, since he had fled her arms that night they had become so passionate upon the settee.

So what was he doing here? she asked herself, and began to get irritated when she could think of no quick answer. Then she noticed what close attention he paid to Reid and Elen. Elen was nearly sitting on the man's lap and kept trying to feed him. Reid was laughing and telling Simon all about the things he had been learning. Simon listened carefully to Reid's words and offered a lot of encouragement and praise. All the while he did so, Simon managed to keep Elen in her seat and food off his clothes with a skill many a mother would envy.

He would make a wonderful father, she mused, and nearly sighed like some love-struck maiden. Filling her mouth with food so that she would not say something foolish, she found that the thought of Simon as a father would not leave her mind. One of the reasons she had been so eager to accept Walter's offer of marriage was her desire for children. Now she could all too easily see Simon as the father of her children, could easily list all the qualities she admired about him that she would like him to teach their children. Of course, she thought with a hidden grimace, Simon was most reluctant to do what was needed to breed those children.

"I have what I believe may be good news, Reid." Simon smiled at the boy and then lightly tousled Elen's thick curls. "And for your sister. I had a word with Sir Donald Chisholm today." He frowned when Reid grew pale.

"Ye arenae going to make him take us back, are ye?" asked Reid in a voice that was high and taut with fear.

"Nay, never. I wouldnae trust the mon with a

mangy dog let alone two fine children like ye and your sister. Nay, I went to make him live up to his rightful responsibilities."

"Oh, how good of ye," said Ilsabeth. "Did ye beat him into naught but a stain upon the floor?"

"Bloodthirsty, arenae ye," murmured Simon, and resisted the urge to grin at her like Reid was doing. "I but punched him once in his nose when he appeared reluctant to do as I asked. I also threatened him a wee bit."

"What did ye ask of him?"

"A dowry for Elen and money for Reid so that he might have a better choice for what he wishes to be when he is grown."

"And he gave ye some?" asked Reid in astonishment.

"He gave me what he had there and has sworn to give me the rest as soon as he is able. I will then see to the care of it until Elen weds and ye, Master Reid, make up your mind as to what ye wish to be and what may be needed to accomplish that."

"Thank ye, sir. I will do ye proud."

"Ah, laddie, ye dinnae need worry o'er that. Just do as your heart tells ye and that will be enough."

Old Bega entered and hurried right over to a yawning Elen, scooping the sleepy child up in her arms. " 'Tis my night to tuck them up in their wee beds," she said as she waved Reid to her side.

"So it is," said Ilsabeth as she hurried over to kiss Elen and Reid on the cheek. "Be good and I shall see ye both in the morning."

Old Bega led the children out of the room, talking every step of the way. Ilsabeth shook her head as she retook her seat and reached for one of the apples set in a bowl in the middle of the table. It was no wonder Elen talked so much, she mused, as she neatly cut and cored the apple, when the child spent so much time with a woman who never seemed to be quiet.

Tossing a piece of apple in her mouth, Ilsabeth looked at Simon. "That was a verra good thing ye did," she said as soon as her mouth was empty.

"The mon couldnae be allowed to shirk his responsibilities," replied Simon, already wondering when he could slip away without offending her too much.

"Many do. Do ye believe he will gather the rest of the money ye demanded of him?"

"I do believe so. Told him I would be watching and if he didnae I would beat him until he couldnae sire any more children."

"A verra good threat."

"Thank ye. And what were ye planning to do with him if ye e'er found him?"

"Beat him o'er the head with something verra heavy until he fell at my feet begging for mercy and then go and speak with his wife."

"His wife may weel be pleased that he is taking his pleasure somewhere else. Those eight children, if ye recall."

"Ah, of course. Weel, yours was still a verra good threat."

"The mon is an utter coward. One didnae need a truly good threat to make him cower but I believe one should always do one's best."

She laughed and Simon's insides tightened with desire. It was such a free sound, so full of honest delight that it acted upon him like a caress. He idly wondered when the last time was that he had made a woman laugh and did not like the fact that no memory leapt to mind. When had he become so somber, lost that sense of fun he could faintly recall having when he was younger? Simon had the sinking feeling that it was yet another thing Mary had stolen from him along with his naïveté and ability to trust easily.

Ilsabeth saw the somber and tense expression rob Simon's handsome face of that light humor he had just displayed and inwardly sighed. It had grown more and more difficult to spend even a few moments alone with the man before he retreated behind that cold, distant shield he had so perfected. Used to a family that did not hide their emotions, good and bad, she was finding dealing with Simon very difficult.

She stood up and moved to stand right next to him. The way his whole body grew tense both amused her and saddened her. It was funny how she, a small woman, could make a man like Simon afraid, but it hurt, too. Ilsabeth knew she loved him. The way her heart had grown so full it hurt when he had announced what he had done for the children told her so. The object of her devotion, however, sat there as if waiting for her to stick a knife in his ribs.

And that, she mused, was probably the problem. Sometime in his past he had been badly used and hurt by a woman. Ilsabeth suspected it was a little more than that, that the incident had been made more than a heartbreak by other circumstances, for Simon was too intelligent to shield himself as he had over one simple heartache when he had been a young man. The problem was, how did she fight that memory, that hard lesson?

"I thank ye for what ye did for Reid and Elen today," she said, and brushed a kiss over his mouth.

Suddenly his hand was at the back of her head holding her in place. A soft groan escaped him and she captured the sound of frustration and desire in her mouth. Ilsabeth was just slipping her arms around his neck to fully savor the deep, hungry kiss he was giving her when she felt him tense again. This time she pulled back, not wanting to suffer another of his abrupt retreats.

"Nay," she said, and started toward the door. "I will be the one to run away—this time. Good sleep, Simon."

Simon stared at the door for long moments after it had closed behind Ilsabeth. She saw him too clearly. That, he decided, was not a good thing. He doubted any man wanted a woman who could see him clearly.

She had it right, however. He did run away. He pulled her close, gave himself a taste of the passion they could share, and then ran for the hills. The fact that Ilsabeth knew he did actually brought the heated sting of a blush to his cheeks and he had not blushed since he had been a beardless boy.

"She isnae Mary, ye great fool," he muttered as he filled his goblet with wine.

A nudge at his leg drew his gaze down to Bonegnasher and he slipped the dog a piece of roasted venison. "There are many reasons I should stay far away from her, my old friend. Many, many reasons."

Bonegnasher rested its head on his thigh.

"But, when I sort through it all, the biggest is

that, if I grab what I want, I fear I will never want to let go. Mary's lies cut me to the bone but it wasnae just her; it was all the other lies and betrayals that happened at that time. I fear that Ilsabeth could do so much worse with naught but a simple smile of regret as she walked away from me and left me all alone."

After kissing the children good night, Ilsabeth started to leave only to have Reid pull her back to his side with a soft whisper of her name. "What is it, laddie?"

"It was verra good of Sir Simon to do what he did for me and Elen, aye?" said Reid.

She sat down on the edge of his little bed and gently brushed the hair from his forehead. "It was verra good of him. He is a verra fine mon."

"If he is so fine then mayhap ye and him would get married and Elen and I can stay with both of ye. And the cat and Bonegnasher."

And that was something she wanted so badly she could taste it, but she would not raise the child's hope. It was difficult enough to keep her own hopes under control. "I wouldnae set my heart on that happening, loving."

"Ye dinnae like him? I mean as a lass likes a laddie?"

"Oh, I like him, but when one is grown, liking isnae enough. Let it be, Reid. What happens will happen nay matter how much any of us want it or dinnae want it. Dinnae forget that I am in hiding and Sir Simon is trying to find proof that I am innocent of what I have been accused of. 'Tisnae a time to be thinking of anything save getting that proof and getting my family free to go back to Aigballa."

"I ken it. 'Tis a nice thought, though."

She laughed softly, kissed him on the cheek, and left to go to her own bedchamber. Ilsabeth moved to the window and stared out at the small moonlit garden at the back of Simon's home. A large part of her wanted to confront the man right in his bedchamber and try to take what her body ached for. That would be bold indeed. Yet, another part of her feared that even then he would flee and her heart would break.

Reid's wish was now embedded in her heart, strengthening the one that was already growing there. Ilsabeth could see it all so clearly, her and Simon wed, Reid, Elen, and their own children by their side. It was a dream that filled her heart with joy but her mind, that part of her that could see beyond the haze of desire in her eyes, was not so certain such a dream could ever come true. Simon Innes was the man her heart wanted but she was beginning to fear that his heart was way beyond her reach.

Chapter 7

Her heart pounding so fast it hurt, Ilsabeth crept through the shadowed alley running between the cooper's shop and the butcher's. She had donned her nun's attire thinking that it would keep her safe, as it had during her journey to Simon, while she went in search of some healing herbs. Poor Elen's throat was sore and Ilsabeth needed something to ease the child's pain, if only to get the child to go to sleep. Such a simple little chore. Ilsabeth did not understand how it could have gone so wrong. At least she had the herbs, she thought, and hastily swallowed the insane urge to laugh. The very last thing she needed to do at the moment was crumble beneath the weight of her fear.

It was all the fault of that foolish mongrel, she thought as she reached the end of the alley. If the animal had not been trying so hard to tear her skirts to shreds, she would not have turned around to find herself staring right into the shocked face of one of Walter's friends. Worse than that, it had been one of the very few who had seen her more than once. The man had even called her by name. Ilsabeth had babbled something she could not recall in French, yanked her skirts out of the dog's mouth, and hurried away. She was not surprised that the man had begun to follow her for she had acted in a way that would rouse anyone's suspicions.

As cautiously as she could, Ilsabeth peered into the street. Simon's house was almost visible but she could not reach it without crossing the street. From what she could see in the fading light, the man hunting her was not on the road, but that did not reassure her much. Taking a deep breath, she touched her wimple to make certain it was still straight, and then crossed the road. Ilsabeth did her best to walk as if she had no cares yet fast enough to get out of the road as swiftly as possible, praying every step of the way that she would not hear that man's voice hail her again.

The moment her feet touched the ground on Simon's side of the road, Ilsabeth gave up all pretense. She quickly looked around and then dashed into another alley. She was going to have to get to Simon's house by the back way. For once, however, luck was with her, and she made it to the kitchen door without anyone else seeing her.

"Here now, lass, just what are ye about?" demanded Old Bega as Ilsabeth stumbled into the kitchen and hastily shut the door behind her. "Ye shouldnae be outside and weel ye ken it. Ye promised Sir that ye wouldnae leave the house."

"Actually, I dinnae believe I e'er actually promised that." Ilsabeth collapsed onto the bench by the old scarred table. "I needed to fetch something that will help to soothe Elen's throat. Such things as a sore throat can easily turn deadly, ye ken."

"Aye, I ken that weel. Lost two bairns to it."

"Oh, I am so sorry."

"T'was years and years ago. As for wee Elen, I think she has just been talking too much."

Ilsabeth laughed as she removed her wimple. "That could be the truth of it. Talking *and* laughing."

"And 'tis a lovely sound to hear those two bairns laughing. That it is. But, himself is going to be verra angry if he kens that ye left the house. Did anyone see ye? I mean, see ye and ken who ye are?"

"Weel, one mon saw me. One brief look he got and I could see that he wasnae sure. He has only seen me a few times in the past."

"That would be enough, lass. Ye cannae hide them eyes."

Ilsabeth did not understand what the woman meant, but she did not argue. She may have known Old Bega for only a week but she had quickly learned that one did not argue with the woman. It was akin to banging one's head against a very hard wall. She reminded Ilsabeth of some of the women at Aigballa.

The thought of her home made her heart ache. Her family was still scattered and hiding, the only good news being that the soldiers did very little hunting for Armstrongs. Ilsabeth knew what soldiers could do to a place they had captured, however. Even if they did not destroy it, they would strip it clean of all valuables, food, and drink. Aigballa could easily be no more than a desolate wasteland before her family could return to it. At the very least, the loss of supplies could mean they suffered badly come the winter. She shook aside thoughts of home and tried to fix her mind on her current problem.

"Aye," Old Bega continued, and Ilsabeth realized the woman had not stopped talking while she had been lost in her thoughts, "if he discovers ye were out and that some fool may have recognized ye, weel," Old Bega shook her head, "I wouldnae want to be ye when he gets home. Nay, I wouldnae."

Ilsabeth prayed that her little foray remained a secret and then got up to make a soothing herbal drink for Elen.

Simon frowned as the usual whispering around the court suddenly increased. He looked toward the man who appeared to have started it all. A tall, thin man with wild red hair, his long arms waving about somewhat dangerously, stood talking to Hepbourn. Curious as to what the excitement was about, even though he knew it could all be just because some fool was seen crawling out the bedchamber window of some other fool's wife, he moved a little closer to two women who were talking with their heads close together. Their postures implied that they had something they both considered important news.

"Sir John is absolutely certain it was her," said the brunette who Simon thought was Ida Chisholm, Sir Donald's maiden sister. "Sir Walter isnae certain he believes the mon, however. But can ye imagine if 'tis true? A murderess! Here!"

A chill went through Simon but he forced himself to remain still and quiet. He needed to hear more. Ilsabeth could not possibly be so foolish as to go where she might be seen and recognized. Since her arrival at his home he had been so consumed with trying to prove her innocence and fighting her allure there could well have been a new crime committed that he was unaware of. The king certainly would not have interrupted his search for traitors just because someone was murdered.

"But, Ida, why would she be dressed as a nun? Isnae that blasphemy?" asked Morag Beaton, a pretty young woman with blond curls who Simon knew was sweet but somewhat witless. "Father Maclean will be outraged when he hears of this."

"Morag, that doesnae matter. What matters is that the woman is a murderess, she killed that sweet boy Sir Ian Ogilvie, and she is running free in our town. Why, we could wake to find that she has cut our throats."

"Ye cannae wake up if your throat is cut, Ida."

If Simon had not become so knotted up with fear and anger, he knew he would have laughed, especially since the younger woman spoke with utter seriousness. "If ye will forgive the intrusion, m'ladies," he said, stepping closer and bowing to them, "might I learn what news is this that near all here are so excited about?"

"Why, 'tis news of that Armstrong lass, Sir Innes," replied Ida Chisholm, giving Simon what she must have believed was a flirtatious smile. "Sir Ian Graham is claiming that he saw her right here, in town, right out upon the road. Aye, met her on the street, he did, and she was dressed as a nun."

"Is that what the mon is saying? 'Tis a verra strange tale." Simon was a little surprised that he sounded so calm, even mildly amused, when inside he was raging with so many different emotions he doubted he could name them all even if he wanted to. "Why would the woman come here, right within the reach of those who hunt her for the crimes of murder and treason?" It was a question he was aching to ask Ilsabeth.

" 'Tis said that she plots to kill our king so would-nae she have to come here so that she could get close enough to him to do it?" asked Morag.

"That is something to consider, Miss Beaton," replied Simon. "Yet, with her plot already discovered, I cannae see what she would hope to gain by coming here. She has to ken that she would ne'er get within striking distance of our liege. That is, assuming that she is a killer and a traitor."

"Why do ye think it is an assumption? Her dagger was found in that poor man's heart. The lass isnae right in the head, is what it is," said Ida. "None of those Armstrongs are."

Simon found he was certainly questioning Ilsabeth's sanity at the moment. "I have no proof save for the dagger and I didnae see her use it, nor does it make sense to me that someone who is clever enough to plot against our king would be foolish enough to leave her dagger in the heart of the mon she killed." He was pleased to see both women frown in thought and decided it was past time to start working harder at sowing some doubt around the court. "I believe I shall go and speak to Sir Ian myself. If ye will be so kind as to excuse me, ladies?"

With every step he took toward Sir Ian and Hepbourn, Simon fought to get his emotions back under tight control. Telling himself that Ilsabeth would not try to flee without the children, and there had been no mention of them, did not help much. He wanted to go home immediately to make certain that she was still there. And, if she was, he was seriously considering chaining her to the wall.

"Ah, Sir Simon," hailed Hepbourn. "Just the mon we need to speak to. My friend here"—Hepbourn hastily introduced Simon and Ian—"claims he saw Ilsabeth right here in the town and dressed as a nun." He laughed and shook his head, but Simon could hear a false note in that laughter. "I cannae see why she would e'er come here, can ye? Nay right into the lion's den."

"I tell ye, it was her," snapped Ian. "A mon doesnae forget eyes like that lass has, nay once he has looked into them."

No he does not, Simon silently agreed. "There is naught here for her except the gallows. It makes no sense for her to come here and then go about the town as if none would see her, disguise or nay."

"There, Ian, isnae that what I have been saying?" Hepbourn patted the other man on the shoulder.

"Then why did she run away from me?" asked Ian.

"Ye probably frightened the poor lass. Nuns are e'er afraid of men."

Simon had the strongest feeling that Hepbourn did not believe a word he was saying. That could only mean that Hepbourn was not sure if Ian was right or not, but was determined to divert the man's attention. All the reasons Simon could think of for the man to do that were bad ones. Nevertheless, he joined in the game. His objective, however, was to divert both men and as soon as he did he was headed home to either hunt down Ilsabeth or strangle her, or even both.

"I find it difficult to believe the woman would come into the very heart of the enemy," Simon said. "Whether she is guilty as accused or nay, she would have to ken that she is being hunted and, if caught, might not be given any chance to prove her innocence."

"Innocence?" Hepbourn laughed. "The woman's dagger was found in Ian's heart. How can ye think she is innocent?"

"I didnae say that I thought her innocent or guilty, just that there is nay any proof to say she is guilty. Naught but that dagger and we all ken how easy it would be for someone to use her dagger to do the killing, kenning full weel that she would be blamed."

Ian nodded slowly. "True. Verra true."

"Ye are both just saying this because she is a woman," snapped Hepbourn. "Women are capable of killing and plotting."

"Of course they are," agreed Simon. "Sometimes with far more stealth and cunning than any mon. But 'tis my way to look for the truth, Sir Walter, and I havenae found any proof that she or her clan are what everyone is claiming they are."

"Weel, ye just keep searching for your cursed proof. The rest of us will search for that traitorous killer."

"If ye feel ye must. I would suggest that ye bring her to the king alive. After all, if she is hastily executed and then proven to be innocent, ye would become the killer, now wouldnae ye?" As Hepbourn stood there speechless, Simon turned to Ian. "Good to meet ye, sir."

That last statement to Hepbourn probably had not been the wisest thing he had ever said, Simon thought as he made his way through the crowd. He did not regret it though. The man was working hard to get a young woman accused, tried, and convicted of crimes Simon was increasingly certain Hepbourn himself was guilty of. If Hepbourn was not so visible at the king's court and so well liked, Simon would have grabbed him, dragged him to a private place and happily beaten the truth out of him. Now, however, he had to get back home and try to calmly talk some sense into a certain blue-eyed woman.

Ilsabeth was just settling herself beneath the warm covers of her bed, mourning the fact that she was doing so alone again, when the door to her bedchamber slammed open. She barely smothered the scream that rushed to her throat as she thought the king's soldiers had finally found her. Just as she leapt from the bed, she realized it was only one man and, in the dim flickering light from the fire that man looked to be a very angry Simon. Somehow he had discovered that she had left the protection of his house.

"Have ye lost whae'er few wits ye may have had in that bonnie head?" he snapped as he shut the door behind him and advanced on the bed.

Ilsabeth was so stunned by this display of hot anger from her cool, often cold, and very con-

trolled man that it took her a moment to understand what he had just said. "Are ye calling me witless?" Anger prodded her to leap back onto the bed
and swiftly cross it until she knelt on the edge,
meeting Simon's glare with one of her own.

"What else can one call a lass who goes wandering about the town e'en though she kens she is
being hunted for the crimes of murder and treason?"

"I needed to get some herbs for a potion."

"I pray it was one to make your wits keener or, at
least, give ye some understanding of the danger ye
are in."

"Elen had a soreness in her throat!"

Despite a pinch of fear for the child who had
quickly wound herself around his heart, Simon's
fury did not ease much. "If they only thought ye a
murderess, it wouldnae be so dangerous, but they
think ye are a traitor, too. Can ye nay understand
that, if they get their hands on ye, I might nay be
able to stop a swift execution? Not everyone cares
that there be actual proof of a crime. The king has
already suffered the bitter sting of betrayal. There
will be little mercy to be found if ye are brought before him."

She knew that, but tried hard not to think of it
too often. The terror it inspired chilled her to the
very marrow of her bones. Instead, Ilsabeth settled
all of her attention on Simon's anger. He was a man
who kept a tight rein on his emotions yet he was
scolding and bellowing at her because he knew she
had put her life in danger. She had to believe that it
was more than a strong sense of responsibility for
her that drove his fear and anger.

The moment she placed her hands on his cheeks all his muttering about foolish women marching blindly into danger ceased. She leaned forward until her body was pressed against his and heard him catch his breath. The stormy gray of his eyes changed into the rich, dark gray of desire. He lifted his hands to grasp her arms, but his hold on her quickly turned into a caress, and Ilsabeth trembled.

"I wore my nun's garb," she said, and brushed a kiss over his mouth. "It was but ill fate that put that fool there to see me."

"He not only saw ye; he recognized ye." He had to struggle to keep his eyes open when she kissed his cheek. "The whole of the king's court was whispering about it. Soldiers will now be looking for a blue-eyed nun."

"And they willnae find her for she willnae be skipping through town again nor at the nearest convent nor anywhere else they might look." She wrapped her arms around his neck and smiled at him. "I wouldnae have done it at all if I had had any other choice. MacBean and Old Bega didnae ken what I needed, where to ask for it, or even which would be the best to select, and I couldnae ignore Elen's sore throat. True, it now appears that it wasnae of much importance, but it could have been a sign of something more, of something deadly."

"I ken it." Simon found it difficult to speak while she was kissing his neck. The warmth of her lips was rushing straight down to his groin. "Ilsabeth, ye should stop. I am nay at my strongest just now."

"Oh, good." Ilsabeth nipped at his chin as she watched his face and nearly grinned when his eyes widened.

"Honor demands . . ."

"Bugger honor."

Simon laughed briefly at her crudity but quickly grew serious again. "Ye are a maid."

"Aye, I am. A maid of one and twenty years. A maid who was betrothed. A maid who suddenly is verra, verra tired of being a maid."

He groaned softly as she unlaced his shirt and kissed the hollow at the base of his throat. Simon ached to grab what she offered, to wallow mindlessly in the passion he knew they could share, but a few shredded tatters of good sense remained. It was enough to keep him from immediately hurling her to the bed, tearing off the thin linen nightgown she wore, and burying himself deep inside her. If he was going to become her lover, he was going to attempt to do so with some finesse. He may have lost the control to refuse what she offered, but he was determined to find enough control to make her first time with a man something she would recall with fondness and pleasure.

"Are ye thinking of running away again?" she whispered by his ear before lightly biting his earlobe.

"I should. Ye can ne'er return to being a maid."

"I should pray not."

Simon pushed her away. The disappointment and hurt upon her face decided him. He might not understand why she wanted him, but she did, and his running each time desire flared between them was hurting her. That he could not do. It shamed him to realize how little thought he had given to her feelings each time he had fled the desire she stirred within him. He started to shed his clothes and the way her eyes brightened with interest stroked his vanity. He just hoped the beautiful eyes considered to view him with favor when she saw his back.

"No running this time?"

Ilsabeth was not surprised to hear how husky her voice had grown, for the sight of Simon's body had her panting like a hard-run hound. His shoulders and chest were broad enough to please any woman. The rest of his tall, lean body was all smooth skin and taut muscle. There was only a small patch of hair on his chest. Her gaze moved down his body until she saw the dark arrow of hair that began below his navel and thickened slightly around his groin. The long, hard jut of his manhood told her that he was more than ready to become her lover. He stood with his legs apart, the hair-roughened strength of those limbs making her palms itch with the urge to touch them.

"Nay, no more running," he said, and nearly grinned at the way her gaze settled on his groin. "Are ye about to run?"

"Of course not."

"Good." His voice came out as almost a growl as he leapt onto the bed and pushed her down until she was sprawled beneath him. "I think I might just chase ye if ye did."

Simon kissed her, savoring the taste of her as he unlaced her nightgown. As soon as he undid the last tie, he pulled it off her and tossed it aside. Her body was far more lushly built than he had imagined during too many sleepless nights, her breast full and high, dark rose nipples hard and inviting. Her hips bowed out nicely from her small waist and her legs looked surprisingly long and well muscled. The sight of the tidy wedge of black curls between her pale thighs had him fighting the urge to bury his face in there. He placed his hands just beneath her breasts and slowly moved them upward until he held the soft flesh in both hands. Ilsabeth gasped and he kissed her again.

Ilsabeth wrapped her arms around him as she lost herself in his hungry kiss. She stroked his broad muscular back and could not halt the way her body briefly tensed in shock. Simon's back was covered in scars. Before she could hide her reaction to them, she felt Simon's body tense as well.

"Can ye abide it?" he asked as he nuzzled her throat and tried to sound as if her answer did not matter to him.

"Aye, of course I can, but, Jesu, Simon, what happened?"

"I will tell ye later. Now that I have ye naked and beneath me, the verra last thing I wish to do is to speak about an old misery."

He kissed his way down to her breasts. The way he was caressing them with his lightly calloused hands, stroking the hard tips with his long fingers until they ached, had her passion running hot. When he took one taut end deep into his mouth, suckling and lashing it with his tongue, Ilsabeth was surprised she did not swoon from the force of the desire that swamped her.

She was just caressing his taut backside when he slipped his hand between her legs. The way he stroked her heated flesh and slipped his finger inside her in imitation of the intimacy they both craved, had her crying out in demand. Ilsabeth was not precisely sure how well they would fit together, but she wanted him inside her. Now.

"Need to go slowly," Simon said, nearly groaning the words against her silken breasts. He slipped another finger inside her and trembled at the way her wet heat closed tight around his fingers. "Need to ready ye."

"I have been ready for days."

Simon choked out a laugh and then began to slowly join their bodies. When he reached the barrier of her maidenhead he took a deep breath, pulled back, and then rammed his way through it until he was fully seated within her. Ilsabeth's soft shriek did not startle him but the sting of her small sharp teeth digging into his shoulder did. It also made his passion soar until he was a hairsbreadth from a complete loss of control. She clung to him with her whole body as he pounded into her, cursing himself as a brute but unable to stop. Her release hit hard and, reveling in her soft cries and the hot, wet clasp of her body, he swiftly joined her in that sweet, rapid tumble.

It took Simon several moments before he could catch his breath enough to ask, "Are ye hurt?"

Ilsabeth thought on her answer for a moment and then said, "Nay. Why? Are ye ready to run again?" She lazily caressed his body everywhere she could reach.

"Nay, and once I regain my breath and my strength, I will show ye that I can do this slowly, too."

"I eagerly await the lesson."

He smiled against her skin. Simon did not think he had ever experienced such passion before. It astonished him that he had held back for so long. A little voice in his head told him that this had been a mistake, that he should not have given in to his desire for a woman who had been put under his protection, but he ruthlessly silenced it. That was a problem to sort out later, after he proved her innocence.

Ilsabeth stared up at the ceiling even though it was too shadowed to see anything. Simon almost idly kissed and caressed her and the spark of desire began to heat her blood again. She should be blindly happy. The man she loved was in her arms.

One little thing dimmed that happiness, however. Simon had not spoken one word about how he felt about her. If he had said anything while they had made love, she had been too blinded by her own passion to hear it, but instinct told her he had not said anything more than passionate words about how she tasted or how soft her skin was. She needed so much more than that.

Patience, she warned herself. She may have known he would be the man for her from nearly the moment she set eyes on him, but not everyone made such an important decision so quickly. Men were also notoriously slow to see where their hearts lay.

Neither was she truly free to follow her heart. It could even be cruel to try and make him love her when she might soon be dead. Ilsabeth had seen enough of the world's injustices to know that just because she was innocent did not mean she would escape punishment.

She also admitted that she was the one who needed this closeness now, whether words of love were spoken by him or not. Hiding, fearing the possibility that she could be dragged off to some deep, dark dungeon at any moment, and afraid for her family, she needed someone to hold on to. For now she would allow that to be enough. She would push her love for him to one side and make no demands. The very last thing she wished to do was send him running again.

Chapter 8

"Where is that child?" demanded Old Bega as she stomped into the hall where Reid and Ilsabeth worked on his numbers. "I cannae find the bairn anywhere. She was with me in the kitchen and then she was gone."

Ilsabeth felt a tickle of worry cut through her high spirits. She had woken up in Simon's arms for the third morning in a row and was finally certain that he was no longer running from her. He had not even crept from the bed like some thief in the night but lingered to make love to her again. She was not fool enough to mistake his passion or sweet words for love, but she was hopeful that she would soon know both. Ilsabeth could not believe that a man could make love to a woman as he did her and hold her throughout the night without feeling more for her than simply passion.

"Mayhap she is but playing hide-and-go-seek with ye," said Ilsabeth. "Elen does love that game."

"I dinnae think so. We had a wee talk about how

she must let us all ken if 'tis time to play that game and she has been verra good at doing so. And she isnae verra good at hiding, is she, yet me and MacBean cannae find her. And Bonegnasher cannae find her either."

That tickle of worry flared up into a chilling fear. The dog was an excellent hunter. It should have had no trouble at all finding a tiny girl who often gave her hiding place away by giggling. The fact that the dog found nothing was alarming.

"Come along, Reid," said Ilsabeth as she stood up, doing her best to hide her sudden fear from the boy. "We need to find your sister."

An hour later, Ilsabeth had to agree with Old Bega. The child was not in the house. Ilsabeth was now fighting the urge to run outside yelling Elen's name. She set Bonegnasher to tracking the child again and the dog ended up at the kitchen door, scratching on the wood and whining. Once outside, the animal went straight to the garden gate, which was wide open, and waited for her to tell him to come back or continue on the hunt. Since she could not loose the dog in the town without someone at its side, she called it back.

"She has gone awandering," said Reid, his eyes wide with fear for his sister. "I have told her again and again that she shouldnae do that and she will be good for a wee while but then she does it again. She could get hurt. I dinnae think she understands that."

"Aye, she could, and the verra young take time to see that there is a lot of danger out there, but we will find her," said Ilsabeth as she hurried back into the house to change into her nun's attire. "Bega,

MacBean," she said as she entered the kitchen, "Elen has gotten out through the garden gate. We shall all need to search for her."

"Nay, ye must stay here," said MacBean. "Ye cannae risk being seen again."

"'Tis nay a risk—"

"It is and dinnae try to tell me it isnae. Ye were seen when ye went out in that nun's gown. That means the soldiers will be looking about for a blue-eyed nun. Aye, them and anyone else who has heard the tale. We dinnae exactly have a lot of nuns about this place, ye ken. We will take the dog—"

"Ye cannae do that. Ye cannae let anyone make a connection atween Elen and Simon. He hasnae said that plain, but he hasnae let anyone ken that the children are here, either. Weel, except for Donald, who willnae dare speak of it, and Tormand, who can be trusted. I am thinking Simon fears I may have been seen when I first came here. Now that ye tell me that ye dinnae see many nuns, I can see that that is a possibility."

MacBean cursed. "Another reason ye cannae start running about the town dressed as a nun again."

That and the fact that she had more or less promised Simon that she would not do so, but MacBean did not need to know that. "Then I shall dress as naught but a poor maid with my hair covered as many of the wedded lasses cover theirs. Verra few people pay any heed to a poor maid."

Ignoring MacBean's stuttered protests, Ilsabeth hurried to her room, Old Bega at her heels. Together they got her dressed quickly, her hair braided and hidden beneath a kerchief. It was a thin disguise but, if anyone was looking for her at the moment, they were looking for a blue-eyed nun, not a servant. The disguise would work long enough for her to find Elen.

Simon was going to be angry, she thought as she headed back down the stairs. For a brief moment she considered sending him a message and waiting for him to come and help find Elen. She quickly shook that thought aside. There was no time. Elen had been missing for too long already.

Both she and Old Bega ignored MacBean's continued complaints. He finally gave up the fight when Ilsabeth sent him and Bega off in two different directions while she and Reid went in a third one. There was a very pretty little girl wandering the streets of the town and they all knew how many dangers such a child could face.

It was growing dark by the time she and Reid saw Elen. Ilsabeth's heart lodged in her throat as she watched the man Elen spoke to stroke the little girl's bright hair. It could be an innocent touch but Ilsabeth's heart and mind were both clamoring *danger.* There was something about the way the man acted with Elen that was just wrong. Elen was not smiling at the man, either, and she smiled at everyone.

Before she could think of a quiet way to extract Elen from the man, Reid started to run toward them. The hard, angry look upon his young face told Ilsabeth that he might well know exactly what sort of danger his sister was in. Ilsabeth cursed and hurried after him before he could start a confrontation that would draw a lot of attention, but feared she would be too late.

"Dinnae touch her," yelled Reid as he grabbed Elen by the arm and yanked her back, away from the man.

"Here now, laddie, what are ye doing?" said the man, his plump face twisting into a scowl. "I was just helping the wee lass. She is lost, aye?"

"She doesnae need your sort of help." Reid kicked the man in the shins, causing the man to howl in pain and anger. "I ken what ye are. Ye were-nae going to help her at all. Ye just wanted to—"

"Reid," Ilsabeth snapped as she reached the boy, and then she gasped as the man backhanded Reid across the face. "Dinnae touch that boy!"

"The wee bastard kicked me!" The man reached for Elen. "And he was trying to steal away with the lass."

"That lass is his sister." Ilsabeth pushed Elen behind her. "We have been looking for her for hours."

For a moment the man just frowned and studied her and Reid, who now stood at her side. Then his too pale eyes narrowed and he gave Ilsabeth a smile that made her skin crawl. She knew what he saw, a woman and two children who clearly had less money and power than he did. He looked at Elen and then back at Ilsabeth. She had to wonder just how many little girls he had gotten his hands on in this way and it made her stomach churn.

"Ach, now, lass, I am thinking ye could use a wee bit of coin, aye? Too many mouths to feed and all that. Why dinnae I just make the burden on your shoulders a wee bit lighter. I will pay ye for the lass here. A wee bit of training and she will make a fine servant in my house."

"I wouldnae sell ye a sick goat, ye pig," snapped

Ilsabeth, trying not to think of how many other little girls he had bought this way, offering a false future for a daughter to some poor mother. "Ye cannae hide what ye are. E'en the lad saw it. Ye ought to be nailed to a wall where all can pass and spit on ye."

The man's face went so red she thought he might collapse at her feet. Instead he swung one meaty fist toward her head. Ilsabeth ducked the blow and pushed Elen toward Reid. Out of the corner of her eye she could see several of the king's soldiers watching them with far too much interest for her liking. At the moment all they could see was her back. If they came any closer they could see her eyes and too many people had told her they were memorable. This was not a good time to test the truth of that. She had to end this quickly and flee but the way the man began to curse her told her that would not be an easy task. Offers of money had not worked and now he was intent upon using intimidation and brute force.

Simon heard the sound of an argument even before he saw who was making all the noise. Shock brought him to a halt as he saw a woman and two children confronting a man who was doing his best to hit the woman or the boy, all the while trying to grab the little girl away from her protectors. The children were easy to recognize and that told Simon who the woman dodging the man's flailing fists was. Ilsabeth had obviously found herself a new disguise but it had not kept her out of trouble any more than the last one had. He was beginning to think she attracted trouble the way a table attracted dust.

This time was worse for there were half a dozen soldiers watching the battle with keen interest.

Cursing as he watched the soldiers start toward Ilsabeth and the others, Simon hurried to get there first. At the moment, Ilsabeth was turned away from the soldiers and that might be all that saved her. He grabbed the man swinging at her by the wrist, halting the blow that had been aimed at Ilsabeth's face. The man tried to wrench free but Simon tightened his grip until the man paled and stood still, finally realizing how close he was to having his wrist snapped. Then he looked at Ilsabeth.

"Thank ye for aiding my children, mistress," he said as he held her gaze, "but I am sure ye have work ye must need to return to. I wouldnae want your charity to cause ye trouble with your mistress. I can handle it all now."

Ilsabeth opened her mouth to argue, but then saw Simon glance pointedly behind her and recalled the soldiers. She curtsied and ran, darting around Simon and the man she hoped Simon would soundly beat. Without stopping, she wove her way through the alleys and back gardens until she reached Simon's home. She hurried up to her bedchamber to wash up and considered all the advantages of hiding there until the anger she had seen in Simon's eyes faded a little.

The thought of behaving so cowardly was enough to stiffen her backbone. No doubt Simon would think she had broken some promise to him by leaving the house again. Ilsabeth doubted he would be able to see all the fine nuances of what she had said. Nevertheless, she would meet him when he returned home. He would have to see that she had had no choice.

Simon looked at the man whose wrist he still held, tempted to break it even though the man was no longer fighting him. It was Colin Rose, the second son of a nearby laird and a man rumored to be very fond of young girls. He then looked at Elen, who peered around an angry Reid. It was all too clear to see that the rumors were true. There was no doubt in his mind what Colin Rose had intended to do with Elen and Simon was even more tempted to snap the man's wrist. The thought of killing the man was even more tempting but Simon could not afford the sort of trouble that would bring him, not now.

"I didnae realize they were your bairns, Sir Simon," said Colin. "I didnae e'en ken ye had wed."

"I havenae," Simon said. "These are my foster children."

The man grew even paler and Simon wondered if Colin Rose was about to faint like some delicate woman. He could not help but think of how Ilsabeth, a woman wrongly accused, had to hide and was in fear of her life, while this man who hurt small children for his own pleasure walked free and unafraid. It was, perhaps, time to make the man taste a little fear.

"They may nay be of my blood, Colin Rose, but they are as dear to me as if they were. I would be certain to harshly punish any mon who harmed them. I have a special distaste for those who hurt children," he added softly. "I shall be sure to keep a close watch on you from now on."

"Ye having some trouble, Sir Simon?" asked the biggest of the five soldiers, who finally stepped forward.

"Not any longer," Simon said, and shoved Colin Rose away from him. "I believe we have come to an understanding." He looked at Reid and Elen. "Shall we return home while ye explain to me why Elen is out and wandering at this time of the night?"

A quick glance behind as he and the children started to walk away revealed the soldiers circling Colin Rose. The men had understood what the man was and why he had tried to grab Elen. Simon knew Colin Rose would be crawling home tonight, broken and bloody. It was tempting to go and join the soldiers in that task but Simon turned his attention back to the children.

"Weel?" He looked at Reid. "Why are ye out here?"

"Elen sometimes wanders, Simon," answered Reid. "I always kept a close watch on her because she is apt to decide to just go for a walk. I didnae think she would keep doing it now that we have a fine roof o'er our heads and so I stopped watching."

"What ye should have done is warned us of this. We would have been able to watch her more closely, made sure all the doors and gates were more tightly latched."

"I ken it." Reid started to look back as he heard a man's cries and the sounds of fists hitting flesh but Simon put his hand on the boy's head and forced him to keep looking forward.

"The soldiers have decided that Colin Rose needs a wee lesson in how a mon should treat children," Simon said.

"Will they kill him?" asked Reid.

"Nay, for they dinnae think him worth hanging for."

Simon picked Elen up after she flung herself at his legs. She was trembling and clung to his neck with a strength that surprised him. Elen might be too young to understand the nature of the danger she had just faced, but she obviously had enough instinct to know that she had been in danger. He just wished that would be enough to make her stop her wandering.

"Has anyone e'er hurt her, Reid?" he asked.

"Nay. There was a time or two when I feared it might happen but, nay, no one has. 'Tis why I stayed in the wood though. Told Ilsabeth it was because I didnae ken where else to go and that wasnae a lie, but I also didnae want Elen in the village where she would be seen a lot and maybe taken."

"Verra wise."

"Are ye going to yell at Ilsabeth again?"

"Ah, ye heard me yell at her that time, did ye?"

"Ye were verra loud."

Simon hoped the child had not heard much more than that. "She shouldnae be leaving the safety of the house. The lass doesnae seem to ken how easily she can be recognized or remembered nay matter what guise she dons."

"Aye, 'tis her eyes. I dinnae think I have e'er seen such a blue. Ilsabeth doesnae ken that there is anything special about her eyes, ye ken. But, she had to help find Elen. Ye can see why we couldnae leave her out on her own."

"I understand but that doesnae mean I like it. If Ilsabeth is caught it willnae go weel for her. She has to remain out of sight until I can find the real killer and the real traitors."

Simon seriously considered locking Ilsabeth in the cellars, perhaps even chaining her to a wall down there. He did understand that she had had no real choice this time. Elen was too small to be walking around the town on her own. It was not just filth like Colin Rose that the child could be in danger from. Understanding did little to ease his fear for Ilsabeth, however.

He found her waiting for him in his ledger room after he had handed the children over to Old Bega. Simon watched her, rather enjoying the faint signs of nervousness she revealed as he poured them each a tankard of cider. She had come too close to being captured tonight. The thought of just how close she had come still chilled his blood.

"Ye didnae heed my words of wisdom at all, did ye?" he said as he sat down and watched her from across his worktable.

"I did, but I couldnae leave Elen out there all alone," Ilsabeth replied.

He sighed and rested his head against the back of his chair. "Nay, ye couldnae."

Ilsabeth was so relieved that he understood that she drank down her cider and then went and sat on his lap. "I thought about sending ye a message and waiting for ye to come and help find her, but then I kenned that would take too long."

"Colin Rose would have had her tucked up in his house by then."

"Is that who that was? Ye ken the mon and what he is and yet he is still walking about?"

"No proof. And a laird for a father. And he will-nae be walking about after tonight, at least not for a verra long time."

"Did ye beat him?"

"So eager ye sound. Nay, I wanted to, but the sol-diers decided to do it. They must have kenned I wouldnae help the mon for they began to beat him while I was still close enough to hear it." He set his empty tankard down and pulled her into his arms. "I kept Reid from looking and just kept right on walking."

"Do ye feel guilty about that?"

Simon thought about that for a moment. "Nay, not a bit." He smiled when she laughed.

"I was so afraid for her, Simon," she whispered.

"Aye, and ye were right to be. She needs to be watched verra closely. I have naught but admiration for young Reid for keeping her alive and safe for so long. She may be the bonniest wee thing I have e'er seen and as sweet as summer fruit, but she is also a great deal of trouble on two wee feet."

"She certainly is." Ilsabeth kissed his throat. "We must needs go and have our meal in but a few mo-ments."

"I was thinking we might have a little something else first."

Wriggling on his lap, she could feel how hard he had grown. "I can tell but it will have to wait until later." She sat up and kissed him before hopping off his lap. "I am certain Old Bega has had a stern talk with Elen but I believe I will add a few words myself. See you in a moment."

Simon watched her leave and shook his head. He had gone from sitting by the fire with a dog and a cat to having a house full. He certainly was not lonely now.

Ilsabeth frowned at the door to Simon's ledger room and wondered if she should go in. MacBean had brought Simon a message and she had not seen the man since. She wished he would share such things with her, but she was not going to try and make him do so, if only because she knew she would be hurt if he refused to do it. She had not even pressed for the tale about how his back had become so scarred and yet he had said he would tell her.

The problem was that, unless he began to share his life with her in more than the bedchamber, it was going to be very hard to win his love. She would be reduced to being no more than his bedmate and that thought twisted her heart. Her parents shared everything as did most of her other married kin. That was what she wanted with Simon but she knew that if she tried to force that sharing it would never be right. It had to be given willingly.

Her only thought was to spend as much time as she could with him when they were not making love. He would have to talk to her then. Once he became more comfortable talking to her, he would begin to share his news, good or bad. At least, she hoped so, she thought, and grimaced as she rapped on the door.

Stepping into the room after he called out permission to enter, she frowned. He was just sitting there with a tankard of ale in his hands. Ilsabeth had the distinct feeling he had just been staring at the walls. She placed the small plate of fruit on his table and smiled at him.

Simon could not stop himself from smiling back. There was something about the way Ilsabeth looked at him that made him happy. He needed that at the moment, too. The king had demanded his presence in the morning and Simon had nothing to report. That always left his liege displeased and a displeased king was not what Simon wanted to face early in the day.

The lack of news to give the king had made Simon all too aware of how little he was discovering concerning the true killer and the traitors. Instinct told him time was running out. He could only pray that did not mean it was running out for Ilsabeth. It was frustrating. All he needed was one hint, one misstep by the guilty ones, and he could unravel the whole twisted mess. Killing Ogilvie had been a mistake but the killer had covered his trail very well.

"If ye are verra busy, I shall leave then," said Ilsabeth.

Simon grabbed her by the hand and pulled her into his lap. "I am never too busy to see you. I was but thinking. I feel I am missing something but cannae grasp what it is."

She turned in his lap and kissed his forehead. "Dinnae think on it so hard then. 'Tis as if thinking on something too hard and long only pushes what ye search for further away. It will come."

"So I should just clear my head then, should I?"

"Aye. Ye can but try."

"I ken just the way to do that, too." He cleared away the things cluttering the top of his worktable, picked her up, and set her on top of it.

Ilsabeth squeaked in surprise when he began to push up her skirts, kissing his way up her legs. "Simon, dinnae say ye mean to do that here?"

"Aye. 'Tis one of the thoughts that was turning about in my mind."

Simon decided that they had been lovers long enough for him to be a bit more daring. He had not lied, either. As he had sat there staring at the walls and his worktable he had suddenly seen Ilsabeth there, her skirts up to her hips and his head between her thighs. It was not something he had indulged himself in very often. In truth, he could only recall one or two times. Most of the women he had bedded had been with a lot of men and he had not been inclined to get that intimate. Learning how to stroke a woman with his fingers had served him well enough. Yet, just thinking of feasting upon Ilsabeth had made him as hard as a rock.

Ilsabeth was torn between desire and embarrassment as Simon kissed her thighs and pushed her skirts up so high she was fully exposed to his eyes. It was foolish, for he had seen all of her in the bed they shared, yet that had never made her feel so brazenly displayed. Then she felt his warm lips touch the heated softness between her thighs and she tensed.

"Simon?" She blushed when she realized she had squeaked out his name like some timid mouse.

"Hush, sweet Ilsabeth. Let me taste ye."

Before she could protest, he did just that. It took

but a few strokes of his tongue and she no longer cared what he saw or did so long as the pleasure he gave her continued. She cried out his name as she felt her body tighten but he ignored her, bringing her to release with his mouth. While she was still reeling from the force of it, he pushed her legs up and thrust into her. Ilsabeth did not even have time to catch her breath before he was sending her spiraling up to the heights all over again but this time he joined her in that blissful fall into passion's abyss.

Simon collapsed on top of Ilsabeth, still shaking from the strength of his release. He could feel her body trembling beneath him, hear the way she struggled to catch her breath, and nearly smiled, feeling very smug and pleased with himself. Ilsabeth was a very passionate woman and he reveled in her warmth, but mostly he liked the way he could drive her wild with desire.

When he was finally able to move, he helped her sit up. The way she blushed as she straightened her skirts amused him, but he struggled to hide it. He leaned forward and kissed her.

"Dinnae fret so, lass," he said. "Ye are beautiful in your passion."

Ilsabeth was not so certain she believed that. She could not see how any woman could be beautiful splayed out on top of a table with her skirts up to her waist. Honesty compelled her to admit that she had found a lot of pleasure in what he had done, however, and was determined to overcome the uncomfortable bouts of modesty. He also looked a little smug so she found it surprisingly easy to push aside her embarrassment.

"I just hadnae realized ye could do such things on a table," she muttered.

"Ah, bonnie Ilsabeth, ye can do this in so many places and in so many ways. I shall enjoy showing ye."

For a brief moment she wondered how he thought he could do that when she could not leave the house for fear of being grabbed by the king's soldiers, but she shoved the thought out of her head. Simon was looking far less troubled than he had when she had first entered the room. She would not remind him that the future did not yet look secure enough for him to be making such plans. Instead she wrapped her arms around his neck and kissed him. The fact that he was thinking of things that would require her to be in his future was enough to please her for now.

"Do ye think we can try one of your many ways in a common old bed next time?" she asked.

Simon laughed, picked her up in his arms, and headed for their bedchamber.

Chapter 9

"Morning."

Ilsabeth smiled sleepily. Simon spoke the word against her neck and the warmth of his breath seeped into her skin. " 'Tis morning so soon?"

"Aye and 'tis time for ye to assist me in greeting the new day in a proper manner."

She slid her arms around his neck and welcomed his kiss. Simon looked so much younger and less serious in the morning. It gave her a glimpse of the man he could be, although she loved the man he was now, too. Ilsabeth just wanted Simon to learn how to enjoy life more.

Ilsabeth knew she should probably go and confess her sins, do her allotted penances, and then stay as far away from Simon Innes as possible. She also knew she would never do that. Nothing she did with Simon felt sinful and she suffered from no guilt whatsoever. Love was what kept her in Simon's arms, in his bed, and she could not see any sin in that. She knew her family would not either.

"I dinnae think this is exactly proper," she said, and gasped in delight as he kissed his way to her breasts.

" 'Tis the best way to ensure that a mon wakes up and goes to his work with a smile upon his face."

Ilsabeth's laughter was stopped by his kiss. She gave herself over to the passion he could so effortlessly stir inside her. Her last clear thought as he joined their bodies was a touch of astonishment that he did not yet see how utterly perfect they were together.

Dressed, his body pleasantly sated, and prepared to leave for the king's court, Simon paused by the bed to stare down at a sleeping Ilsabeth. She was sprawled on her stomach, her tousled hair covering most of her face. It was a mistake to keep crawling into bed with her but he doubted he could stop even upon threat of dismemberment by her family. He needed her and that frightened him in so many ways he dared not count them. The most important was that she brought a joy into his life that had been missing for too long.

What did he know about keeping a woman like her, a gently raised laird's daughter from a large and loving family? What did he have to offer her to make her want to stay with him once she was free of the danger she was in? He was a king's man but that could change at any moment, the position lost in one misstep, one wrong word, or even his liege waking up in a sour mood. He did not even have a clan to call his own any longer. Even if he used his money to buy some small manor or the like, he knew nothing about how to make it profitable enough to keep her in the manner she was accustomed to. The honorable thing to do was to send her home as soon as it was safe to do so and that was going to tear him apart.

Shaking his head at his maudlin thoughts, he brushed a soft kiss over her shoulder and left the room. He had told her that the king had demanded his presence. Simon had the strong feeling that he was not being summoned so that he could be praised for all his hard work. There were too many rumors whirling around the court, ones that put his integrity into question, and the king was neither deaf nor blind. As he began the long walk to where the court was being held, Simon tried to think of answers to some of the many questions he was sure he would be asked.

By the time he was shown in to see the king, Simon believed he could soothe any suspicions or anger raised by all the rumors. One look at his king's angry face told him that he might have allowed himself to be a little too confident about that. He wondered if he had missed hearing some of the rumors, ones far more damning than the ones he had heard. The anger stirring within him over being questioned about his integrity, his honesty, after so many years of faithful service and proving himself, was not easy to tamp down.

"I dinnae like what I have been hearing, Simon," said the king.

"Rumors have always flown about the court like flies o'er a carcass, my liege," Simon said, swallowing the insult given by the lack of an invitation to sit down.

"Not ones that have me wondering if the mon we all look to for justice has been corrupted."

Simon struggled to hide the fury that swelled inside him. "I havenae heard those rumors yet, sire."

"Nay? 'Tis said that ye are verra close to the Murrays, a clan now tainted by their association with those traitors the Armstrongs of Aigballa. 'Tis said that the woman who murdered Ian is running about the town freely yet ye dinnae seem to be able to find her. It reminded me of how ye have twice removed yourself from my court to run to the aid of a Murray accused of murder. What do ye believe I should think of all that? Is it nay enough to make any mon begin to question if ye are able to be fair in all of this, if ye can truly look beyond friendship to find the truth?"

"My liege, I did indeed help exonerate both James Drummond and Tormand Murray. There is no denying that. I can only swear to ye upon my honor that, if either mon had been proven guilty of the murders they were accused of, I would have led them to the scaffold myself." Simon could tell by the narrow-eyed look the king was giving him that his words were being carefully weighed if not fully believed. It was also possible that the anger churning in his gut had seeped out into his voice. "I *will* find the one who murdered your cousin and who plots against ye. Ye have my word on that. Aye, nay matter who that might prove to be, he or she will be brought to ye to face justice."

The king sighed and rubbed at his temple, briefly revealing the strain he was under. "Why is that woman roaming freely about the town and dressed as a nun, for sweet Mary's sake."

"She isnae." At least not at the moment, Simon thought, and hastily sent up a prayer that that remained true. "One mon saw a nun with blue eyes. His insistence that the nun was Ilsabeth Armstrong has caused many to think they have seen her round every corner and down every shadowy alley. I dinnae believe she is roaming about the town but I have my men watching for her."

"A nun was seen entering town with two children and 'tis said that ye have collected up two children in town. Ye were heard to claim them as your own."

Simon silently cursed. Someone had seen her arrive. His only solace was that the king's question made it clear the one who had seen Ilsabeth had not seen her come to his home nor looked closely at the children. Whoever had spread that tale was clearly trying to tie him to Ilsabeth and cause him too much trouble to continue his search for the real traitors.

"The mon I was confronting at that time was trying to take the small girl child away with him. Her brother and some maid were trying to stop him. I but claimed the child and her brother to keep him from doing so. He wasnae taking the little lass away as a kindness, sire.

"If those two children are the same two who came to town with the nun, they havenae said so. The maid also fled without claiming them. I ken who fathered them and tossed them out, and he is from this town, but I will ask them about a nun. My housekeeper, Old Bega, has taken them under her wing so they now reside with me."

"Simon, ye have been unrelenting in finding justice and seeking the truth from the first day I met ye. Dinnae allow these rumors to continue and put a stain on a glorious past. Get the one who killed Ian and find me the traitors. And do so in a way that allows no one any leave to question the justice of it."

Simon left the king's chamber in a fury. He tried to smother it, to hide it from the ones he walked past, but it had settled into his heart and mind with a strength that was hard to shake free of. The best he could do was hide it and he could almost feel his face harden into a mask of empty courtesy.

He wanted to hit something. When Hepbourn stepped into his path causing him to have to stop, Simon had to clasp his hands behind his back to keep himself from satisfying the strong urge to do violence by beating Hepbourn until the man was no longer so pretty and never would be again. The way Hepbourn took a quick step back told Simon that not all of his anger had been hidden away.

"Do ye wish to speak to me, Hepbourn?" he asked the man.

"I just thought that ye might wish to ken what is being said about ye," replied Hepbourn.

"I have heard the rumors. What do they matter to me? There are always rumors winging their way through the court. Few of them ever prove to be true."

"Nay? There must be some good reason for them to start and to keep being repeated."

And that reason is that ye will not let them die, thought Simon. In truth, he suspected the source of many of them was Hepbourn or one of his lackeys. "Then I am to believe that ye ease your grief over the betrayal of your betrothed in the arms of Alice Mure, Janet Cumyn, and Margaret Skene?"

He got a twinge of pleasure when he saw how un-easy Hepbourn became. Since Janet and Alice had two hulking great husbands, Simon suspected that Hepbourn feared he would be made to pay dearly for his stolen pleasures.

"As ye say, there are always rumors about. Have ye found that blue-eyed nun yet?"

"Nay. We are looking for her. Since this town has verra few nuns wandering about its streets and none of my men have found her, I begin to question whether she even exists. Or she was but passing through here on some business. Mayhap e'en on a pilgrimage. The verra religious are quite fond of pilgrimages."

"Ah, 'tis possible."

"Quite possible. Now, if ye will be so kind as to excuse me, I have work to do."

Simon left the court and started walking. By the time his anger had eased enough for him to see clearly, he was deep into the wood at the edge of town. The way he was breathing so heavily made him aware that he had run the last mile or so.

Was it only a few hours ago that he had re-minded himself how easily he could lose his place as a king's man? Simon had not realized how deeply that would cut. He suspected it was the hint of his having been corrupted, the unsaid slur against his honesty, that bit the deepest. For years that had been his creed, justice, and truth, and he had proven himself again and again. Yet a few ru-mors, ones undoubtedly spread by Hepbourn and his minions, had been enough to put years of cold-eyed honesty and the meting out of justice into question.

"Bastards," he muttered, and kicked at the ground, sending several small pebbles flying.

He took a deep breath and let it out slowly. With his hands on his hips he stared up at the cloud-covered sky. There was nothing to gain in having a childish burst of anger. He had dealt in the politics of court for too long to be surprised by this.

A part of him wanted to pack up his household and flee, to hide away with Ilsabeth until the true traitors showed their faces. Simon knew he would not do that, however. He wanted her free and that would not happen until the men who tried to use her to cover their trail were caught and punished. Now, he also wanted to stay so that he could prove himself. It did not matter if he had done so before, time and time again. He refused to flee leaving anyone questioning his honor. His good name, the reputation he had built, were all he had and he would not allow them to be taken from him.

A little calmer and determined to prove himself yet again, Simon began the long walk back to town. He was just negotiating his way through a thick tangle of brambles and saplings when he heard voices. Just far enough so that he could not hear exactly what was being said, two men were talking. Deciding it was an odd place for men to meet unless they wanted to talk of something they did not want anyone to hear, Simon slipped silently through the tangle until the men came into view. Crouching down, Simon smiled. It was Hepbourn and a man Simon suspected was the David they had been looking for.

"I tell ye, Walter, I am being watched!"

"David, watching isnae such a danger. Just accept

that 'tis true and be cautious." Walter patted his cousin on the back. "T'will all be over soon. I just got word that Henry is on his way with his men."

"That is good news but it doesnae help me much, does it?" David snapped, and began to pace. "Ye would find it hard to believe what a tortured route I had to take to get here. I tell ye, I think 'tis worse than being watched. I would swear that I am being hunted."

Perhaps David was not a complete fool, Simon mused, making careful note of what the man looked like, even down to the way he walked. A look at the anger on Hepbourn's face told Simon that the man was not accustomed to David complaining. Dissent amongst the ranks was something Simon found very promising.

His men were doing their job well, too, he decided. They had put the chill of fear into David and made it difficult for Hepbourn and his lackey to meet in comfort. Such small inconveniences could disrupt even the most well thought out plans, although it appeared the plot was still on course. The guard around the king would need to be increased.

"David, calm yourself," said Hepbourn. "This agitation could prove dangerous and ye ken weel that Henry willnae tolerate it." Hepbourn nodded when David stopped his pacing and grew pale. "Exactly. Dinnae e'er forget how he treats those he no longer trusts. Wheesht, or those who just make him angry."

"How can one forget? The mon made sure all those who were joined with him saw and learned the lesson weel. Are ye certain he is the right choice?" David took a deep breath and blurted out, "Aside

from what he did to those two men who thought
they could just walk away from all this, I have heard
some hard things said about the mon."

"It wouldnae do us any good if we had a weak
mon to lead us, would it?"

"Nay, nay. Of course not. But, 'tis said he killed
his own bairns."

"They were lasses. His wives have always failed
him in that. Every mon wants sons."

"Aye." David nodded but his expression revealed
his unease.

"If ye begin to have doubts, David, I would advise
ye to swallow them. Henry will be here soon."

"How soon?"

"Three, four days. 'Tis hard to say. He sent his
mon ahead to tell us so that I can ready some ac-
commodation for him and his men, but the trip
from Lochancorrie isnae an easy one and there is
much that could delay him."

Simon nearly leapt to his feet and demanded
Hepbourn tell him all he knew. Just hearing the
name Henry had sent a brief shiver down his spine,
but this chilled him to the bone. There could not
be too many Henrys from Lochancorrie yet Simon
did not want to believe that his own brother was involved in a plot against the king. The Inneses of
Lochancorrie might not be a big, rich, or important clan but, until Henry had begun to rule it with
an iron fist, it had been one many had been proud
to belong to.

His home could be lost, Simon suddenly realized. If Henry truly was part of a plot to steal the
throne and murder the king, and if that plot failed,
then all of Lochancorrie would suffer. The king

would have every right by law to take it from his family and give it to someone else. Henry was vain, brutish, and cruel, but Simon was finding it difficult to believe his brother, and laird, would risk all he held to grab for something he had no right to.

"Aye, I ken it. It was a miserable journey the last time we made it. I best go as the men watching me may wonder if I slipped away when I dinnae appear outside the inn soon. That would mean e'en more trouble for me as it took me quite a while to slip around them this time. 'Twas more luck than skill, I am thinking, so I dinnae think I will be able to do it again."

"I will meet ye in the tavern tomorrow eve."

"But, if I am being watched . . ."

"I am doing naught wrong in going to a tavern to have some ale and a tumble with some wench and none can say otherwise. Go, David. I will see you on the morrow. And regain your faith in what we plan, cousin. I swear, Henry can smell a weakness or a doubt on a mon."

Simon sat still and silent until he heard two horses ride away. To be certain he would not be seen, he remained where he was for a full hour. He needed the time to think, anyway.

"Henry, I kenned ye were a vicious, coldhearted brute, but I ne'er thought ye would be a complete fool," he muttered, and ran his hand through his hair.

While it was true that he had not been near Lochancorrie for ten long years, Simon found the idea of the lands being taken from the Inneses too much to bear. There was some proud history in those stones. Good men had lived and died at

Lochancorrie for years before his father and then his brother had stepped up as lairds. Simon did not want to see it gifted to some court lackey whom the king felt he owed a favor.

Standing up, he brushed his clothes off and resumed his walk back to town. He needed to find more proof that his brother was in with the traitors. David and Hepbourn were cautious in their speech even though they had thought they were not being listened to. Neither one of them openly spoke of a traitorous plot or murder. It was even more important to get his hands on David now. The fact that David was beginning to question the rightness of the plot, of their leader, could only work in Simon's favor.

He needed to talk to his men and not only to get them to place themselves in every tavern in town in order to watch David and Hepbourn meet. He needed to know what, if anything, they had heard about the man Henry. If they had heard something, if Simon gained some proof no matter how thin, that his brother was part of this plot, he would have to move fast to try and save what he could of Lochancorrie.

"He was in the woods?" asked Peter, one of the men Simon had placed to watch David.

"Aye," replied Simon, and waved to the tavern maid to bring both him and Peter some ale. "He met with his cousin there."

"Wheesht, I am that sorry, sir. I ne'er saw him leave."

"Dinnae blame yourself. Ye were watching him

closely. Sometimes one of them just gets a wee bit of luck and slips right by a mon. E'en he sounded surprised that he had managed it."

"Aye, but 'tisnae comforting to ken that he has realized we are on his trail."

"Doesnae matter. It is making him uneasy and that can only be in our favor. We will take him up soon. I but need a wee bit more ere I dare kidnap the fool. The king is beginning to question why we havenae found the traitor yet." The foul curse Peter spat out eased a little of the fury just speaking of the king's inquiry roused in Simon.

"We *have* found him. 'Tis that fool Hepbourn and his weak-chinned cousin."

"Oh, aye, that it is. But, Hepbourn isnae without power and coin and he is weel liked at court, e'en by the king. More is needed to point the finger at him. Especially when the king is convinced it is the Armstrongs of Aigballa. They make a much better clutch of villains than Hepbourn and his foolish cousin. If naught else, there willnae be many who complain about the fate of that wee clan for too many Armstrongs are weel kenned to be thieves and rogues. And, we need to find the one who is the leader."

"Are ye certain it isnae Hepbourn?"

"Verra certain. Hepbourn himself says so. I do, however, have a name now. I need to ken if it is the right one, and if he is the leader. What was said by David and Hepbourn in the woods didnae make that all that clear. If I didnae feel certain that I was weel hidden, I would think they had seen me—their talk was so carefully worded."

"Who is it?"

"Sir Henry Innes of Lochancorrie."

Peter stared at Simon in silent shock for a moment and then cursed again. "He is your kin, isnae he?"

"He is my brother in fact. My elder brother. If he hadnae banished me from the clan, he would be my laird."

"Jesu, Simon, this becomes dangerous for ye now. Mayhap ye should step back a wee bit. E'en better, go far, far away so that when this is all discovered, no one can point any fingers at ye."

"I cannae." He prayed Ilsabeth would understand why he could not leave even though the net of suspicion was tightening around all of them now. "'Tis my clan."

"And your blood, your own brother."

"Nay, Henry isnae any brother to me. He didnae have to banish me for I had ne'er meant to go back there. But there are good people there. Old Bega and MacBean were born there and still have family there. The ones who came before my father and brother were good men and they built something worth saving. I cannae let what Henry does stain the honor they showed all their lives or the honor that was Lochancorrie's before my father and brother sat in the laird's chair."

Peter nodded. "The stain spreads wide when one of a clan dishonors the name and that isnae fair or just, but 'tis how it is. Especially if 'tis the laird who spread the stain. So, I am to watch for Henry Innes, laird of Lochancorrie. His looks?"

"Much akin to mine only he is heavier, broader, more muscular and with a thicker neck. I havenae

seen him for near to ten years but I dinnae think he
will be difficult for ye to spot. He has but one eye
and a vicious scar running down the right side of
his face. A gift from his first wife. He claims she attacked him in a fit of madness and then hurled herself out the window. He ne'er did explain why she
was in the highest of the tower rooms, the one
Henry used as his private den so that he could de-
bauch all the maids in peace.

"But I am thinking it will be the way he behaves
that will give him away the most. He doesnae act
like the laird of a small, remote clan. He acts just
like a mon who thinks he has a right to steal a throne."
Which was one reason Simon could not immediately discount the idea that his brother was head of
the group of traitors. "He is brutal, uses fists ere he
e'en thinks of using words, and he takes to bed
whate'er lass catches his eyes whether she wishes to
be taken or nay. If ye ken any lasses in this town ye
care about, Peter, best get them hidden. Henry sees
rape as a mon's right."

"Are ye certain ye were bred from the same
seed?"

Simon laughed briefly and even he could hear
the bitterness in the sound. "Aye, I fear I am certain. My father was a brute as weel, but nothing like
Henry. In the end, my father e'en feared him and
he may have been right to do so. There is a verra
good chance that it was Henry who killed him. Be
verra cautious around Henry, Peter. He may act like
some brute from a distant past, all brawn and brutality, but he has wit and cunning. He also has skill,
fights like one possessed, and prefers to kill all enemies as slowly as he can."

"There is a monster coming to town then, isnae there?"

"Aye, there may be. I am still hanging on to the hope that Hepbourn is wrong, confused, or has been lied to by someone. The possibility that he is right gives me e'en more reason to find the traitors, prove they are as guilty as sin, and prove that I deserve the reputation I have made for myself. Win the king's favor all over again, if ye will. If I can do that then I may be able to keep the clan from having to pay for Henry's idiocy. I may e'en be able to keep the lands."

"Then ye would be a laird."

"At best I would be guardian of Henry's son for I wouldnae wish a child to pay for the sins of his father, either."

"Does Henry have a son?"

"He has certainly done his best to breed near every woman for miles so I cannae see why he wouldnae. Ere I left he had buried two wives and three of the four daughters they had given him. The other was barely more than a child and he sold her in marriage to a mon who was old enough to be her grandfather. If Henry finally had the son he craved, from his third wife or one of his lovers, 'tis something I shall deal with when this is done for there are too many things that could go wrong." Simon stood up and clapped Peter on the back. "Heed me in this. Be verra careful if my brother does come into town. If ye miss him slipping out on ye, ye will pay for it with your life, for he will come up on your back and cut your throat."

"Do ye have any other family?" Peter asked, his smile a little crooked.

"Three younger brothers and two sisters. My sisters have long been married and I believe they are content. I dinnae ken where my other brothers live, but they left home at a young age just as I did. I pray that means that they havenae been infected by the taint that twisted my father and brother. Take care, Peter. I will meet with ye again, same time and same place, in two days unless something happens that requires we meet sooner."

Peter held his tankard up in a silent toast and Simon headed for home. He realized he had a need to be with Ilsabeth and the children. He was feeling sick to his soul over the chance that his own blood would be a traitor. Despise Henry as he did, he still found it hard to believe that the man would turn against his own king. As far as Simon knew, there was no real reason for Henry to do so. Henry had been banished from the court but he suffered no other ill, and he had well deserved to be banished.

What would he do if the leader of the traitors were Henry? Simon cursed softly. He knew what he would do. He would hand his own brother over to the king for punishment. It would be hard, and not because he had any care for the man, but because he was blood, his own laird despite throwing him out of Lochancorrie.

As he stepped into the house and heard Elen laughing, there was a lightening of his heavy mood. This was what he needed, Simon thought as the little girl appeared in the doorway to the great hall and smiled at him. He caught her up in his arms when she ran toward him, her little arms outstretched and bellowing his name in a surprisingly loud voice. The sight of Reid and Ilsabeth standing inside the door to his hall only added to the easing of his spirit. As he moved to join them he decided there was no harm in losing himself in the sweet honesty and laughter of Ilsabeth and the children. The troubles he had to deal with would still be there on the morrow and he needed this reprieve.

Chapter 10

Ilsabeth awoke with an uneasy feeling flowing through her veins. She was not sure where it had come from. Her cheek was warmed by the heat of Simon's broad chest. His strong, slender arms were wrapped around her, holding her close to him. Nearly all was perfect in her world for the moment. So why did the bitter taste of fear sting her tongue? She clung to Simon a little more tightly as she struggled to recall the dream she suspected was the cause of her uneasiness. Just as she began to grasp a thread of it, Simon pushed her onto her back and kissed her, wiping all other thought from her mind except for the taste of him and how much she craved the pleasure he gave her.

Simon nuzzled Ilsabeth's neck as he struggled to regain his breath after a greedy bout of lovemaking. Ilsabeth was still sprawled beneath him, her own breathing still fast and uneven. Her passion was a gift. He just wished he had more time to enjoy it, but he needed to leave the warmth of their bed.

"Good morn, sweet," he said, kissed her lightly, and then sat on the edge of the bed to stretch. "I wish I could linger here with ye for a few hours, mayhap e'en all day, but I must meet with Tormand in the wood north of town soon." He gave in to the urge to kiss her again before finally getting up.

"I pray he has more news, useful news," she said as she sat up, tucking the linen sheet around her. "I do like to hear that none of my family has yet fallen into the hands of the king's soldiers, but that isnae truly helpful."

She smiled when all she got in reply was a grunt as Simon slipped into the small room attached to his bedchamber where he could relieve himself and wash in some privacy. Even though he showed no qualms about striding around the bedchamber naked, he clearly preferred some moments of privacy. Ilsabeth admitted that she appreciated that small room as well.

"The message Tormand sent me implied that he had discovered something of importance," said Simon, answering the question she had asked before he had left the room as he stepped back into the bedchamber and began to get dressed. "He also said that Morainn had seen something."

"Tormand would have said if she had given him a name or the like, aye?"

"Aye, but in her visions she doesnae often see things like names. What she does see, however, can ofttimes show me a verra clear path to follow to what I need."

"I hope that is true this time." Ilsabeth grimaced when she realized she had not kept all of her growing frustration out of her voice.

Simon sat on the edge of the bed and caressed her cheek. He could understand her frustration; he shared it. He was not the one accused of crimes that could lead to a very unpleasant execution, however. Nor was his beloved family forced to hide in the hills. Each day had to be a torture of waiting for her.

"Dinnae lose hope, Ilsabeth."

"Nay, I willnae. I but grow so verra weary of it all." She placed her hands on his newly shaven cheeks and stared at him, idly wondering how she had ever thought that his eyes were cold. "I woke uneasy, Simon. I dinnae have dreams or visions as Morainn does, but ye ken that many of my kin have gifts. Some have nay more than a verra strong instinct, some have much, much more. I am nay sure what I have but something troubles me about today, something concerning ye. Be verra careful today. That is all I ask. Watch your back."

"I always do, love," he said, and kissed her before he stood up and left, warmed by her concern.

Ilsabeth stared at the door for a long time after it closed behind Simon. She wished she could recall her dream more clearly but she trusted how it had left her feeling. That uneasiness and touch of fear the dream had left behind were warnings. She could only wait and pray that Simon heeded them.

Simon reached the meeting place Tormand had indicated early but did not mind. He sat on a log and enjoyed the warmth of the sun, something he rarely had the time to do. There was a peace within him that he had not experienced for longer than he cared to recall, a peace that Ilsabeth had given him.

He wished he could ease her growing frustration but finding the truth took time. She worried about her family while he worried about her. All the frustration he suffered was born of his intense need to see that Ilsabeth was safe and that could not happen until the true killer of poor Ogilvie was found and the real traitors caught. He was certain now that Hepbourn was one of them but proof of that was elusive. No matter how deep his conviction was that the man was guilty, he refused to send the man to a certain death without proof. Vague overheard conversations were not enough and, even though Ilsabeth had heard condemning words from the man's own mouth, he could not use her as a witness.

"Am I late or were ye early?"

Simon shook free of his thoughts and smiled at Tormand. "I was a wee bit early. I was just enjoying a rare sight of the sun. So tell me, what has our Morainn seen then?"

"*My* Morainn," Tormand said as he sat down on the log next to Simon. "Eager, are ye?"

"This game grows verra tiresome. I find I lack the patience I usually have."

"Because ye worry over Ilsabeth?"

The way Tormand looked at Simon told him that the man suspected something was going on between Simon and his cousin. Simon had no intention of admitting to anything, however. If Ilsabeth wanted any of her family to know they had become lovers, she would tell them herself.

"She needs to be free of this burden, as does her

family," he finally said, and scowled when Tormand just grinned. "What was it that ye thought I needed to hear about?"

"Morainn is certain that ye hunt the right men—Hepbourn and his cousin. She cannae see how to trap them though. She said that could be because it needs to be done with no warning, that ye can and will do it without any help. Vanity and cowardice. That is what her vision revealed as their weaknesses. I believe I can easily guess which goes with whom."

"As can I. We had already guessed most of that but 'tis good to have it all confirmed in one of her visions. And, I now ken where David is and that he is definitely part of Hepbourn's plans. Ilsabeth told me so but I needed to hear it for myself as I cannae use her word for it, can I? I heard enough to tell me that they plot all this together although David is already showing signs of unease about the plans being made. I but wait to grab him for I think it may help if I let that unease brew for a wee while."

"How did that piece of good fortune happen?"

"Quite by accident. I stumbled across him and Hepbourn meeting in the woods."

"Lucky. Morainn did say something else was shown to her. She said that one of your own is the head of the snake."

"One of my men? Nay, I cannae believe that. I would trust them with my life and dinnae question their loyalty to our liege. Morainn must have mistaken what she saw."

"I dinnae think so." Tormand sighed. "She didnae mean one of your men. She meant one of your blood. She says it is one who already has a lot of blood on his hands. Morainn also said that included yours, but that makes no sense for ye are still here. So, mayhap she has misread what she has seen."

"Nay, she hasnae. I nearly wasnae here," Simon whispered, shock stealing the strength from his voice. Morainn's vision only confirmed what he had overheard David and Hepbourn say, that Henry was involved in the plot to kill the king.

"What do ye mean, ye nearly were not here?"

Unable to sit still as he revealed what he saw as his idiocy and his humiliation, Simon stood up and began to pace in front of the still-sitting Tormand. "I ken that I once told ye that the last time I went home was to see my father buried, but that wasnae the truth. I was drawn back to Lochancorrie one more time. Ten years ago to be precise. By a woman."

"Ah. And this woman is the reason ye havenae been back or even spoken of your kin since then?"

"Aye. Her name was Mary. She was my brother Henry's third wife. Henry brought her to the court with him once, when he was allowed to still show his face there. I was there as weel, with my foster father, and acting as his squire. Part of my training. It wasnae easy, but I did my best to stay out of Henry's sight and reach. Mary found me instead."

"This tale doesnae end weel, does it?" muttered Tormand.

"Nay, not weel at all. Mary was beautiful and she stirred my blood until I was crazed with lust for her. Jesu, I was but a green lad of eighteen with verra little experience of women and she was a weel-practiced seductress of five and twenty. She also filled my ears with tearful stories of how cruel Henry was to her, how desperately she needed to get away from him. She was certain that he would kill her one day. At least in that she spoke the truth. I got word that she drowned about five years ago. The mon who gave me the news hinted that few of the people at Lochancorrie believed it was an accident. He also implied that no one truly cared if she was murdered or nay. They were just pleased that she was gone."

"So she seduced ye and it wasnae out of love. Why? Revenge on Henry?"

"Nay. She and Henry were much alike, in truth. She wanted a son. She had already given Henry two daughters and he wasnae verra pleased by that. I fear they, too, may be dead for Henry's daughters dinnae live long, either. I only ken of one who lived to marry, although in truth she was still little more than a child when she was sold off to an old mon.

"I discovered later that Mary chose me to breed her because she wished to be certain that the child looked like Henry. That was Henry's plan as weel, although I was stunned that he would e'er accept that he was unable to breed a son.

"Weel, Henry discovered we were lovers and beat me near to death. My back is badly scarred from the whip he used and he peeled most of the skin off my back with it. My foster father didnae hold much hope that I would survive until weeks later. He said he had ne'er seen anyone so torn up. He ne'er got over his astonishment that I had had the strength to crawl back to our rooms."

"What did ye do after ye healed?"

"Fool that I was, I went back to Lochancorrie. I feared for Mary's life, didnae I. I had some grand plans about rescuing her from my brute of a brother. Henry's wives didnae live long although no one could e'er prove that he killed them." Simon scowled as he recalled all the painful truths he had uncovered on that last visit to his birthplace.

"Ye dinnae need to continue, Simon."

"Aye, I do." If only to learn how to tell the tale when I finally answer Ilsabeth's question about what happened to cause the scars, he mused. "Instinct made me cautious. I at least retained enough sense to ken that I couldnae blindly rush to the fair maiden's rescue, that I needed to plan. So, I watched and I listened. Disguised, I e'en got inside the keep a few times. That is how I discovered that Henry had sent her to seduce me. I willnae trouble ye with all the things she said save to say that she didnae do it for love or e'en fear of Henry. Henry's outrage over finding his wife in my bed was false although he admitted that he enjoyed beating me. Called me a self-righteous little bastard."

"Do ye think he is expecting ye to come after him?"

Simon stared at Tormand for a minute and then cursed. "I cannae say. I didnae want to believe it when I heard Hepbourn say his name. Couldnae believe that Henry would risk all our forefathers built, all he has claimed and lived off for years. It just makes no sense. But it seems that he has."

"Some men cannae resist the lure of power."

"There is naught in our history or bloodlines that should have given him the insane idea that he has a right to the throne. Not one cursed thing."

"All he needs is a thirst for power, Simon. Ones who get that thirst will justify all of their actions until they believe they are right in what they think and do. Mayhap ye should step away from this. I suspicion ye have no care for your brother, but all the rest? Aye, I think ye care that he risks Lochancorrie and its people. Yet, there is no ignoring that he is blood and, if ye get the proof ye need to reveal him as a traitor, he will be facing a verra hard death."

"That willnae trouble me all that much. The mon has killed and is long overdue for a hanging. As Morainn saw, the mon has a lot of blood on his hands. Aye, it willnae be an easy death he faces, but he chose his path. I doubt many of the others at Lochancorrie were asked their opinion and yet they will all lose."

"Aye and that is why I think ye may be too close to all of this."

"I have a small hope that I might yet save Lochancorrie. If I am the one who brings the traitors to justice, I may weel be able to ask a boon."

"And that boon will be the lands, aye?"

Simon nodded and leaned against a tree facing Tormand. "'Tis all I might be able to save. E'en if I step back, Henry will be found out for the traitor he is. At least if I stay and try to bring him to justice I have a chance of keeping others in the clan from suffering for his idiocy. And did ye forget that your kinsmen sent Ilsabeth to me to protect? That they are looking to me to prove her innocence?"

Tormand cursed. "For a moment, aye, I did. So ye must see this out until the end." He stood up and briefly clasped Simon's arm. "Take care, friend. I dinnae want to see ye place more scars upon your soul. And tell my cousin that her family remains safe and free." He started to walk away. "I am at your service if ye need me." He stopped and looked back at Simon. "What are the names of your other brothers?"

"Malcolm, Kenneth, and Ruari. Why?"

"No particular reason. Ye arenae the only one who suffers from the bite of curiosity. And, mayhap it will help ye do what ye must if ye think on how ye will be trying to save Lochancorrie for them as weel."

He watched Tormand disappear into the wood and sighed, thumping the back of his head against the tree a few times. The thought that his brother was a traitor, that he planned to kill their liege lord, was more than Simon could bear. There was so much anger churning inside him, he felt ill. There was only one path he could take and that was to bring the traitors to justice no matter who they were. And he had lied to Tormand. It would trouble him to send Henry to a traitor's death despite all the ill will that lay between them. Henry might be a brutal monster in a man's skin, but he was still blood, still clan, still his brother.

Simon stood in the great hall where the king was holding his court and watched Hepbourn. The man was still busy slandering the Armstrongs and spreading the subtle rumors that had made the king question Simon. The man was relentless in his pursuit to destroy the Armstrongs all the while saving his own hide. For the first time in a long time, Simon wanted to beat the truth out of someone.

This is what his brother wanted? To rule over these adulterers, gossipers, and sycophants? Simon had seen what the king had to deal with every day, the weight of some of the decisions the man had to make, the idiocy and the arrogance he had to suffer through, and he could not see Henry wanting any part of that. Henry was obviously thinking of only the power and wealth he would gain.

The thought of Henry sitting on the throne of Scotland was a chilling one. Simon knew his brother would use his new power to make a lot of blood flow. Anyone who disagreed with his plans, or just looked at him wrong, would be killed and there would be little anyone could do to stop it. In truth, Simon was certain that, if by some miracle Henry won the prize he sought, there would be war and the ground would soon be soaked in blood.

This was a bad place to come and try to calm his tumultuous emotions, Simon decided. He was so filled with anger that the people around him made his head pound and his fists clench with the need to hit someone. As if in answer to his need, Hepbourn walked over to him.

"The search still nay going weel?" Hepbourn asked. "'Tisnae such a big town. I cannae see how one small lass can hide in it so weel."

"Unless, of course, she was ne'er here to begin with," drawled Simon.

"If she plots to kill the king she will have to come here at some time, will she not? She cannae kill the mon without drawing close to him. Mayhap ye would serve our liege better if ye ceased trying to find the traitors and guarded the king. Then they will have to come to ye, aye? And then ye will finally have them."

Simon's hand tightened so much on the tankard

of ale he held that he was surprised it did not
buckle. Hepbourn was growing bold. No longer satisfied with questioning Simon's skills behind his
back, Hepbourn was doing it right to his face.
Taunting him. The man was beginning to feel dangerously confident. Simon tried hard to restrain his
urge to beat the man for this was just what he
needed. A man who was too confident of victory
made mistakes.

"And what if they come with an army, Hepbourn? Nay, 'tis best to stop the threat before it
draws too near to the king. I will find my answers. I
am a patient mon. I ken how to wait and watch."

Realizing he was too angry to be cautious about
what he said, Simon nodded to Hepbourn and
walked away. He needed to get out, to get away
from all the empty words and false smiles of court
life. Simon strode through the crowd, sullenly
pleased by the way they hurriedly moved out of his
path, and went outside. Just as he had done when
he had first heard Henry's name connected to treasonous plots, he walked until his legs ached. Only
then did he turn around and head home. This
time, however, the hard walk had not eased him or
cleared his mind.

He was still too angry to think clearly. Somehow
he had to shake free of the fury gripping him so
tightly. Simon knew he could all too easily make a
mistake if he did not get his emotions under control.

The house was quiet when he entered, the children already abed. He suspected Ilsabeth was in
bed, too. His body was eager to join her there but
he fought the temptation. He feared his anger was

still so great and so uncontrollable that he could hurt her. There would be some relief to be found in the sweetness of her passion but he knew he would be rough in the finding of it.

As he entered his ledger room, he thought on how Henry had managed to ruin the one good thing Simon had found. With a soft growl, Simon picked up the oddly patterned rock Reid had gifted him with yesterday and hurled it at the fireplace. It hit the mirror hanging over the mantel and loudly smashed it. The abrupt act of violence brought him little ease.

"Sir?" asked MacBean as he opened the door to look in shock at the broken mirror.

"God's tears, mon, why do ye never knock?" Simon hurled himself into his seat and put his head in his hands.

Ignoring the scolding, MacBean drew near. "What ails ye? Shall I have the old woman brew ye up something?"

"Nay, I dinnae need some potion." He sat back. "I am attempting to rein in the rage that is near to choking me."

Simon could see that he was alarming MacBean. The man was used to an even-tempered master, a man who got, at his worst, a little broody or irritable. "I have found out who leads the traitors. The mon should arrive in town within three to four days."

"But, isnae that good news? Isnae that what ye have been looking for?"

" 'Tis what I have been looking for and yet, 'tis nay what I expected."

"So who is it? Anyone we might have met?"

Simon laughed and even he had to wince at the harsh bitter sound of it. "Aye, MacBean, we ken the mon verra weel indeed. 'Tis Henry." For the first time since he had known the man, MacBean was struck speechless.

"Nay, that cannae be."

"So I said when I heard the first mention of his name. But I fear it was the truth I heard. After all these years spent searching for the truth, ye would think I would recognize it when I heard it, but I hesitated."

"Your brother plots to kill the king? Why? What does he mean to gain?"

"The throne," replied Simon. "My dear brother has obviously gained some high ambitions over the years. Instead of just killing wives and daughters and the occasional poor fool who displeases him, Henry seeks to kill the king. And, even more astounding, the mon seems to think it should be him who sits on the newly emptied throne."

"Sweet Jesu, the king will send soldiers to Lochancorrie. People will be killed."

"Go, MacBean. Just go. If there is someone ye feel compelled to warn of the trouble headed his way, do so, but do it as secretly and subtly as ye can. It would not do us any good if Henry gets word that we have caught on to his game."

"Simon," MacBean began, his voice softened with concern.

"Nay, just go. I am so filled with fury that my head aches and my stomach churns. I am nay good company this eve. I need to think, need to get rid of some of this anger that is making me lose all my wits. If I dinnae, then I will nay be able to work.

Henry could win and then all of Scotland will suffer."

Simon winced as the door shut behind the departing MacBean. The man had called him Simon. MacBean had not done so since Simon had been a beardless boy. He must be in a far worse condition than he had realized.

"I think I need to get drunk. I need to drink until I fall on my face and my mind ceases to work," he said as he stared up at the ceiling.

A bad idea, he decided a moment later. Drink might put him down for a while, but it would take some time for it to do so. Simon did not want to consider what he might do when that drink mixed with the fury inside him. He could wake in the morning, head aching, to discover he had done something very foolish or taken his anger out on some poor fool who crossed his path.

What he did not understand was the depth of his anger. He had not seen his home for a very long time and he had few good memories of it. The despair he suffered over its impending loss made no sense. There were good people there, ones like MacBean and Old Bega, but he had not seen them in ten years, either.

That left Henry as the cause of his fury. Henry, who had tormented all of his siblings with brute force and rages. The man had even slaughtered Simon's first dog and tossed the carcass onto his bed while he was sleeping in it. Henry never discussed anything. If a person did not agree with his opinion or plan, he beat them until they did or they died, whichever came first. Henry was not particular. Simon decided that there was where his fury was born, in the knowledge that Henry was still destroying all that had been good at Lochancorrie.

Perhaps he should just hunt his brother down and kill him. That would put an end to the danger to the clan and its land. Once Henry was dead the other traitors would be easy enough to catch and punish. A small, still sane part of Simon was dismayed by how reasonable that sounded to the rest of him. The boy who had grieved over his dog and the young man who had dragged his bleeding, ravaged body back to his foster father both liked the idea.

A madness had seized him. It was the only explanation for how he was feeling and the things he was thinking of. Simon knew he had to get some control over himself. He just did not know how; he had never felt such anger before and no skill in caging it.

Perhaps there was more of Henry and their father in him than he had realized. The mere thought that he might carry some of that tainted blood chilled Simon so deeply that, for a brief moment, his anger eased. He shook the thought out of his head, refusing to believe it.

The sound of soft footfalls caught his attention and he braced himself. He knew who was coming down the stairs and walking to his door. The breaking of the mirror must have roused Ilsabeth. His lover who was hiding from false accusations because his brother thought he had a right to be king, he suddenly realized. His own blood had had a hand in bringing her such trouble.

That was the source of at least some of his anger. Because of Henry's ambitions, Ilsabeth could not go home nor could her family. She had to hide in Simon's home while her family hid away in the hills around Aigballa. All she had suffered was because of his family, his blood. Simon did not know if he could face her now that he knew the truth.

Her soft rapping at the door stirred him to answer. He wanted to tell her to flee, to just yell it through the closed door, but Simon knew he owed her more than that. He just did not know how to explain that the root of all her troubles was her lover's brother.

When she stepped into the room in answer to his invitation, he nearly cursed. She looked still warm from their bed. Her hair was uncombed and there was still a sleepy look in her wide blue eyes. His body hardened. She was what he needed. Ilsabeth had the soft touch to soothe his fury, he was certain of it. He would have left her alone tonight if she had stayed in bed. But, she was near, standing by his worktable and looking at him with concern, and every tortured part of him wanted to reach for her.

Chapter 11

The sound of breaking glass yanked Ilsabeth from her rest. She reached out for Simon but found only the chilled linen. For several moments she lay still, listening carefully. There was the murmur of voices coming from below and, although she could not hear what was being said, she could hear the sharpness of anger behind some of the words. Then she heard MacBean's distinctive tread, one that was very nearly a stomp, disappearing into the back of the house. A door slammed and then there was silence.

She closed her eyes and told herself to go back to sleep, but that proved to be impossible. Something had upset Simon. Ilsabeth was certain of it. She had to go to him, she decided, as she climbed out of bed and donned a robe.

It was not until she stood before the door to his ledger room that she hesitated. If he truly needed her or wanted her he would come to her. Simon was such a private man and so proud of his control, he might not wish anyone to see him so out of control now that he was breaking things.

Ilsabeth was just about to turn around and quietly retreat to her bedchamber when her courage returned. Simon might not see it yet but she knew they were destined to be together. She could not keep slinking away for fear that she would breach one of the many walls he kept around his secrets and emotions. Ilsabeth knew that even though she loved Simon, she would never survive a life with him if he kept himself so locked away. She needed to be part of his life, not just the woman who stood beside him. She rapped on the door and, when he called out for her to enter, she did so without any hesitation.

Until she saw him. The door was closing behind her and she had the sudden feeling that she was now trapped in a room with a wolf. This was a Simon she did not know. There was no calm, no restraint in his expression. He was not just angry, he was absolutely enraged.

"Simon?" She tried not to look as timid as she felt as she cautiously stepped closer to him.

"This isnae a good time for ye to come to me, sweet," he said as he slowly stood up and started to walk around his worktable.

He prowled toward her. It was the only word that truly described the way he moved. Like some large predator on the hunt. Ilsabeth fought the urge to run. She experienced a tickle of fear even though she knew he would never hurt her. Pure lust swamped that unease, however. Ilsabeth could not understand how having a furious man stalk her could make her desire for him rise so swiftly it made her a little light-headed.

"Nay? I heard a crash." She glanced at the broken mirror before meeting and holding his sharp, heated gaze. "Something troubles ye, Simon. Can ye nay allow me to help ye?"

"Och, aye, ye are about to help me verra much indeed."

He lunged and Ilsabeth could not fully smother a cry that held an odd blend of fear and excitement. When Simon grasped her around the waist and pulled her hard against him, her feet dangled off the floor and she wrapped her limbs around his lean body. He gave her a kiss so fierce and demanding it bordered on painful. Ilsabeth knew she ought to protest such rough handling but she did not really want to. A Simon not in control of himself, even if it was because of an anger he had not yet explained to her, was proving to be wondrously exciting.

She shifted her position in his arms just enough to press her aching womanhood against the long hard length of him. The way he shuddered excited her even more, giving her a delicious sense of power. Even the noise he made stroked her desire. It was a low growl that reached deep within her and demanded that she meet, and equal, the wild passion he was revealing to her.

Simon moved toward the wall with Ilsabeth curled around him. Each step he took caused her to rub against his throbbing erection. He knew he was caught up in some lust-induced madness, but now that he held her in his arms, could sense her eager welcome, he could not leash it. That small, still sane part of him that fought valiantly against the fury that held him captive began to pray that he did not hurt her.

When he got her securely trapped between his hungry body and the wall, he gritted his teeth against the fierce need to thrust deep into her heat and pound out the fury enslaving him, to release it along with his seed. He wanted to bury himself in her moist fire until it burned away his raging anger. Panting like a dog caught out in the summer sun for too long, Simon kept a death grip on the last tiny shred of sanity he retained and slipped his hand between her slim thighs, determined to at least ready her for the onslaught. He found her already hot, wet, and welcoming.

Cursing softly with impatience, he yanked her nightgown up to her waist, loosed himself from his clothing and thrust home, all within such a short period of time, he knew his sane self would probably be utterly mortified later. This wildness was unlike him but he was sunk too deep in the pleasure to care.

Ilsabeth clung to her lover and allowed him to take her on a savage journey to that sweet bliss only he could give her. The words he growled against her ear, her throat, her mouth, thrilled her and added to the passion already thundering through her veins. He spoke of his need, his passion, his delight. And it was all for her.

Such words could not be taken as words of love and she knew it. Her mother had told her that a woman should never believe that flatteries and declarations of desire could be seen as more than they were. Pretty words, words to warm her, but still only words. The vows a man might utter while caught up in passion's fury should be taken no more seriously than the vows of a man lost to drink. Not unless you knew he loved you. Her mother had also said that it was safe to accept such pretty words as flatteries she could treasure if she wished. And Ilsabeth did wish to do so. Simon's words stroked what little vanity she had but, more importantly to her, they gave her the confidence she needed to be Simon's lover, and to be one that he could not forget or set aside.

Her body tightened and when her passion crested in a wild rush of blood-pounding delight, she cried out Simon's name. He thrust into her like a man possessed, withdrew and left her almost empty, and then hurled himself back inside her again. Twice. Then his whole body tensed, became as rigid as a stone, and he called out her name in a voice so thick she barely understood him as he poured his seed deep inside her. Despite how weak and unsteady Ilsabeth was, she continued to cling to him as he sagged against her, his hands pressed against the wall on either side of her head, his sweat-dampened forehead touching hers.

"Jesu, Ilsabeth," he muttered when his mind finally began to clear. "I took ye so roughly, like some beast in rut. I am so verra sorry."

"Oh, I didnae mind." When he raised his head to look at her, making a careful study of her face, she smiled at him. "I suspicion I wouldnae wish to do it too often though," she said when he slowly pulled out of her and stepped back, steadying her until she no longer trembled and could stand on her own. " 'Tisnae all that kind to a certain part of me." She grimaced and rubbed her backside.

Simon grinned at her, but it was such a brief flare of good humor she could have missed it if she had blinked. Then all the dark storms that had clouded his eyes before returned in force and she could feel the chill of the fury he was battling as it surged through his body again. Something or someone had torn free the reins of Simon's anger so completely that he was having a great deal of trouble grasping hold of them again.

Ilsabeth gently stroked his arm. "Simon, ye are so troubled I can almost taste it in the air. Your fury is so completely unrestrained and, I ken I havenae been with ye long, but I am sure this isnae like you. I also cannae e'en begin to guess why."

"Nay matter what troubles me, I shouldnae have taken ye up against the wall like the lowest of tavern wenches."

"I truly didnae mind. Do ye think me so meek I would accept any physical abuse from ye silently and without at least trying to pay ye back in kind?"

"Och, I would ne'er call ye weak, lass."

"Then dinnae mark me as too frail of mind and heart to listen to what troubles ye either, to hear what causes the anger I can see in your eyes, and in the way ye stand."

"The way I stand?"

"Ye stand as if ye are searching for someone to fight with."

"I am. Ye have the right of it." He took a few steps farther away from her when the urge to take her again, right there against the wall, wove seductively through his veins. "Mayhap ye should leave."

"Nay. Ye are so tangled up, aye, knotted, that I

fear for ye. Nay matter what it is, I will listen without flinching away or swooning like some fine lady."

Simon dragged his hand through his hair and began to pace the room. "I ken who the leader of the traitors is now. S'truth, I kenned it the other day but I did my best to shake aside the truth of what I had heard, denying it and arguing it away in my mind."

Ilsabeth would have thought that such news would have made Simon happy for it was what he had been searching for so diligently, but there was no joy to be seen in him over the successful end to his work. "Who is it?" she asked, but was dreading the answer.

"My brother."

"Jesu," she whispered. "Are ye sure?"

"Aye, I heard David and Hepbourn speak of him when I caught them meeting in the woods. That was the truth I was trying to deny. Weel, there is no denying it now. Morainn had a vision. In it the mon who leads all these fools is one of mine, she said, one of my blood. She said he had a lot of blood on his hands, including mine. Kenning that she saw that then made it impossible to ignore what I heard David and Hepbourn say. My brother Henry, the laird of Lochancorrie, is the one leading the plot to kill the king and take the throne. He will be here in three days."

"He put those scars on your back, didnae he?"

"Aye. Ye asked how I got them and I have done my best to avoid telling the tale for 'tis of a young mon's folly." He took her by the hand, sat in his chair and tugged her down onto his lap. "I suspicion ye have heard a few of those."

"Aye, but they didnae usually end with the laddie being scarred for life."

"Nay, but few deal with my brother Henry and walk away whole. And that is if they are fortunate to walk away at all." He took a deep breath and told her about Mary.

Ilsabeth listened and heard things Simon did not say. A lonely young man with a strong sense of justice, a natural born protector, seduced and used by his brother and his brother's wife. Mary had known just how to pull Simon into her net. The woman may not have known it when she started the evil game but she had seen into the heart of the young Simon very quickly.

As for Simon's brother Henry, Ilsabeth had no words. She pressed closer to Simon and absently patted his chest as she thought of the man who now plotted to be made king. That Simon had emerged from that family with so much honor in him was a miracle and a testament to the strength of his soul.

Simon waited for Ilsabeth to comment on the sordid tale he had just told her, but she remained curled up tightly against him, patting his chest. He did not get the sense that she was outraged over his affair with the woman who had married his brother and laird. In truth, he was more concerned that she saw him as a fool. Then he smiled as he glanced down at the small hand still patting his chest. She was soothing him, he thought, and smiled.

It was at that moment that he realized his anger had eased. It was still there but now it was controllable. He knew he had a right to be so furious but it had troubled him that he could not stop himself from aiming it mindlessly at anyone who crossed his path.

"Ilsabeth, ye can cease petting me," he said. "I am saner now."

Ilsabeth peered up at him and knew he was telling the truth. His eyes did not hold the turmoil they had before. He even smiled a little as he put his hand over hers and stopped her stroking of his chest.

"Ye are verra quiet," he said. "Have ye been shocked speechless then?"

"I was just wondering if there was a good way, one that isnae too offensive, to tell ye that someone should have strangled your brother Henry at birth."

Simon laughed and hugged her. "The truth is always the best and, aye, someone should have put an end to him a long time ago. Many lives would have been saved." He kissed the top of her head and frowned. " 'Tis odd, but Henry has always had an unerring sense of who just might be thinking of doing exactly that."

"And so he killed them first."

"Aye. Morainn was right in saying he has a lot of blood on his hands. The mon kills on a whim, for the smallest of reasons. At times I would get the feeling that he sometimes killed because he enjoyed it. As with my poor dog."

She sat up and looked at him. "What dog?"

"When I was home for Michaelmas at the age of ten, I found a ragged wee dog and took it in. I planned to take it back to where I was being fostered. Henry killed it and tossed its gutted body on top of me as I was sleeping. Henry was always cruel, e'en as a boy."

"Simon, that was far more than cruelty." Just the thought of that poor young boy waking to find his dog's bleeding corpse on top of him made her want to retch. "There is something verra wrong with that mon. I thank God ye got away from him and stayed away."

"As did all three of my brothers. They were fostered out just before my father died."

"Also a good thing. If ye and they hadnae gotten away, I suspect all of ye would have joined your father in the ground. Nay, Simon, I think ye have seen enough of the ills of the world, of the horrors one person can inflict on others, to ken that Henry is mad."

Simon grimaced. "I think he might be, that he was born twisted in some way. Yet, he doesnae rant or rave. He is cold and calm, has a sharp wit and is a verra good soldier if ye dinnae mind how many dead cover the field."

"Madmen dinnae have to dance about and froth at the mouth. They can be verra calm and cold. The madness is there, however. 'Tis seen in how they treat people. Aye, and how they treat animals. Treat anyone they think is weaker than they are. Can ye stop him from trying to steal the throne?"

"Aye. And ye are right. Henry is mad. He always has been. I always had the feeling that he killed our father simply because he believed it was his turn to be laird and so the old mon had to go. I should have gone and taken care of him, ended his brutal reign a long time ago."

Ilsabeth kissed him. "Dinnae try to weight yourself down with a guilt ye dinnae deserve. He was the laird by birth so ye couldnae change that. And ye were naught but a boy when ye left. Ye were nay skilled or strong enough to deal Henry the justice he deserved."

"But, I have been big and strong for a few years now," he drawled.

"Which may be why ye havenae been able to prove Henry has killed anyone since that day ye got big enough to beat him." She felt him tense and nodded. "I think he has been watching ye. He may e'en be one of the reasons I was pulled into this. Ye can be certain that Mary told him how she slipped beneath that honor of yours, the one that should have kept ye from touching another mon's wife."

"So he heard Walter had a bonnie wee neighbor and decided she was the way to get me distracted." He cursed. "Put an innocent in danger and Simon will mount his great white steed and do all he can to save her."

"No need to sound so disgusted. I think that sounds verra nice and have been grateful for that knight."

"It isnae just ye who have been used, is it? I have been as weel."

"But he wasnae quite so clever this time, was he?"

"Nay? Ye are running for your life, hiding here, and I am doing little more than running about in circles."

"Simon, the very reason he would toss a lass in danger into your path is the reason he has made a verra serious mistake. Aye, ye are running about trying to get the proof needed to have me declared innocent, but what is needed for that is also what is needed to prove Henry and the others are guilty. Now, Henry might be thinking to get ye out of his way ere that happens," she muttered as she began to think it through, not liking the possibilities that were coming to mind.

"Enough, Ilsabeth," Simon said, and kissed her. "The moment I realized he was part of that I understood that I was in danger. For some reason Henry hates me more than he did any of our other siblings. I dinnae think that has changed. And, who kens better than I how dangerous the mon is. I will be watching my back verra closely."

"Mayhap ye should keep a few of your men at your side from now on," she said.

Simon laughed and stood up with her in his arms. "Now it appears it is I who must do a little soothing and petting. Ye are becoming unnecessarily concerned."

"I dinnae think anyone could be unnecessarily concerned about a mon like Henry," she said as he walked out of the room and headed up the stairs to their bedchamber.

"Nay, true enough." He lightly tossed her onto the bed and then began to undress. "If he had used his wits and strength to do good things, he could have become a great mon, weel honored and weel liked."

Trying not to get too distracted by Simon's fine strong body, Ilsabeth nodded. "He prefers to be feared."

The way Simon stared so intently at her as he tossed aside the last of his clothes and climbed into bed began to make Ilsabeth nervous. "What are ye looking at?" She rubbed her nose. "Do I have a smudge?"

"Nay, and even if ye did ye would still be the most

beautiful lass I have e'er seen. Ye have a way of seeing things that can be helpful in searching for the truth." He grabbed her around the waist, rolled onto his back and set her on top of him. "Ye can see into the heart of a mon."

"I am nay sure I want to see into the heart of a mon like Henry."

"Nay, but ye can take the fact that he has a verra black heart and then see how someone like him might do things. 'Tis a verra useful thing."

Before she could thank him for the compliment and suggest that he allow her to help search out the truth about Henry and his plots against the king, he kissed her. Ilsabeth knew she was being diverted, but decided not to complain. The moment he ended the kiss, she sat up straight and slowly removed her nightdress. Simon's gray eyes went so dark they were nearly black and she could almost feel the heat of his desire when he looked at her.

"Ye are so beautiful, wee Ilsabeth." He stroked his hands up her stomach to cover her breasts. "So soft." He sat up and licked the taut end of her breast.

Ilsabeth lost all concern for the plots and evil of others. Such dark things did not exist when she was in Simon's arms and he was warming her whole body with his passion. Before she lost all of her wits, however, she intended to pay Simon back for something, and pay it back in kind. She pushed him onto his back and, before he could grab her again, she began to kiss her way down his long, lean body.

By the time she had kissed her way to his taut stomach, Simon had a good idea of what she was planning and stopped all attempts to regain control of their lovemaking. He silently prayed that he was right about Ilsabeth's intentions. If she did not do what he was anticipating the disappointment could kill him, he thought wildly as she nipped the inside of his thighs.

Her long, soft hair brushed across his groin in a silken caress. The hard tips of her breasts scraped over his legs in a way that made him ache. But it was when she touched her tongue to the base of his hard length and slowly dragged it all the way up to the tip that he shuddered from the force of the pleasure she gave him. He groaned and, to his dismay, she pulled away. Simon looked at her sitting between his legs, her long hair draping her lush curves in a vain attempt to preserve her modesty, and had to bite back a sharp command for her to continue.

"Ye stopped," he muttered, his heart pounding so hard in his chest he was surprised she did not hear it, and he frantically tried to think of a polite way to ask her to return to what she had been doing.

"Ye groaned," Ilsabeth said, but could tell by the look on his face that the sound he had made had not been one of discomfort.

"Aye, because it felt that good. I can be silent if I must."

Ilsabeth quickly swallowed the urge to laugh. Simon looked somewhat desperate even as he looked annoyed. "Any rules?"

"No biting. At least, nay hard."

This time she did laugh. "Fair enough."

When she kissed the tip of his manhood and slowly circled the head with her tongue, Simon clapped a hand over his mouth. He did not want to make another sound that might have her stopping again. A moment later, he decided she had understood that he wanted her to love him with her mouth for she did not hesitate at all when she heard him groan out a curse. Simon grabbed all the control he could and held on tight, wanting to savor the pleasure she was giving him so freely for as long as he could. Freely and with surprising skill, he thought as he bowed up off the bed after she did something quick and clever with her tongue that sent a blinding rush of heat through him.

Simon knew he was not going to last as long as he wanted to when she slowly took him into her mouth. His body began to tighten almost painfully with a need for release as she loved him. The sight of her between his legs was enough to bring him close to release.

He finally grabbed her beneath the arms and pulled her up his body until she sat astride him. Not only was he pleased to find her wet and eager for him because he so badly needed her to be, but the realization that she had been aroused by what she had done to him nearly sent him over the edge. He thrust inside her, trembled at the way her damp heat clasped him tightly in welcome, and then lost himself in their blind rush to find their release, reaching it as one and clutching each tightly as it raged through them.

With limbs still drained of strength from the force of his release, Simon shifted their bodies around until her slim back was tucked up to his front. He wrapped his arms around her and rested his cheek against her hair. Ilsabeth had been an innocent but she was proving to be the best lover he had ever had. Simon suspected the feelings he had for her added to the pleasure she gave him, but he knew the way she so freely gave of herself was what added to it all.

And just what did he feel for her? he wondered. He wanted her right where she was, in his arms and in his bed. The question was, for how long? Simon pulled his thoughts away from that path. This was not a good time to walk it. Not only was she not free to consider any future yet but his brother Henry was about to arrive in town. Matters between him and Ilsabeth could change a lot when she saw the sort of blood he sprang from.

She was right when she said that Henry was a madman. Simon suspected his elder brother had been born mad. He did not think it right to blame others in a family for the crimes of their kinsman, and so he was a lot fairer in his dealings than others were. Many believed that madness ran in the blood, and sometimes it did, but Simon had seen proof that it did not have to. It was not until he faced the fact that his brother was mad that Simon realized his opinion on that was not as firm as he had thought it to be.

Was there madness in his blood? He had not seen his younger brothers for years, not since they were bairns, but, in what little information he had gathered on them, he had not heard anything that indicated they suffered from any madness. Then again, Henry's insanity was not clear to see right away.

"Simon, ye are going all tense again," murmured

Ilsabeth, her husky voice thick with oncoming sleep.

"Do ye think madness is in the blood?" he asked, and then cursed himself for the weakness that prompted such a question.

Ilsabeth turned until she could wrap her arms around him and rest her cheek against his chest. She was so sleepy; she did not really wish to discuss madness, bloodlines, and such things that required sharp wits to talk about clearly. Yet, she understood Simon's uneasiness. He may have seen the madness in Henry for a long time but he had only just openly accepted it.

"Some is, some isnae," she said. "Whatever madness has Henry in its grip isnae in ye, Simon. Henry doesnae care about justice or helping the innocent. He cares only for Henry. He enjoys giving pain and ye dinnae." She yawned and rubbed her cheek against him.

Simon kissed the top of her head and began to lightly rub her back. "Sleep, Ilsabeth. I but suffered a moment of weakness. I can list the differences between me and my cursed brother all by myself."

"Ye do that."

A heartbeat later he felt her grow limp in his arms and nearly laughed. When Ilsabeth was tired she often went to sleep just like an exhausted child. He was not sure why he found that endearing, but he did.

He did what she had told him to, listing the many differences between him and Henry. It helped a little but he knew the seed of doubt had rooted itself deep in his heart. Simon was just not sure if he could dig it out or how it might affect his life.

When he looked down at the woman asleep in his arms his heart cramped in his chest. Something else he was going to have to do soon was decide what he wanted to do with Ilsabeth Murray Armstrong. Every instinct he prided himself on said that the end of this trouble was coming soon and he would not be able to avoid thinking about her and the future too much longer. Simon was not sure why even the thought of making a decision about her, about her place in his life, made him sweat but he thought it was probably not a good sign.

Chapter 12

"Evening, Master Hepbourn."

Simon could not completely subdue the smile he felt curving his mouth. It had been so easy to take the man. David had been ambling along through the shadowed alleys on his way back from a toss with a tavern maid and walked right into their arms. One little tap on the man's head and it had been ridiculously simple to spirit him away to this secure room in Peter's house.

David was now staring at him and his companions with the dazed look of the newly conscious. He also clung to the arms of the chair they had put him in as if he feared someone was about to steal it out from beneath him. Simon idly wondered how long it would take David to realize just how much danger he was in. At the moment he just sat there, stiff and wide-eyed.

Then, abruptly, his eyes cleared of the dull haze of astonishment. He leapt to his feet and tried to run. Simon was not sure where the fool thought he was going as there was only one small window high up on the rough stone wall and one door. One of Simon's men stood guard at each. It might be a little cruel to just stand and watch as David darted from window to door and back again several times, but Simon suffered no guilt for enjoying the man's panic. This was one of the men who did not care if an innocent woman was condemned and executed for a crime he knew she had not committed. Letting David taste a little of the helpless fear Ilsabeth had been living with was only just.

"Have ye worn yourself out yet?" he asked David, and could swear the man's chin quivered exactly like Elen's did when she was about to let go an ear-splitting howl. "Sit down."

David hesitated only a moment before he stomped back to the chair and threw himself down into it. Despite the man's childish display of anger, Simon knew David was terrified. It was there to see in his stare, which remained too widely open and showed far too much of the white of his eyes. His skin had grown very pale and Simon could see the beads of nervous sweat forming on the man's brow.

"Why are ye detaining me?" David demanded. "This is unacceptable. Ye may be a king's mon, Sir Simon, but that doesnae give ye the right to snatch people right off the streets."

"Actually, it does."

David ignored him. "Just who do ye think ye are?"

"The mon who just might be able to save ye from your own folly. At this moment ye are doomed to die a traitor's death right alongside your vain cousin. Ye do ken what they do to traitors, dinnae ye?"

When David just stared at him, Simon continued, "First they chain ye in the deepest, darkest prison they can find and then they begin to torture ye. Ye might ken a few things they need to learn about the others or they might just feel ye need it for thinking ye had a right to kill a king. A wee bit of stretching on the rack and, when ye can hear your own joints on your legs and arms pop from the strain, they will quickly find another way to cause ye as much pain as they can. The king's torturers are verra skilled at their job. They have whips, chains, knives, hot pincers. And they can wield them all with precision. They like to have a go at the softer, more tender parts of the body. The eyes, the nose, the balls."

Simon stepped back from David. The man had gone a little green. He decided he had described enough of the horrors the man would face, although David had revealed little stomach for the thought of his own pain. He had thought to turn the man craven with such talk but it would do him no good if David ended up too terrified to even talk. He could still take David to the court and hand him over to the sheriff. Simon had the feeling that, if he indulged in his planned talk on the various tortures David would have to endure, he would be handing the sheriff no more than a babbling idiot.

"I dinnae ken why ye would taunt me with such horrors," David said. "I have done ye no wrong."

"Enough, David. We both ken what ye have al-

lowed your cousin to lead ye into." Simon stepped
back close to the chair David cowered in, placed a
hand on each arm of the chair, and leaned forward
to stare right into David's pale eyes. "He will lead ye
no more. Dinnae think he will come to save ye, dear
cousin to him that ye may be. That mon will toss ye
aside as swiftly as he can, no doubt parading about
the court denouncing ye as he has already de-
nounced me and mine. The moment he is certain
that all see ye as the foul traitor he claims, he will
leave ye to suffer. Hell's fire, he will be sure there is
no mercy for ye by the time he has finished telling
his lies."

"Walter is an honorable mon who cares weel for
those he calls friend and kin," David protested, and
glared at Simon when he snorted with laughter, a
laughter echoed by the others in the room.

"Listen to me, ye miserable wee worm," snapped
Simon, his humor vanishing to be replaced with a
cold fury. "I heard ye that day ye met Walter in the
wood. Ilsabeth heard ye and Walter the day she had
to flee for her life, heard ye and the honorable Walter speak openly of treason and murder."

"And ye believe her word o'er that of a mon, a
fellow knight? She points the finger of guilt at us
and tries to make us bear the weight of her sins.
Walter ne'er should have become betrothed to the
wench, ne'er thought of tying his good name to
those reivers, the Armstrongs. If ye wish to find
your traitors, then go and find her, find one of the
Armstrongs of Aigballa, or even one of their kin the
Murrays. There are enough of that cursed clan that
e'en ye should be able to find one. They breed like

rabbits. Go and find my cousin," David demanded. "He will vouch for me."

"Vouch for ye? Ye expect me to accept the word of a traitor? Didnae ye listen to what I just told ye? Ye have condemned yourself with your own mouth. Walter is in this plot as deep as ye are. Deeper, or I wouldnae be considering helping ye stay alive."

Simon continued to listen to David's denials, meeting each one of them with the sure knowledge of David's guilt. Each time David demanded Hepbourn's presence, Simon met the request with cold contempt. He did, however, begin to think David had more backbone than his reaction to talk of torture had implied.

If nothing else, the man was certainly loyal to Hepbourn. Hepbourn would toss David to the wolves without a moment's hesitation. David needed more than Simon's word to believe it, however, and Simon did not have the time and inclination to spend hours trying to wear David down. He needed the break in the man's composure to come quickly, preferably without any of the horrendous tortures he had mentioned to him.

"Ye are so verra certain Hepbourn will come to your aid, are ye?" asked Simon, and watched David glance down at the floor before looking back at him and nodding. He had watched David closely for long enough to recognize that moment of doubt. "So be it. Peter, find something for this trusting fool to write on so that he might send a plea to his loving cousin."

Once David had written out his message, Simon found a boy to deliver it and wait for a reply. After the first hour of waiting David no longer looked so confident of rescue. The boy did not return with a reply until almost three hours had passed, saying that Hepbourn would not answer until he realized the boy would not leave. Simon suspected Walter had needed time to think of what served him best in the matter. The look on David's face as he read the reply was painful to see. David silently handed it to Simon.

Simon read, *It grieves me more than I can say to learn that my own cousin is part of the treasonous plot against our beloved king. You have been as a brother to me and I loved you as one, but I cannot defend your actions in this. I hope this stain upon the name of Hepbourn does not spread and I will pray for your soul, cousin.*

"I have followed him since I was a child," David whispered. "Heeded his every word. When he started to speak of being rid of the king, I was unsettled, but he presented such logical reasons to me that I was soon swayed. What a fool I have been. I have tossed my life away for the sake of a liar."

Simon pulled a chair close to David and sat down to face him. "Mayhap. Mayhap not. If ye give me the names I want, all the information ye have concerning the many twists and turns the plot will take once it is set in motion, I will fight for ye. As I told ye, I overheard ye and Hepbourn speaking in the woods the other day and ken weel that ye are uncertain about this, uncertain about the leader. Ye may nay fully appreciate the tale I spin to save your life, but I believe I can weave one good enough when this is over. I believe our liege will be merciful since ye will have helped us put an end to this plot to yank the throne out from under his arse."

"His cold, dead arse," David murmured. "They dinnae want to simply remove him from the throne; they want him dead. They believe that will be enough to make the mon's followers readily bow to the new king."

"And ye dinnae believe that."

"Nay, but I became verra good at ignoring such talk. And, when I did express some doubt or unease Walter was verra quick to smother such qualms beneath a flood of praise and reasonable explanations." David shook his head as he glanced at the note. "I can see now that he ne'er cared for me for all he claims he loved me as a brother. The few lessons I recall as a child are the ones that tell ye to look up to the mon who puts a roof o'er your head, food in your belly, and clothes on your back. He isnae that many years older than me, but that was what Walter did for me.

"But, my God, I was willing to let that lass die for Walter." He shook his head again. "I kept dreaming of her being dragged to the execution block and would wake in an agony of fear or guilt, but I still followed Walter, didnae I?"

"Aye, and for that alone I would be willing to watch ye die an ugly, painful death, but I need what ye can tell me more than I need that moment of revenge."

David stared at him for a moment and then nodded. He started to talk and kept right on talking, answering any and all questions put to him. Simon wondered when Walter would realize what a grave mistake he had made in spitting on this young man's devotion and loyalty. If Walter survived to stand trial, he would see it clearly enough, for Simon was going to make good use of this witness.

"That Walter is an idiot," said Peter as he and Simon shared an ale by the fire in the small main hall of Peter's home. "I think that boy considered Walter all the family he had. Father, brother, uncle." Peter shrugged. "I can see how the boy could be pulled into this mess."

"So can I, which is why I will do all I can to see he survives his stupidity," said Simon. "And because I also believe that, from the time he was a small child, David was trained to be Walter's ever faithful minion. David's real mistake was to think that Walter returned any of that care and respect."

"What do we do now? Do we begin to arrest any of the people he told us of?"

"Nay, not yet. We watch them. If we gather them all up now we will lose the chance to get their leader."

"Who is your brother, if David is to be believed."

"I think David told us everything he knew or was told. And, aye, the leader is my brother. Do ye think that will be a problem for me? That I will hesitate?"

"Ne'er thought ye would hesitate," Peter said. "Just that it will be hard, I should think, to mark your own brother a traitor."

"It willnae be easy but nay for the reason ye think. There is no love between us. If Henry thinks I ken what he is about, he willnae hesitate to try and see me dead. I will continue with this because I have some hope of saving Lochancorrie. If I am the one to bring all of these fools to justice, even the one I must call brother, then the king may weel leave Lochancorrie in Innes hands."

Peter slowly nodded. "He could also wonder if ye conspire with your brother."

Simon grimaced and took a deep drink of ale. "I believe I can bring forth enough witnesses to make the king see that that would never happen."

"I pray ye are right. I would hate to see all the good work ye have done for the king and the people of this country demeaned or forgotten just because you have a fool for a brother."

"Oh, Henry isnae a complete fool. I dinnae ken what has possessed him to think he has any right to the throne, but dinnae think ye will be dealing with another Walter. Henry is cunning and brutal. If he didnae have such idiots as Walter in his traitorous little army, he could well have gotten just what he wanted."

"Wheesht, ye werenae lying when ye said there was no love lost between the two of ye."

"A close watch needs to be kept on David. I should have been more careful when the message went to Walter and the answer sent back. Someone could easily have followed the boy. Walter may have enough family feeling, or be confident enough of David's undying loyalty, to think nothing needs to be done save let the mon be tried, convicted, and killed as a traitor, but my brother will quickly see that David is a weak link."

"So ye think someone will be trying to get to David to shut his mouth, nay kenning that 'tis already too late to stop up the flow."

"I have nay doubt about it. We have a wee bit of time. Henry willnae be here for another day or two.

But I think we best find a safer place to put our witness. The moment Henry hears that David has been taken up by us, he will be wanting the mon dead and buried."

Peter rubbed his chin and asked, "Do ye think that is why the lad looked so afeared even though ye told him ye would save his life?"

"I believe so. He said he didnae trust Henry, that the mon didnae seem the sort of mon one would want as king." Simon grimaced. "David kens I heard him and Walter speaking that day in the wood so he kens I heard how Henry makes sure no one wants to leave, that every mon who kens about the plot will stay with it until the bitter end. Seems Henry butchered one who sought to walk away from it all and did so in front of all the men gathered there that day. Kenning Henry as I do, I suspect it was a show to put the fear of God in every mon there."

"I just cannae see ye and this mon ye speak of as having the same blood."

"I wish we didnae. Now, I need David to be carefully watched tonight. Walter may suddenly realize that he cannae leave his cousin in our hands if only because doing so will enrage Henry. By the morrow I will have found another place to put David."

"Agreed. And what of the other men he named? The ones that are here?"

"We watch them."

It took several hours to plan the best way to keep a watch on the traitors already in the town. Most of the names David had given him did not surprise Simon. They were men who felt they had been slighted or even cheated by the king, or ones who felt some convoluted bloodlines gave them more of a right to the privileges others enjoyed and were looking to take them as soon as Henry sat on the throne.

They did not know Henry well, Simon thought as he left for the court. Henry would share nothing. He might give away a few things if he thought the man who wanted them could be helpful, but only a few things. The ones who demanded some recompense for helping him get that throne would quickly be silenced. Simon doubted that David would have survived long after Henry became king for the man did have a conscience and Henry would have been able to sniff that weakness out.

Simon was rounding the corner in the road that led to the keep where the king's court was being held and found himself facing six men. One look at them, even in the dimming light of evening, told him they were hired swords. Walter was probably trying to get rid of him before he could spread the word of anything David might have said.

"Evening, gentlemen," he said, his hand on his sword. "May I assist ye in some way?"

"Aye," said a burly dark-bearded man, his sneer revealing that he had long ago lost most of his teeth. "Ye can die."

"Eventually, aye, I suspicion I will. Doesnae everyone?"

"Ye will be doing so a lot sooner than most."

"May I ask why?"

"Ye can ask but it willnae get ye any answers. Mon who hired us didnae say why he wanted ye dead. Doesnae make no mind to me why he does. Coin was good."

"Was he tall, fair of hair, somewhat handsome, and with an air of overweening importance?"

"Mighta been. Told ye, the who and the why dinnae matter."

"Nay sure of that, Mac," grumbled an extremely filthy man whose belly showed that he had too great a love for food. "He kens who hired us."

"Weel, he would, wouldnae he," snapped Mac. "No one wants a mon they dinnae ken murdered, do they? Ye have to ken a mon to be wanting him dead."

"I dinna ken who ye are and I am already wanting ye dead," spoke the tall man who stepped up beside Simon.

Simon sighed and glanced at Tormand, who probably thought he was in disguise again. His eyes could not be hidden, however, no matter how thick he grew his beard or what color berry juice he rubbed into his beard and hair. Tormand seemed to suffer Ilsabeth's difficulty in understanding that there were just some eyes that people did not forget. Beautiful, big blue eyes and mismatched eyes were among them.

"Ye are a wee bit too close to the fire here, friend," Simon said, and drew his sword.

"I am in disguise," said Tormand.

"As what?" Simon spared a quick glance at Tormand's rags. "A beggar?"

"Exactly. No one looks at beggars. So what do these fools want from ye?"

"Ye heard him. My death. I can explain it after they go away." He looked at the men. "I suggest ye give this up. Take that fool's money and run. Verra far away." The men started to have a whispered conversation, although one of them always kept his gaze on Simon, so Simon looked at Tormand again. "My friend, ye can dress in any ridiculous outfit ye like and grow that beard down to your knees but any who look into your face for but one moment will ken who ye are. The eyes, ye fool. No one forgets those eyes."

"Ah, hell's teeth. Cannae do anything about them save for squint a lot. Nay sure I would want to do anything about them either. My Morainn is still trying to decide which one she likes better. She stares into them sometimes and tells me it is difficult to ken when they are both so beautiful." He grinned when Simon groaned. "Heads up. They have come to a decision."

"We think ye ought to give us some money," said Mac. "More than the other fellow gave us. Then we can honestly tell the mon that we couldnae do as he asked because ye paid better."

"He is a marvel, isnae he, Simon?" Tormand laughed.

After a lot of bickering and bartering, the men left, their pockets a little heavier. Tormand continued to occasionally chuckle over the matter as he and Simon made their way to a small tavern. Despite the way the tavern maid eyed Tormand with disgust, Simon was able to get them to a small table tucked far in the corner. As soon as he and Tormand each had a tankard of ale, Simon told him everything he had learned from David.

"Walter made a verra big mistake there," said Tormand, who grinned at, then winked at, the horrified tavern maid.

Simon needed only one peek at Tormand to

know what horrified the woman. "I hope whate'er ye have put on your teeth will come out." They looked as if they were stained with something vile that was oozing from his gums.

" 'Tis naught but some herbal mess Morainn mixed up. It doesnae taste bad. Although, it doesnae go with this ale verra weel." Tormand set his tankard down and looked at Simon. "So ye are truly going to stay with this until the bitter end."

"I have to, Tormand."

Tormand nodded. "I can see it. So could Morainn. She says all will be weel at Lochancorrie. Couldnae tell me if that was because ye took on the land or because whoever the king gifted with a traitor's goods was a good laird, but she thought ye might like to ken that the future is nay all death and misery for your home."

Simon thought about it for a moment and nodded. "It is good news. It takes away a worry and that can only be good at this time. Things are beginning to fall into place."

"Morainn also said that ye will face a great trial and have to make a painful choice, or something akin to that. Mayhap it was that ye make the wrong choice and it is painful." He shrugged when Simon glared at him. "She wasnae sure, either. Just that there will be something painful for ye when all else is right. I told her a few more specific dreams might be better but she told me to tell ye this one."

"That is verra vague e'en for Morainn."

"So I thought but she wouldnae tell me anything else and insisted I come and tell ye that. Good thing I did, too, or ye would have been dead on the road to the king's court."

"I could have beaten them." Simon ignored the mocking sounds Tormand made. "I will think on it for a wee while and mayhap it will make more sense in time."

"Nay so sure of that. Just why were ye headed to the court again? Now that ye are so close to capturing these traitors and all, I would have thought ye would wish to start avoiding that place again."

" 'Tis hard to abide it, but I must speak to the king as soon as possible if I want any chance of saving Lochancorrie."

"Go then. I will wait here for you. As soon as ye can, come back and tell me what ye learned and what the king said."

Simon hesitated for only a moment and then he hurried off to get to the court. He would not stand around waiting to get in to see the king, he told himself, because there was nothing to gain from leaving Tormand wasting time at the tavern while he wasted time in an unanswered bid to see his liege lord. To Simon's relief, and surprise, he was escorted into the presence of the king only moments after he arrived. He bowed before the man he had sworn his sword to.

"Ye have some news for us, Simon?" the king asked.

"We have captured one of the men who was dragged into the plan." Without naming anyone, Simon told him about David, stressing the fact that David had long been caught firm by the other man's lies.

"Weel, if that mon ye hold helps ye bring the traitors to justice before I am killed, he will be freed."

"Thank ye, sire. There is one other thing, ere I return to the business of capturing these men."

"Best speak now whilst I am in a good humor over seeing the end of this plot."

"I fear one of my blood may be involved."

"Ah, a shame, but ye dinnae need to worry that I would blame ye for the act of some kinsmon. Are ye asking to have someone else step in to end this? I would prefer that ye do it as, if men who are liked and respected are involved, your word of their guilt will be held in high esteem. And no one who kens ye would think ye had ought to do with any bad seed in your family."

There was something in the way the king stared at him that told Simon his king had a good idea of which one of Simon's family might be a traitor, but neither of them acknowledged the truth that lay between them. "Thank ye, my liege, but I wish to see this through to the end. What I ask is that, if I am proven right, ye might consider me for the one to take o'er the forfeited lands."

"Of course." He looked at his clerk, who sat at a small table at the far end of the room. "Ranald will see to that, willnae ye, Ranald."

Ranald nodded and Simon could not believe the ease with which it was done. He knew the king could yet change his mind, but the fact that the king had already told Ranald to see to it was reason to hope that Lochancorrie could be saved. After a short while of answering the king's questions yet not giving the man the names he wanted, Simon left and hurried back to the tavern where Tormand waited for him.

" 'Tis strange to see ye sitting all alone in a tavern," Simon said as he sat down.

"I am a married mon," said Tormand.

Simon wondered if Tormand would ever tire of saying that and somehow doubted he would. It made him envious. "And ye have oozing teeth. Why do I think that was Morainn's idea?" He shook his head when Tormand grinned, displaying those horrific teeth.

"Weel, did ye get to see the king?"

"Aye. He was pleased to hear this is all nearing an end, but I think he started to become annoyed that I would nay give him any names until I had the leader in my hands. He did sympathize with me o'er the chance that one of my blood may be involved. In truth, I think he kens exactly who may be involved but naught was said. What he did do was say I could have the land if it was forfeit. He even told old Ranald to see to it."

"Again—a large concern lifted." Tormand finished his tankard of ale and stood up. "I wish to be home now. I but stayed to hear what news ye might have from the king. It will be good to have this at an end soon. Ilsabeth's family can regain their home and Ilsabeth can join them. And ye, my friend, can return to the life ye had ere she tripped into your home with those two foundlings. Rest weel."

"Ye, too," Simon grumbled.

He would not have been surprised if Tormand grinned all the way home. Simon could tell by the look his friend gave him as he had spoken of life returning to normal that Tormand knew Simon did not truly want that. What Tormand could not know was that it might be all Simon could allow. Ilsabeth had a large, loving family eager to take her home. Simon had a mad brother and three missing ones plus lands that had been held under Henry's boot heel for too long. It could be that there was no sane way to put two such disparate people together in any more than a brief affair.

Chapter 13

Humming quietly to herself, Ilsabeth washed the floor in the entrance hall of Simon's house. She was going to have to speak to Simon about hiring a maid to help Old Bega. Although the woman was strong and healthy, there was too much work for just one woman to do. MacBean helped but having some girl come in from town every day would make a great deal of difference. Ilsabeth resolutely silenced the voice that said she would be the one to make such decisions. Simon had given no indication that she would be.

For the moment, Ilsabeth did not mind working hard and for long hours. In truth, she welcomed it. When Simon had first captured David, she had been elated. Common sense told her she had been a fool to have thought capturing the man would put an end to her and her family's suffering, but she had thought it anyway. Now, three long days afterward, she was more frustrated than she had been before David had been taken. Simon was not telling her much except to warn her not to speak of the fact that he held David, and that silence did nothing to help ease her frustration.

She forced herself to look at all the activity that had been going on since Simon had grabbed David right off the streets near the inn where the man had been staying. Simon's men were in and out of the house at all hours, running in to speak to him in urgent tones and then disappearing again. And Simon worked day and night, although he still managed to find the time to make love to her, she thought, and suddenly grinned.

"Ye are happy to be working like some lowly kitchen maid, are ye?"

Ilsabeth's good humor faded so quickly she was astonished she did not cry out at the abrupt loss. Instead, she looked up and met the hard gaze of Sir Walter Hepbourn. There were six of the king's soldiers with him. Ilsabeth did not even think. She leapt up, kicked Walter in the knee and then fled to the back of the house.

"Get back here, ye traitorous bitch!"

One quick glance behind her showed Walter signaling to the soldiers to go after her, and then limping along behind them. When Ilsabeth reached the door to the garden she thought she had made good her escape. She was not sure where she would go, but Simon's house was no longer safe for her. Yanking open the door, she took one step into the garden only to see two of the king's soldiers running into the garden through the gate. She turned to go back into the house, thinking there might be a place to hide, but one look inside told her that there was no safety to be found there. Old Bega and MacBean were trying to hold the soldiers back with a broom and a spade and she feared they would get themselves killed.

A hand closing tightly around her arm reminded Ilsabeth that not all the king's soldiers were in the kitchen. She turned so quickly the man had no time to defend himself against the punch she aimed at his nose. Ilsabeth cursed almost as vehemently as the soldier did when her fist connected with his long nose. Her hand hurt so badly she was not sure if that cracking noise she had heard as her fist struck the man was her fist or his nose breaking.

"Run, Ilsabeth!" yelled Reid as he leapt onto the back of the second soldier and began to pound on the man's head with both of his small fists while Elen skipped around kicking the man in the legs. The soldier she had struck held on to his bleeding nose and moaned. "Run!" Reid yelled again. "Ye can get to the gate now."

To use two children to help shield herself felt wrong but Ilsabeth knew she could not risk being taken prisoner. It was clear to see that the soldiers that Walter had chosen were the kind of men who could not bring themselves to hurt their elders or children for none of her stalwart defenders were hurt yet they were not being so gentle with the soldiers. On the other hand, those same soldiers were trying to drag her away to be imprisoned and then tried, convicted, and executed. Ilsabeth knew she had no choices left. Simon would have to clean up the mess she left behind. That would be far easier for him to do than getting her free of the king's soldiers and dungeons. She turned and ran for the gate.

"Stop, Ilsabeth!" yelled Walter.

"Ye have no say o'er me." She reached out for the latch on the garden gate.

"Oh, aye, I believe I do."

The icy smugness of his tone sent an abrupt chill of alarm down Ilsabeth's spine. Walter sounded very smug indeed and that was never a good thing. She also noticed that everyone else had gone very quiet. It was possible the quiet was just everyone waiting to see if she would obey Walter, but she doubted it. He had some plan he felt certain would bring her to willingly walk into his grasp. Ilsabeth looked down at her hand on the gate latch and then sighed, turning to look back at Walter.

Her heart leapt up into her throat so quickly she nearly gagged. A smiling Walter held a wide-eyed Elen with one arm curled around her middle. In his free hand was a very large, very sharp knife. It was pressed against the child's throat. Ilsabeth was terrified. Elen was too young to understand the need to keep as still as she could. At any moment Elen could begin to squirm and easily end up with her throat cut.

" 'Tis just a bairn, sir," said one of the soldiers, a big, heavily muscled man who watched Walter and made no attempt to hide his disgust. "I dinnae abide with using a wee bairn to threaten someone."

"And I cannae abide failure or traitors," snapped Walter. "This woman killed the king's cousin and is plotting to kill the king."

"All by her wee self or are the bairns going to help her?"

"Best ye watch yourself, Gowan. 'Tis ne'er wise to speak to your betters that way, laddie."

Ilsabeth chanced a glance at the soldier who so openly disagreed with Walter's actions. It was obvious the man was biting down hard on his tongue so that he did not blurt out his opinion of who was the better man. The other soldiers said nothing but looked as if they agreed with Gowan. Elen remained remarkably still while a white-faced MacBean stood in the doorway, his gnarled hand patting the shoulder of a weeping Old Bega. Reid stood utterly still right in front of Walter, his gaze fixed unwaveringly on his sister. It had to be Reid who was keeping the ever busy Elen so still, Ilsabeth was certain of it, but he could not do it for hours.

"Put her down, Walter," Ilsabeth said in as cold and calm a voice as she could muster. "The child has done naught to ye. She is no part of all this."

"We make a trade. Ye for this child. Ye step o'er here and I will set the lass down so that she can run to her brother. If ye keep refusing, I will cut her wee throat."

"Bastard."

There was no other choice for her to make. It was her or Elen. There was something in Walter's gaze that told her he was not bluffing. That Walter could even think of killing such a small child just because he did not wish to fight for his prize made Ilsabeth ill. What had she seen in such a man? A better question might be, how could she have missed this ugly side of him?

Praying that Simon was close to bringing this man to justice, Ilsabeth marched over to him. "Put her down now, Walter. And if there is e'en one drop of blood on her, I will eviscerate you."

Walter snorted in crude derision of her threat. "Ye? Wheesht, ye havenae got a warrior's skill or heart, lass."

He set Elen down. Reid grabbed his sister and ran to MacBean and Old Bega. Ilsabeth waited until Walter looked at her and then she punched him right in his lovely bright smile. She heard one of the soldiers mutter that he could have told the fool Ilsabeth would do that and she suspected it was the man she had punched in the nose. While he stood there trapped by a sense of shock, she took full advantage of it and rammed her knee into his groin.

As Walter fell to his knees retching and moaning in pain, Ilsabeth looked at the soldiers. They eyed Walter with a man's sympathy for the pain but little else. She took a cautious step toward the door. They all shifted position just enough to keep her trapped in the kitchen. They might not like Walter or agree with all he did, but they were loyal to the king and she was an accused traitor. There was no escape.

"Ye bitch, ye bitch, ye bitch," Walter said, his voice growing louder with each word as he staggered to his feet. "God's tears but I will enjoy watching your execution."

That scared her nearly witless, but she pushed away the horror of what she might yet face if Simon could not save her in time. "We will see who will watch who die," she said quietly.

Walter reached for her, but Gowan grabbed her by the arm and yanked her out of the way. "She is the king's prisoner, sir."

"Ye are protecting this traitor?" Walter said, glaring at the man.

Gowan did not even blink. "I am holding the king's prisoner, sir. One the king himself is eager to speak to. I am thinking he would like her to be able to speak. In your anger ye may do something that will prevent that. Shall we go?"

"Ilsabeth," Reid said, his young voice shaking with the tears she knew he would fight not to shed before all these men.

"Hush, Reid," she said, and smiled at him. "Ye will be safe here."

"I will go and fetch Simon."

"Aye, ye do that, laddie," said Walter. "He has a few questions to answer. The first being why he was hiding away a woman wanted for treason."

"He was protecting the king's prisoner," said Ilsabeth. "When ye came I was scrubbing the floor, Walter. That is hardly the act of a woman creeping about and ready to flee. And ye do ken that Sir Innes would ne'er turn a person o'er to trial and execution until he was verra sure that was what was warranted. Mayhap he just feared that he wouldnae be given the chance to find out the truth ere some zealous fool executed me."

"Get her out of here," he snapped at the soldiers, and then he glared at MacBean. "Ye best tell your master he has some explaining to do. The king will be verra interested in where we found this traitor."

"She isnae a traitor," yelled Reid as the soldiers escorted Ilsabeth out of the house, Walter limping behind them. He looked at MacBean after the door shut behind the men. "She isnae."

"Of course she isnae, laddie," said MacBean. "Best ye and I go and hunt down Simon. He needs to ken what game is being played now. I am thinking he will also be in need of a few calm heads about when he hears this."

Ilsabeth stared at the king, idly thinking that he did not look any different from any other man yet not sure why she had ever thought that he would. What he did look like, however, was an angry man and this one had the power to cause her some real harm. Walter stood near her, but she noticed that Gowan managed to always keep himself between her and Walter.

"She was found in Sir Simon's own house?" the king asked.

"Aye, my liege," replied Walter. "He was hiding her beneath his own roof."

The king leaned forward in his chair and studied Ilsabeth, frowning at her water-stained and worn skirts. "He wasnae keeping her verra weel, was he? What is that on your skirts, woman?"

"I was scrubbing the floor when the soldiers arrived, my liege," Ilsabeth replied, and watched Gowan nod when the king glanced at him for confirmation.

"No guards? No bonds?"

"Nay, sire," replied Walter.

"I was asking the lass here, Sir Hepbourn." The king looked at Ilsabeth. "Weel?"

"No bonds, sire, but MacBean was my guard," Ilsabeth said.

"I see. And how long have ye been there, living under Sir Simon's roof?"

"Since three days after I had to run from my home, sire."

Anger tightened the king's features. "After ye stuck your dagger in my cousin."

"Nay, sire. I ne'er even met your cousin. I have no idea how my dagger ended up in him but it soon became clear that I wasnae going to have a chance to find out or defend myself."

"So I am to believe that ye didnae kill Ian and ye arenae planning to kill me. Ye and your family are all innocent, are they?"

"Aye, sire."

Walter snorted. "No Armstrong has e'er been innocent."

Ilsabeth glared at him. "Ye still have all your cattle, dinnae ye?" She heard one of the soldiers snicker, then hastily smother the noise after one glance from the king.

"Weel, I think I must speak to Sir Simon. I must say I am disappointed that he didnae tell me he already had ye in his possession. It makes me wonder what game he is playing and I grow verra weary of games."

"Sire, all he does is seek the truth," Ilsabeth said. "My kin asked him to find the truth about the accusations against us. That is all he has been doing."

"We shall see. Take her and lock her up."

Ilsabeth fought the urge to try and wrestle free of her guard. It took all of her willpower but she managed to leave the king's presence with her back straight. That strength waned with every step they took down into the bowels of the castle. She prayed that Simon could help her soon for she was not sure how long she could remain sane in such a desolate place.

Simon tensed with alarm when MacBean and Reid arrived at the little cottage where they were now keeping David. He had told MacBean where it was so that he could be reached in an emergency. The fact that Reid looked as if he had been crying only increased his alarm.

"The soldiers came to the house today," said Mac-Bean. "Sir Walter Hepbourn brought them and they have taken away Ilsabeth."

For a moment not a single thought went through Simon's head. Then fear rushed through his body and he began to move to the door, his speed increasing with every step. He was about to open the door when MacBean and Peter leapt on him, holding him firmly to the floor as he thrashed and cursed them. It took him more minutes than he cared to consider before his fear receded and his mind cleared.

"Let me up," he demanded.

"Ye arenae going to go racing off to rescue her, are ye?" asked MacBean.

"Nay just yet," he said and, after Peter and Mac-Bean got off him, he stood up and brushed off his clothes.

"What do ye mean by nay yet?" demanded Peter.

"I mean that I will do all I can to bring the real traitors to the king and get her out of the prison she now sits in," Simon replied. "But, if there is a trial and it even looks as if she will be marked for execution, I will get her away from here."

"Fair enough," said Peter, and moved to pour MacBean an ale and get Reid some cider.

"Tell me exactly what happened," Simon asked MacBean, and listened carefully as MacBean and Reid told him everything they had witnessed.

"Gowan is a good mon," said Peter.

"Aye, he is, and I can find some comfort in the fact that he kens she is there as weel as the sort of mon Hepbourn is." Simon dragged his hand through his hair. "I misjudged the man. Somehow he found out where Ilsabeth was. He kenned she had been seen about town but I cannae see how he would feel sure enough that I sheltered her that he would drag the king and his soldiers into it."

"That is something only he can answer."

"And I will ask him when 'tis my turn to question him. But now I had best go and see the king."

"May I come?" asked Reid.

Simon stared down at the boy for a moment. Reid was a handsome little boy and it was clear that he loved Ilsabeth. Simon also knew that the king had a soft heart when it came to small children. It might not help Ilsabeth much for the king to see the foundling boy she had taken in, but it certainly could not hurt.

"Do it," said Peter. "It may help if he sees that she has the heart to take in a child and that the child loves her. 'Tis the way of some men to believe that a lass who can love and be loved by a child couldnae possibly do something like kill a mon or betray a king."

Simon took Reid with him, swinging the boy up into the saddle of his black gelding and then mounting behind the child. Reid was silent and Simon appreciated the boy's quiet for he had to think. He was sure that Hepbourn would have taken full advantage of the fact that Ilsabeth had been hiding in his home, making sure the king heard it and heard it again. Simon knew he was going to have to have a very good explanation for something that could easily put him in with the traitors, at least in the king's eyes.

As they walked through the court, Simon actually felt an urge to smile. Reid's eyes were huge as he stared around at the grandeur and all the well-dressed people. His amusement was fleeting, however, for he recognized what the sly glances and whispers meant. Hepbourn had already begun to spread his lies.

It was not encouraging that he was immediately admitted to the king's chambers. There had been a brief argument with the guard for the man wished to hold Reid back. When Simon faced the king and saw the anger in the man's eyes, he wondered if he had made a mistake in fighting for the boy's presence at his side. The way Reid slipped his small hand into his told Simon that Reid had also seen that anger.

"Ye brought a child with ye?" demanded the king.

"He was the one to bring me the news about Ilsabeth Murray Armstrong's arrest and he was hoping to hear what has happened to her, sire," Simon replied.

"She is in the dungeon. Where else would she be." The king frowned at Reid when the boy gasped. "I hope ye dinnae mean to start crying."

"Nay, um, sire," said Reid. "I just thought someone would talk to her first and then they would see that she couldnae do anything as bad as what they say she did."

"I talked to her, ye impertinent whelp," the king said, but Simon could hear a touch of amusement in his voice. "I havenae decided on her yet so she will stay where she is until this is all settled." He looked at Simon. "It is where she should have been from the beginning."

"I decided that, if all she told me was true, she could be in danger," replied Simon. "Nay from ye but from the ones who marked her as a killer and a traitor."

"So there are traitors in my court."

"I think ye always kenned that there were, sire."

" 'Tis nay so bad to hope one is wrong. She stays where she is, Sir Simon. Now that she has been found, that is how it must be."

"For how long?"

"As long as needed. Ye said ye are close to getting my traitors. Best ye work a little faster. The lass seemed honest enough whilst Sir Walter Hepbourn makes my skin crawl, so I am favoring her at the moment. If that begins to look like a weakness I willnae do it anymore but will start a trial."

Simon desperately wanted to blurt out every name he had and let the king send his soldiers out but he bit his tongue to stop the words. That would allow too many to escape and he wanted them all, especially the ones allied with his brother, who had begun the whole plot. He just prayed that Ilsabeth would understand why he had to leave her there.

"May I speak with her, sire?" he asked.

The king studied him for a minute in a way that made Simon a little uneasy. "Nay, not yet. Mayhap that will prod ye onward and settle this matter more quickly. Dinnae look so insulted. I dinnae think ye have joined the ones plotting against me. That doesnae mean I am certain ye havenae been fooled by a bonnie face. I also ken why ye willnae just give me names, but I would weigh the worth of their lives against the only one we have even the smallest proof against."

"As ye wish, sire."

"Go. Go and do what ye do best. I ken ye are near the end of this. End it soon, even if ye have to be a wee bit less meticulous."

"She didnae do it," said Reid. "Sire," he mumbled, and blushed.

" 'Tis in her favor that she has taken ye and your wee sister in. It wasnae in Sir Hepbourn's that he captured Miss Armstrong by holding a knife to a bairn's throat. I havenae allowed him to see that displeasure yet," the king said as he returned his gaze to Simon. "Again, see this ended soon. If nay for her sake, for yours and mine. I am ignoring the whispers about ye, considering the source, but if they arenae proven completely wrong soon, your ability to do the job ye do so weel will be harmed. Mayhap beyond repair."

"Understood, sire."

The moment they were out of the king's chambers, Reid said, "I dinnae understand. Why would ye nay be good at what ye do anymore?"

"To do what I do I must be believed to be above corruption, above most everything that can weaken a mon into making a wrong judgment. Ilsabeth is the sort of woman who can make a mon lean toward making a wrong judgment. Once people begin to think I was turned from my usual insistence upon the truth by a bonnie wee lass, they will begin to doubt every judgment I make, everything I say or do to prove a mon guilty or innocent."

After a moment of frowning silence, Reid said, "They will think that ye lied for her and if ye lied for her, ye may lie for others."

"Aye, exactly."

"Ah, there ye are, Sir Simon. I have been meaning to speak to ye."

Simon turned to look at Hepbourn. The man looked so pleased with himself Simon longed to punch that look right off Hepbourn's face. "What do ye want?"

"An answer to the question near all at court are now asking. Why was that woman hiding at your house? That seems a most questionable act by a mon who swears he is all about finding the truth and protecting the innocent."

Simon could see some of the other courtiers edging closer. It would not be wise to take Walter by the throat and choke the life out of him. Too many witnesses, he decided. Instead he leaned nearer to the mon and asked, just loudly enough for all close at hand to hear, "I will answer your question, if ye answer mine. Just what were ye doing at my house holding a knife to the throat of a wee lass of two years?"

There was a flurry of whispering and gasps of outrage from several of the women. Walter glared at Simon. "Unlike ye, sir, I have a care for our king. Ye were doing naught to catch these traitors so I kenned I had to act. That woman ye were hiding injured me in all her attempts to escape. I had to do something or she would have disappeared again."

"Aye, I heard she had kicked your balls up into your throat. With such a wee foot as she has I am surprised she could hit a target as small as that."

Ignoring Hepbourn's sputtered outrage and the snickers of those around them, Simon took Reid away from the court and tossed him up into the saddle. He was angry at them all now, even the king. Years of hard work, of unquestionable honesty and dedication, and this was his reward. He wanted to bellow out the truth about what he thought of most of the ones lurking around the king hoping for some small gift or step up in power and prestige. Leeches, the whole lot of them.

"Can ye find the bad men, Simon?" asked Reid as Simon swung up into the saddle behind him.

"I can and I will. I ken who most of them are but, at the moment, the best I have is the word of one traitor pointing the finger of guilt at another." Simon looked down at the boy's head, knowing Reid was struggling to understand. "I must set aside my own vanity and just do the job. Find the men, arrest them, and drag them before the king. Then I must pray that what proof I have stands up firm against the power and coin some of these men have. To be honest, at this moment, I dinnae care if some of them slip the noose and later try again to kill the king."

"One of them is that Sir Walter, isnae it? 'Tis what Ilsabeth says."

"Aye. It is and he will be caught. Even if I must give up some of the others because I am now pushed to do this quickly, Hepbourn willnae be one of them."

"Good. I want him punished. He held a knife to my sister's throat and I had to stand there and hope that she didnae wiggle or try to get down and that knife was so close it would have cut her. And he is still trying verra hard to get Ilsabeth hanged for his crimes."

"Have no fear, lad. He will soon be paying dearly."

Chapter 14

One thing Ilsabeth truly hated about being imprisoned was the smell. She was no delicate lass. She knew the scent of blood, the scent of the winter slaughter, the scent of human and animal waste and even the scent of death, but this smell made her stomach curdle. It was the scent of despair, she decided. Despair, lost hopes, fear, and resignation. She was probably adding to the wretched miasma clouding the dank air. Ilsabeth did not want to consider how many of those who had come here to die, their sorrow still mired in the stone, had been as innocent as she was.

Where was Simon? she asked silently. She was headed into her second full day in this hell. The dark, the occasional rattle of a chain, the intermittent screams, told her others were there with her but nothing could help her stop feeling so utterly alone. Her family would rush to her side if they knew where she was, but that would only get them captured and tossed inside with her. No, it was Simon she really needed, so where was he?

The light suddenly grew brighter around her cell and Ilsabeth sat up on the rat-gnawed pallet she had been given to sleep on. Then she heard footsteps. Two men, she decided, listening closely. Ilsabeth prayed that one of them was Simon. When Walter and a larger man came into view, she cursed, her disappointment so sharp she was surprised she was not bleeding from it.

When the two men stopped in front of her thickly barred cell, she sent Walter a look of utter loathing before studying the man he had brought with him. There was something very familiar about his height and shape, the broad shoulders and the long legs, but she decided that should not surprise her. Within her own family there were a lot of broad shoulders and long legs. Then Walter, wearing that smug look that always made her so nervous, held his torch a little closer to the man, shedding more light on his face, and she frowned in concentration while studying that face even more closely.

A gasp escaped her as she found what she had blindly been seeking, the reason she felt she knew him, as her gaze was caught and held by a familiar shade of gray in the man's one eye. Ilsabeth began to reach out to the man but her good sense and caution returned quickly. She yanked her hand back inside her prison, suddenly glad of the cage she was in, just as the stranger reached out to clasp her hand.

"So ye have brought Henry, the beast of Lachancorrie, with ye, have ye, Walter?" she asked even though she knew that was who the gray-eyed man was. "Trying to better yourself in his eyes by showing him how cleverly ye have escaped punishment for your crimes. How wondrously brave ye are, to make certain a wee lass takes all the blame. Lies, deceit, murder, betrayal. Ye have been a verra busy boy gathering all the weaponry needed by a knight of the realm. A tale to tell your grandchildren for certain, aye? Ah, but if I happen to escape ye will have no bairns for I will find me a verra sharp knife and kill your progeny at the source."

Walter looked as if he tried to glare at her yet appear untouched by her insults and threats. It was an odd look. Simon's brother was silently staring at her in cold, hard fury. There was something ugly deep in the man's one good eye. Ilsabeth could not believe she could have, even for a moment, thought they resembled Simon's eyes. Unlike Walter's expression, Henry's sat easily on his scarred face. The man looked ready to chew through the bars to get to her. She did not even want to think about what he would do if he got his hands on her.

"I hear ye are the woman my brother is bedding and risking his precious good name for," said Henry.

He looked her over in a way that made her want to slap him and then go and bathe. For the second time since she had been tossed into her cell she was heartily glad for the thick iron bars between her and Henry, both times inspired by him. They stopped her from attacking the man who had caused Simon so much pain and they stopped Henry, laird of Lochancorrie, from breaking her neck or inflicting some other horror on her.

"Whate'er your brother and I might be doing is really none of your business," she snapped at Henry, suddenly realizing that every time she looked at Henry all she could see in her mind's eye were the scars covering Simon's back. "I suggest ye give up your traitorous plots and run along home, Henry. The boy ye tried to beat to death ten years ago is a mon now and that mon willnae rest until he has ye tried, convicted, and executed for the traitor ye are. Mayhap, if ye cease, if ye just go away, ye can keep all ye have now—your life, your lands, your whips, ye filthy bastard," she ended in a furious hiss. "Did all your clever planning get ye the son ye wanted?"

"Nay. I got yet another cursed, useless daughter." He smiled and Ilsabeth decided it was the coldest thing she had ever seen. "Sad to say, she was weak, just like her puling excuse for a father. She died."

Ilsabeth prayed Simon never found that out. "Do ye ken? I believe someone should have hunted ye down years ago and killed ye. I ne'er thought I would say this, as I believed I held all life sacred, but ye are a mon who sorely needs killing." Oh, aye, Henry would dearly love to kill me or at least make me pray for death. "My mother would say that ye are a mon who has no other purpose in life but to destroy things, people, a young lad's pet."

She looked at Walter again. "Say what ye want and go away. Your company grows tedious."

"If ye were one of my women, I would beat ye, but I would do it so verra slowly, breaking one bone at a time," Henry said.

That was truly terrifying, she decided, especially when the man saying the words spoke in such a slow, considering way one could imagine him savoring the pictures they painted for him. When she had first seen Henry, she had let anger rule her tongue, not fully considering what she was saying, but now she thought she may have been very close to the truth. There was something very wrong with Henry Innes. She prayed his plot to steal the throne from the king failed miserably because, if Scotland ever came under this man's rule, it was doomed to fall into a bloody, cruel time from which it might never recover.

"How verra intriguing. Most would just snap my neck," she said. "Like a twig is often how they put it, I believe."

"Ilsabeth, ye should watch that sharp tongue of yours," warned Walter.

"Why? If your great plan succeeds, I will soon be dead. If it fails, I will be dead. What difference can it make what I say now?"

" 'Tis in the manner of the killing," said Henry. "I can make it verra painful."

"That is a skill to be so proud of. Henry, if I am declared guilty of all this fool"—she jabbed a finger in Walter's direction—"has seen that I am accused of, my death is already destined to be verra painful. Unless the two of you and whatever poor fools ye have drawn to your cause, succeed, I dinnae have to worry o'er who can kill me in the most painful way possible." She looked at Walter again. "I am certain ye didnae come just to gloat so what do ye want?"

"I wish to speak to Ilsabeth in private, Henry," said Walter, "if ye would excuse me for just a moment."

Henry shrugged and, after a final chilling look at Ilsabeth, walked away. "Ye are a fool, Walter," she told her former fiancé, "to risk everything ye have because that mon wants to be king. He will kill ye as soon as possible after he dons his stolen crown."

"Of course he willnae," Walter snapped, "but I didnae come to talk about Henry. Ye do ken what ye are facing, dinnae ye?"

Ilsabeth thought that was a rather witless question. Her insides were knotted with a terror she tried to fight back with every breath she took. In fact, only the anger over how she had been used by this man kept it from overwhelming her until she was no more than a shivering, wretched creature curled up babbling in a corner.

"A knighthood?" She wished she could see the sneer she was giving Walter for she was sure it was one of her best.

"I ne'er truly realized what a sharp, irreverent tongue ye had. No matter, that can be mended. So can this in a way. I ken a way to get ye out of here, Ilsabeth, to free you."

"Nay, ye dinnae mean to free me. Dinnae try to lie to me, Walter, ye festering scab." The way his eyes widened was proof enough that her fury was revealing itself in far more than her words. "Ye wish to put me in a wee cottage in France, a mistress ye can force to your will because her only other choice is death. Weel, this woman would prefer the torturous death of a traitor to that."

"How do ye ken about my wee cottage in France?"

"How do ye think I kenned enough about your plans to run and hide? I heard ye and David, didnae I? I was but yards away when ye sat in that garden and spoke of killing kings, laying false accusations, and saving me from execution by slipping me away to France to await your pleasure."

"Ye were creeping about my house like a thief, were ye?"

"Oh, go away, Walter. Ye are as doomed as I am. Ye have tied your fate to a mon who beats his own brother nearly to death, who kills his own wives because they give him no sons or just because they irritate him, and who kills his own daughters because he thinks them naught but useless. A mon who killed his own father because he thought the mon had been laird enough and now it was his turn. And ye believe he willnae kill ye? Nay, Walter, ye may be even more doomed than I. Go. Away."

"I think ye are the fool. Weel, if ye finally come to your senses and choose life, ye ken where to reach me."

"Aye, in the gutter. Your mother would be so proud."

She sighed when he finally marched away. Walter just refused to see the monster he had tied himself to. She could only pray that Simon succeeded in ending this plot. The thought of Henry sitting on the throne was too horrifying to contemplate for too long.

Then she frowned and looked toward the direction Walter and Henry had gone. It was not the usual way one entered and left the dungeon. And why had there been no guard with them? There was always a guard when someone came down into the dungeon.

The soft scrape of a boot on stone drew her out of her thoughts. She looked up to find Henry leaning against her cell and smiling at her, that smile that made her fear of her coming execution seem petty. He was back, without Walter and without a guard. The man who wanted to steal the throne, a man all knew had been banished forever from the court, should not be wandering around in the dungeons with no guard keeping an eye on him. Ilsabeth hid that knowledge quickly and eyed him as she would any unwanted guest.

"I think ye could be one who would give me a son," he said.

Ilsabeth almost gagged, not only at the thought that this man would have to touch her to accomplish that but that any child of hers would be close to such a man. "Let me think. I can stay here and meet the torturous death of a traitor. Or, I could allow Walter to steal me away to play his mistress in France. Or, I could allow ye to breed a child on me. Has a woman e'er had so many wondrous choices? My bounty is overflowing."

"Your father didnae beat ye enough." He frowned. "And he has let ye run free for far too long, too. I think ye are twenty, mayhap a year or twa more. Ye should have been wed with half a dozen bairns by now. It is time I had another wife. Ye would do."

She glanced around wondering if she was actually still asleep. "Do ye or Walter e'er hear what ye say? He wants me to whore for him in France until he tires of me and then he would probably sell me or send me back here to face the same thing I am facing now. Ye speak of making me your wife so that I can breed ye sons but ye must ken that I have heard what happens to your wives and your poor wee daughters. So ye offer me a few years of servitude to ye until I prove I cannae breed a son or ye tire of me whereupon I will be killed. And that after I may have had to watch ye kill a child or two of mine because it wasnae born with the right dangling part. What have I done to make ye and Walter think I am that dim-witted?"

"Actually, I think ye may be very sharp of wit. Too sharp. 'Tis a dangerous thing for a woman to be sharp-witted but 'tis something I would like to have in a son of mine. Aye, I believe I will consider this more. The added joy of taking ye to wife and breaking ye to my hand is the knowledge that ye belonged to Simon."

"Why do ye hate Simon so? What has he e'er done to ye?"

"He lived. He grew up and watched me with my own eyes at every turning and he judged. No one judges me."

"I see. Weel, it has been a pleasant time talking to ye as I dinnae get many visitors down here, but 'tis time for my rest. Have a pleasant journey home."

Henry shook his head. "Enjoy your foolishness as ye will. Ye will soon do as I want." He leaned very close to the bars and said in an almost friendly voice, "Ye have a weakness, lass. Ne'er forget that. Think hard on what that weakness is and ken weel that I will use it to make ye do as I want, e'en if it means I get a wee bit of blood on my hands." He started to walk away. "The sweetest blood is said to be that of the tender wee lasses. It runs smoothly and brightly o'er the hands."

His horrible words echoed in the dungeon long after he had walked away. It took Ilsabeth a moment to realize that she was panting with fear, her heart pounding so hard she felt faint. Staggering back to her wretched pallet, she tried to make herself believe it an empty threat, but she could not. This was a man who—barely into what some called youth and others called manhood—had slaughtered his brother's dog and draped it over him as he slept. Three years later he had murdered his own father. She would be a fool not to take any threat he made very seriously indeed.

Ilsabeth looked around her cell and nearly screamed out her frustration and terror. Her weaknesses all lived at Simon's house, the man Henry loathed and badly wanted dead. Henry knew about the children. She wrapped her arms around herself and rocked slightly on the pallet. There was nothing she could do until someone came with the pitiful meal and sour water they delivered once a day. That was hours away yet and Henry was wandering freely around the very heart of the king's home. He would find getting into Simon's house and getting to the children no trouble at all.

And Simon, she thought, and shivered. He was after her Simon. He was also a weakness with her, but she suspected Henry would try to kill Simon simply because he wanted to.

Ilsabeth began to pray for Simon to come to her. She understood why he had not for there were many good reasons. He was trying to bring the real traitors to the king so that she would be free. He could have also been forbidden by the king to come to her. But, still she prayed, for he was the only hope she had to try and keep Henry from doing any of the things he threatened to do.

"Find a way, Simon. Please, please, find a way to come to me."

Simon jerked awake and wondered why he felt so afraid. He was sleeping in the chair in his ledger room, which was uncomfortable but no cause for alarm. The children were in bed and he could hear the faint sounds of MacBean and Old Bega arguing about something just down the hall.

Probably him, he thought, and grimaced as he rubbed a hand over his face and listened to the rasp of his beard. There was a little time for him to clean up before he made his way to the court and tried yet again to get permission to speak to Ilsabeth.

He tensed as the dream that had yanked him out of his much needed sleep came rushing back into his mind. He could see Ilsabeth, huddled on a pallet, her arms wrapped around her legs, rocking slowly back and forth. She had been so clear to see in his dream that he had reached out to her.

Simon frowned, thinking hard and forcing more of the dream to come to mind before it faded into the mists of his memory. There was something important there that had forced him to wake alert and feeling as if he needed to get to her quickly. He could still feel the urgency thrumming inside him.

Deciding he would go to the court and press harder to get permission to see her if only for a few moments while heavily guarded, he leapt up and hurried to the door. He opened it to find Peter there with his hand raised to knock and nearly groaned. Duty called and Simon knew it was an important one. It would save the king's life, but more importantly, it would save Ilsabeth's.

"Come in then," he said, and went back to his chair to sit down.

"I hope I dinnae look as ragged as ye do," said Peter as he sat in the chair facing Simon.

Looking his friend over, Simon said, "Aye, I think ye do. Do ye have anything?"

"Weel, Henry is certainly in the town. 'Tis proving difficult to track the mon, however. We lost a mon last night, name of Frazer. He was following Henry round the taverns and ended up dead in an alley near where Henry was last seen taking his pleasure with a tavern maid."

"How was he killed?"

Peter grimaced. "Throat cut but I think he may have welcomed it by then. He was slowly mutilated, his mouth gagged so tightly I doubt anyone e'en heard him while he screamed. If he was tortured for information, they must have had to tug that gag off now and then to hear his answers."

"Do ye think he talked?"

"I would have to say aye but I hate to demean his death. 'Tis just that he had to have been in such agony he could have said anything and everything without truly kenning he was doing it."

"Henry is verra good at that."

"So ye think he did that to Frazer?"

"From what ye describe, aye. Thank ye for nay telling me all the ways my brother hurt the poor mon. I have seen it but that was years ago and I suspect he has perfected the skill by now. So what did Frazer have knowledge of?"

"Nay much at all. I still moved David to another

place. He went verra willingly when I told him why I was doing it. He is terrified of your brother."

"For a fool he can show surprising touches of a sharp wit." Simon lightly drummed his fingers on the table. "I am thinking I need to move the children away from here."

"Aye, I think that might be a good idea. I hate to think that any mon would hurt children just to get at a mon but your brother isnae like any mon I have e'er dealt with." Peter shook his head. "I listened to your warnings, but I think I just put them aside, mayhap e'en thought they were the memories of a bullied child. But seeing what was done to poor Frazer made it all too easy to ken that Henry is a verra dangerous mon."

"Send the children to Tormand and Morainn. Be verra sure no one is following ye and warn them of who may be hunting them. Tomorrow is soon enough."

"Nay, Morainn says to get them to her tonight. Have MacBean and Old Bega come as weel," said Tormand as he walked into the room.

"What has Morainn seen?" asked Simon.

"That the children need to be hidden away." Tormand frowned. "She said they will become both a weapon and a tragedy if they stay here."

"Does that make any sense?" asked Peter.

"In a way," replied Simon. "I think she means they can be used to make someone do what they— or he—wants. Or someone wants to kill them or use them as bait. I suspicion they are to be bait. For me or for Ilsabeth. So, aye, we will take them to your place tonight."

"MacBean and Old Bega will be enough help for

that," said Tormand. "Morainn says ye must go to see Ilsabeth and quickly. She says Ilsabeth kens something verra important."

"What could Ilsabeth ken? She has been imprisoned in the dungeon for two days. There is naught one can learn down there except how to keep the rats at bay."

"I just tell ye what I am told. Wheesht, Simon, ye ken as weel as I do that poor Morainn cannae always understand what she sees, that 'tis more often just pictures and some words. And Ilsabeth needs ye to come to her because she has important information. Morain said Ilsabeth spoke to her in the visions. Ilsabeth said, 'Find a way, Simon. Please . . .'"

"Please find a way to come to me," Simon finished, and suddenly knew what had ripped him out of a sound sleep. Ilsabeth's fear and grief. She was terrified of someone. What he had felt had not been just the terror some can suffer when put in the dungeon. This had far-reaching consequences.

"Ye heard it." Tormand looked at Simon with a faint smile. "Mayhap ye have a gift."

"Mayhap 'tis Ilsabeth who does. Coming from the family she does, it shouldnae be a surprise."

"That is true. I think whate'er has frightened her or made her so urgent to see ye caused her to, weel, send out a call. Doubt she even kens that she did it. But ye say it was what woke ye and Morainn says it was clear in her vision. Go and get yourself presentable for court while we get those poor bairns out of their nice warm beds and take them to Morainn."

Simon clapped Tormand on the back as he hurried out of the room to go and get ready for court. He was washed, shaved, and dressed so quickly he briefly worried if he had forgotten something. When he hurried back down the stairs he met with the others, Tormand holding a sleepy Elen and Peter holding a wary Reid. Simon went and kissed each one on the cheek. Elen had returned his kiss with a loud, somewhat wet one of her own before turning her attention to charming Tormand. Reid allowed the kiss but grabbed Simon by his hair to stop him from walking away.

"Reid, ye shouldnae do that," he said as he untangled the child's fingers.

"Why are ye giving us away?" Reid asked. "Isnae Ilsabeth coming back?"

"Nay!" Simon took Reid from Peter's arms and, holding the child close, stepped away from the others so that Elen could not overhear them. "Nay, I am not giving ye away. Ye ken weel that this is a dangerous time, aye?"

"Aye, so we should stay with ye to make sure ye are safe."

"Reid, the mon who is putting us all in danger isnae like those soldiers ye tried to stop from taking Ilsabeth. He is like the one who held a knife to Elen's throat but even worse than that. Tormand's wife, Morainn, has dreams and most of them tell us things that will be, but that can also be changed by acting wisely. She sent Tormand here because she said ye must come to them tonight."

"Because this really bad mon might come here to hurt Elen?"

Simon opened his mouth to say the bad man

would hurt Reid, too, but abruptly saw the way to get the child to do as he should with no more complaint. "Aye, and mayhap e'en MacBean and Old Bega. Ye dinnae think I am giving them away, do ye?"

"Nay. But ye will come and get us when the danger is gone, aye?"

"Aye, as soon as it is safe again."

"Ye swear?"

"I swear that ye arenae being given away and that ye will see us again. Come, lad, do ye think Ilsabeth would let me give ye away e'en if I wanted to?" He was pleased to see Reid smile. "Now back to Peter here and do as they tell ye so that ye can get to Tormand's safely."

They left the house as secretly as possible, but Simon still kept a close watch for anyone following them. If Henry had already decided to hurt the children as Morainn's vision implied, he would have some men watching for them at the house. Simon watched the others until they were out of sight, constantly sweeping his gaze over all the hiding places someone could use while they tried to follow people. He was just about to turn away when he saw a slight movement in a small alcove between two old crooked houses. A moment later a man slipped out of the niche and hurried along the same path Peter and Tormand had taken his family.

His family, he thought, as he slipped his knife from its sheath and crept out of the house to follow the man he had seen. The word fit, rolled from his tongue with ease. It was the threat to his family that had him creeping behind a man, his knife ready to be used to kill.

Just as he drew close enough to grab the man, his prey turned around. Simon hesitated because he recognized his old childhood friend from Lochancorrie. "Ye are leaving the chase too early, Wallace," he said. "And ye cannae think that Henry will believe ye lost them. Ye were always the best of trackers, e'en as a child."

"Simon?"

The tall, young man with thick, curly, red hair lowered the knife he had held in the ready to strike Simon. Simon took it from the man's shaking hands. The Wallace he recalled would never have gotten mixed up in such things as treason and murder. He had been a gentle boy who loved animals, a risky love around Henry.

"Aye, 'tis Simon. What are ye doing here, Wallace? Do ye ride with Henry in this treasonous folly?"

"I ride with Henry because his men hold my wife and bairn. They will kill them if Henry but says the word."

"He cannae say it from here, can he? Nay without reducing what few fighting men he brought with him. And, with so many of the king's soldiers about, Henry willnae risk being undermanned."

"Then he will do it when he gets back to Lochancorrie or send that word when the fighting stops."

"When the fighting stops, and my plan is to have as little fighting done as possible, Henry will be going nowhere but to the dungeons, a swift trial, and an execution."

"Ye sound so certain of that. I want to believe ye, but, if ye were able to take Henry down, why havenae ye come home and done it?"

"I will explain that as I can. Just come with me. Ye

ken that Henry will ken that ye didnae follow your quarry as ye were told to. He will kill ye and then kill your wife and bairn at his leisure. If ye are standing with them, ye will die there. As I see it, ye have nay choices left to ye. Come with me."

"Aye, for ye are right. I am dead nay matter what I do and all because I couldnae follow them, nay kenning that Henry wanted to hurt that wee bairn. I dinnae suppose ye will give me my knife back, eh?"

"Later, after we talk. For right now I mean to leave ye with a mon who guards my house. He can decide if ye should have a knife or nay. Heed him, for he is a skilled soldier, as most are who live to a great age."

"Aye." When they reached the door, Wallace paused and looked at Simon. "This will cost Lochancorrie dearly, aye?"

"I am doing my best to see that all Lochancorrie loses is its laird."

"Then God be with ye, Sir Simon, for that will be the greatest blessing to befall the clan in years."

Chapter 15

Simon followed the guard down into the bowels of the castle. The damp chill of the place grew worse with every step he took and he knew the hard toll it could take on a body. Ilsabeth was so small, so delicate, and unused to such harsh conditions. Fevers lurked in these dark places, ones vicious enough to down a big, battle-hardened warrior. He had to get her out of here.

He was ready to ease his harsh rules for finding the guilty. Simon knew he could be too stern, too exacting. The many times he had seen the innocent pay while the guilty slipped free had made him so. He had more than enough to bring in Walter, Henry, and half a dozen others, all the important ones who had done all the planning and found the soldiers needed to back them up and fight the real battles for them. Simon was sure that his brother would fight any battle and do so with great enjoyment, but a lot of the others he had drawn into his plan were not great warriors.

And then there were ones like Wallace, who was pulled in because Henry needed fighters, threatened to fight a battle they knew was wrong. Or David, who had been trained from childhood to follow Walter wherever he led. Simon knew he had more than enough reasons to want Henry stopped but Wallace's plight only added to that need. Even though he knew Henry was bad, he had been shocked to hear Wallace say his wife and child were being held hostage to his cooperation, but then had he not just hidden his own children away? Women and children were a weakness and Henry was never reluctant to use a weakness.

The guard nodded toward the cell Ilsabeth was in and then handed him a torch. Simon could not hide his surprise at this easing of the watch and the guard just smiled. "Gowan says she is a good wee lass and he thinks someone has done her a verra bad turn. This wee kindness is the best we can do. I will settle myself in back where I showed ye the wee guard post and ye come by when ye are done visiting." He then handed Simon the key.

"Thank ye."

"Oh, and tell her that wee potion she told me about worked on my son. He is already showing signs of getting better and we had thought we would be burying the wee lad soon."

"Of course." Simon watched the guard walk away and shook his head.

Ilsabeth could not even stay in a prison without reaching out to others. He could not believe he had ever been suspicious of her. He had grown cynical as well as unbending, he decided. It was to be expected for he often saw the worst people could be or do to each other. When one was surrounded by crime and deceit, one soon saw it everywhere.

Then again, he had believed in Wallace's innocence quickly. Simon silently cursed. Wallace was not a beautiful woman who made him harden with lust with just a smile. It was apparent that he had also become very cynical about the innocence or honesty of women. Perhaps when this was all over, he would find the courage to swallow his pride and apologize to Ilsabeth for that because he knew his distrust had hurt her.

He stepped up to the cell and set the torch in the holder on the wall. "Ilsabeth?" he called softly as he unlocked the door.

Simon was just stepping into the cell when she flung herself into his arms. He felt her shaking and feared she had become ill already. He touched her forehead and cheeks but found no heat of a fever. He did find them wet with tears, however.

"Ilsabeth, love, what is wrong?"

"Walter came to see me and he brought a guest."

"Who?"

"Henry."

"Nay, Henry has been banished from the court. That happened years ago and it was a banishment that made it verra clear he was not to come to court as long as this king ruled." He thought about that for a moment and then cursed. "Damn. Ye dinnae think this is all about Henry's stung vanity, do ye?"

"I dinnae ken but, Simon, if Henry is banished how did he get into the dungeons? How did Walter get him in? They had no guard with them." She frowned. "Neither do ye."

"I was given a gift because Gowan thinks ye have

been wronged and the guard who brought me here thinks your potion saved his son."

"Oh, I am so glad wee Alek is getting better." She grabbed Simon by the hand and led him over to her tiny bed. "But listen, Simon, it was more than the fact that Henry should ne'er have been in here. He and Walter came in the wrong way. I havenae seen that many people come down here but even the guards come in the same way ye did. Walter and Henry came in from the opposite direction and left that way, too."

Simon stared at her in shock. That shock caused her words to circle in his mind for a moment, unable to settle. This was a major breach in their defense of the king. Henry could have walked in any time he chose and slithered close to the king with little more opposition than the king's personal guard. How had all of them missed such a thing? Even more important, who inside the keep had helped the enemy find it?

"God's blood, this is what Morainn meant."

"Morainn had a vision?"

"Aye, and she told me to get down here to see ye as ye had some important information. It was about this creeping into the dungeon. Those men ken a way to get in and out without being seen. Weel, I doubt they will come back today for they must have accomplished what they set out to do, but a guard will need to be set. I will look into that when I leave."

Ilsabeth wrapped her arms around him and pressed her cheek against his chest. He smelled so clean she was suddenly, embarrassingly, aware of the fact that she did not. She started to pull away but he held her close and rubbed his cheek against her hair.

"Simon, I am verra dirty," she protested, "and who kens what has crawled into my hair."

"Ilsabeth, ye have only been here two days. Ye dinnae smell dirty at all."

He kissed her on the neck and nipped gently at the tender skin there. Ilsabeth was so glad to have him with her but she knew she could not enjoy his company until she told him about Henry's threats. She needed Simon's assurances that the children were safe.

She leaned back in his arms until she could see his face. "Simon, just heed me for a moment. 'Tis about your brother. He . . . he threatened the children." She watched his eyes narrow and saw a glint of that anger Henry always brought into Simon's eyes. "He told me that he kenned I had weaknesses and he kenned what they are. He said I should think on that ere I refused him."

"Refused him what?"

"Ne'er mind that. He threatened the children. I wouldnae be surprised if he was threatening Old Bega and MacBean, too. He said I should think hard on those weaknesses and how he will use them to make me do what he wants e'en if it meant he got a wee bit of blood on his hands. But, the worse was that he said, 'the sweetest blood is said to be that of the tender wee lasses. It runs smoothly and brightly o'er the hands.' He meant Elen, Simon. He meant our wee sweet Elen. Ye have to get the children somewhere safe."

He pulled her back into his arms and rubbed his hand up and down her back. " 'Tis done, love. They have been sent to Tormand and Morainn this verra night. Morainn saw the need for that, too. She didnae name a threat but when she says something about having to get the children to her now, ye do it."

"Oh, thank God. I was so afraid. There was no one to tell, no one to come and take a message to ye."

"In truth, Ilsabeth, ye sent me and Morainn a message." He grinned when she looked at him in shock. "Aye, I was yanked out of a sound sleep and was trying to understand what had done that, but all I kenned for sure was that I had to get to ye and naught would get in my way. Peter came then and told me that one of our men was butchered in a way that is my brother's favorite so I was distracted from that urgency for a while. A short while later Tormand arrived and said Morainn wanted me to get to ye now. He began to repeat what message Morainn had heard and I finished it, suddenly able to recall the words that had slapped me awake. I think ye yelled it out so loud it did get sent and ye didnae e'en have to write it down."

"I might have a gift?"

She looked so delighted at the thought that he had to smile. Holding her close as he was, however, his thoughts swiftly wandered to how long it had been since he had last held her. The guard was being kind, but Simon was certain that the man would grow uneasy if he stayed with Ilsabeth for too long. He wanted, needed, to steal some of that time to love her, hold her, and savor the passion they shared. Try as he did to ignore it, a little voice in his mind kept warning him that what he shared with her might not last much longer.

"Shouldnae ye be trying to see where it was that Walter and Henry got in unseen?" Ilsabeth asked as Simon pushed her down onto the rough pallet.

"There is time to do that," he replied as he started to slide his hand up beneath her skirts. "Right after I feed a hunger that has gone unfed for far too long."

"Only two days," she murmured, although she shared his hunger.

"Far too long."

"Ye mean to make love in a dungeon?"

"Aye."

"The guard . . ."

"Handed me a torch and the key and told me to fetch him when our visit was over. Now, hush," he whispered against her mouth, and then kissed her.

Ilsabeth hushed. She was hungry, too. She had missed Simon, missed the way his big, warm body curled around her as they slept. Most of all she had missed the way he made her feel safe. She was desperate to feel safe, even if only for the time she was in his arms. Safe and warm, she thought, even as she lost herself in his kiss.

It took only a kiss to cause their passion for each other to run wild. Simon was starved for her, but part of what had him so desperate to bury himself deep inside her was his fear for her, a fear that had been eating at him from the moment he had been told that Walter had taken her. Suddenly, his house was empty, his bed was empty, and, he realized, a large part of him was also empty without her. When he finally thrust inside her, he stilled, savoring the heat of her and a deep sense of belonging.

"Simon?"

"It feels so good," he whispered.

"Aye, it does."

Ilsabeth did not know how long she could wait for Simon to give her what her body was crying out for, however. It moved her that he found the way their bodies joined together so perfectly, the way that joining brought them close in so many ways, something to savor. Any other time she would savor it, too, be pleased with sharing a time that was both sensual and peaceful. This time she needed more; she needed fire and rough passion.

"I think today it might feel a wee bit better if ye moved," she finally said.

Simon looked down at her and grinned as he slowly pulled back until he was nearly free of her body and then ever so slowly pushed back in as deep as he could go. "Like that?"

Ilsabeth looked at that grin and narrowed her eyes. Then she smiled and dragged her fingernails down his back, no longer afraid that she would hurt him. The first time she had done it in a moment of heightened passion he had shuddered as he did now and she had quickly apologized. Simon had explained to her that he needed the rougher touch, that the damage done by the whip Henry had so viciously wielded had made it difficult for him to feel a soft caress.

Now she took full advantage of the fact that he found her scratching his back intoxicating, relishing the fact that he felt anything at all. She did it once more and finally received the hard loving she needed. They raced toward that bliss she craved as one, and when he joined her in that release from a blinding need, their voices blending as they cried out from the force of it, she prayed she would soon be free to enjoy this as she had before Walter had dragged her away to this dark place.

Appreciating how long he held her close after their lovemaking, Ilsabeth made no complaint when he finally straightened their clothes and tugged her to her feet. "Time to go, aye?" she asked as he brushed a kiss over her mouth.

"Aye," he replied. "Soon, Ilsabeth. I will have ye free of this place soon."

He kissed her again and started toward the door, hesitating and sending her a tortured look when he realized he would have to lock her in. Ilsabeth walked over, pushed him out of her prison, and closed the door. He had to stop the men planning to kill the king and, in truth, with Henry still running free, she knew she was safer right where she was.

"Lock it, Simon," she said. "I ken ye will solve this trouble soon and that my stay here will be a short one." She leaned against the door as he locked it and then smiled at him. "And, I was just thinking that Henry cannae reach me here." The expression that crossed his face and the way his eyes narrowed told her that that might not have been the wisest thing she had ever said.

Simon locked the door and looked at her. "What else did Henry threaten ye with?" When she just shrugged and tried to step back, he caught hold of her hand and pulled her closer, only the bars separating them. "Ye cannae slip back and hide away, nay with these fine new doors the king had put on these cells. Do ye ken why he had them built? Too many guards were hurt by the prisoners because they couldnae get a good look inside there before they had to step inside. E'en the prisoners who were chained could prove dangerous. The king decided the guards needed to see the whole of the inside. So, I can easily see that ye are hiding something no matter where ye stand in there. Tell me, what else did my brother threaten ye with?"

"It will only make ye angry and there is naught ye can do about it anyway."

"Ilsabeth, I can stand here waiting for a verra long time."

"Aye, I suspicion ye can," she muttered and sighed. "He thinks I can give him a son."

She winced as his grip on her hand tightened. Ilsabeth could see his fury tighten his face and darken his eyes. A part of her was very pleased by this sign of possessiveness, maybe even jealousy, but she knew it was a waste of their time. Henry could not reach her in this prison; he could only threaten her. Simon needed to use his anger and need to protect to capture his brother and put an end to the man's evil games. The expression on Simon's face told her that it was not going to be easy to get him to ignore Henry's talk.

Simon took a deep breath and let it out slowly, easing the grip he had on Ilsabeth as well. For a moment all he had been able to think about was killing Henry. He had had to fight the urge to run right out into the town and try to find his mad brother and end his life. That would solve nothing. Planning was needed if he was to catch a villain as wiley and brutal as Henry and he could only plan well with his head clear.

He had to wonder if Henry had said such a thing knowing Ilsabeth would tell him. It would be the sort of thing Henry would do. It did not mean that Henry had lied, however. Ilsabeth would be the sort of woman Henry would want to take and, if the man had seen her strength and wit, he just might believe she was the type of woman who could give him a son.

"He will never touch ye," he said.

Simon's voice was hoarse and deep and Ilsabeth knew anger had a strong grip on him. "He cannae reach me here, Simon. I am safe and now the children are, too. Wheesht, ye are the only one still in danger. Henry hates ye, Simon. He said it was because of the way ye used to watch him with his own eyes, judging him. Henry doesnae think anyone has the right to judge him."

Just as she had hoped it would, telling Simon why Henry claimed to hate him had tugged at that curious part of his mind enough to pull him free of the tight grip his anger had on him. The anger was still there, but it could now prove more of a strength than a weakness. Ilsabeth realized that she needed Henry gone for more reasons than his threat against the king, against her and her loved ones. She needed him dead so that Simon could shake free of the past, of all that pain that roused such fury inside him whenever Henry drew too near.

"If I watched him too much it was just to ken when it was time to run or when to get my brothers out of Henry's way." Simon shook his head. "And a mon needs a guilty conscience to fret o'er being judged for who he is or what he has done. I would-nae have believed Henry could feel guilty about anything he has done."

"The mon is mad, Simon. The mad probably only make sense to themselves at times." She reached through the bars to stroke his cheek. "Get him, Simon, and worry o'er why he is what he is, later. Stop him now."

He kissed her palm, released her hand and left, searching out the guard. The anger that had swept over him when Ilsabeth had told him what Henry had said was leashed now, but not gone. Simon knew he had to stop allowing what Henry did or said to enrage him so. That rage came from old wounds, from the fact that Henry was the one responsible for Simon's loss of a true family, for the man had driven away everyone close to them, or killed them. It was time to pull free of that past and deal with the traitorous game Henry played now.

The guard was quick to understand the threat posed by the ability of men to come and go from the bowels of the keep unnoticed and unguarded. In a short time there were guards, soldiers, and some of Simon's men searching every prison cell, every wall, and every twist and turn of the labyrinth below the keep. Simon worked with Gowan, planning a way to set a trap for Henry and Walter once they found the way the men were secretly slipping inside.

Ilsabeth watched the men searching and waited patiently for a cry of discovery. When it came she breathed a sigh of relief. There would be no more visits from Henry. She knew it was important for the safety of the king, but that did little to dim the pure selfishness of her relief. Henry terrified her.

She smiled when Simon appeared at her cell door. "Ye found it."

"Aye, and 'tis because of ye that we e'en kenned a need to look," he said. " 'Tis an old bolt-hole. It was sealed and they did their best to make it look as if it still was. It was Gowan who felt the slight movement of air where there should have been none. We are setting a trap now."

"Ye think they will come back?"

He heard the fear in her voice and reached through the bars to take her hands in his. "Aye. Once my head cleared of my anger at Henry, I recalled that Walter also had a reason to see ye here. He still wants ye to run to France, aye?"

Ilsabeth grimaced and felt herself blush. "Aye. I confess, Simon; I angered both men with my sharp tongue. I dinnae think Walter kens Henry's plans for me, either."

"We are close to ending this, Ilsabeth. Verra close. And then ye willnae have to fear either mon again."

Ilsabeth hoped he was right. She was tired of being afraid. Part of her saw it as a weakness but she knew that was foolish. She had good reason to be afraid and it would keep her wary and alert.

"I pray ye are right, Simon, but dinnae let concern o'er me take up too much of your thoughts. I am safe here and weel ye ken it. Go and finish this."

It was a little awkward but Simon gave her a kiss

through the bars and then walked away. There were plans to be made. He intended to make more than the one plan to capture Henry and Walter as they tried to sneak back inside through the old bolt-hole. Simon knew that, no matter how good their trap was, how well it was set, there was a chance the men they wanted could escape. He wanted to be absolutely certain that there was a second plan ready to be set in motion immediately.

Simon cursed long and viciously as he looked around at the dead and wounded men, most of them Walter and Henry's men. He recognized a few men from Lochancorrie. Many of the others looked like men who wielded their swords for anyone with coin enough to pay for their skill. Two days of planning and lying in wait and all they had were the soldiers hired or coerced by the traitors.

"More of your clan?" asked Gowan, studying the six battered men huddled together against a wall.

"Aye. I suspect they are more men like that lad Wallace I told ye about, who did such a poor job of trailing after the children. I will talk to them but they have all probably been forced into this in the same way Wallace was. None of them put up much of fight, did they?"

"Nay, although ye think they would fight rather than get caught and chance being tried and excuted as traitors. That would scare many a mon into fighting to the death."

"Henry probably scares them more. This way he will be thinking they were killed here and, if Henry holds a sword at the throat of their loved ones, it might ease now. Or that is how they will think. I dinnae think many of those at Lochancorrie believe anyone can do anything to rid them of Henry."

"Weel, I will leave ye to decide what to do with them."

"Thank ye. I will speak with them."

Gowan looked around. "Most of these others are naught but swords for hire although I can see a few from houses I ken weel and have been watching for a while. They dinnae have the look of hopelessness your lot does so I am thinking they didnae disagree with what was asked of them. Some men think much akin to the laird they serve. But, we didnae get Sir Walter or your brother."

"Nay. I suspicion they sent their men in first to test the water and have left now that they ken the way in was discovered."

"Think they kenned the lass might have guessed about the bolt-hole?"

Having talked to Ilsabeth several times, Simon believed he now had the whole truth about all that had been said between her and Walter, and her and Henry. "Not Sir Walter because, fool that he is, he would ne'er think she had the wit to ken it, being a mere female and all that." He nodded when Gowan snickered. "My brother, however, would have anticipated the possiblity after talking to her for a moment. He might think her unnatural, for Henry thinks verra little of women, but he would have quickly guessed at her intelligence."

"So the men we set outside will have caught no one or will be dead."

"Aye, I fear so. Henry may be mad enough to think he can kill the king and set his arse on the throne, but he is sharp-witted and a fighter to be wary of."

"I want this mon, Sir Simon," Gowan said in a hard, cold voice. "Him and that fool Hepbourn. I want them to pay full toll for this plan against the king."

Simon was a little surprised by the vehemence in Gowan's voice, but nodded. "Oh, ye will have them soon. Weel, if my brother doesnae kill Hepbourn first."

"What do ye mean Ilsabeth told them of the way in?" Walter slid off the winded mount he had been riding hard for miles. "How could she have any idea about that old bolt-hole?"

Henry dismounted and stared at Walter. "Ye ne'er really kenned her, did ye? I said I wanted a lass to dangle before Simon, one he would feel the need to protect. Ye decided to play your own game and try to rid yourself of the Armstrongs. Wanted their lands, too, didnae ye?"

"And why not? They abut mine."

"Of course. Weel, if ye had looked a little more closely instead of praising yourself on your cleverness, or trying to get beneath her skirts, ye might have seen that the lass has a verra sharp wit."

"A sharp tongue, most assuredly. I cannae believe I didnae see that, but she was probably just on her best behavior so that she could catch me as her husband." He screamed when Henry slapped him so hard he fell to the ground, and stared at Henry in fear.

"Dinnae be any greater a fool than ye have to be," Henry said. "That lass is quick, and nay just with her sharp tongue. She kenned something was wrong and she thought on it. It didnae take long for her to realize we had come in the wrong way, unguarded. If ye had kenned her as ye claimed, I would ne'er have made such a mistake."

"Weel, we have more men." Walter cautiously got to his feet.

"And we had best get to them."

"Why?"

"Because, ye fool, my cursed brother will be right behind us. He set up that trap because he had the sense to heed his woman when she told him something wasnae right about our being there. He will also have a plan ready to come after us because he wouldnae have set all his hopes on catching us as we tried to get back into the dungeon." He looked back in the direction they had just come from. "Simon is coming and this time I will kill him. And then I will take his woman."

"I thought she was going to be my woman." Walter stepped away from Henry when the man stared at him. "Weel, she is yours then, although after feeling how deep her sharp tongue can cut, I cannae see why any mon would want her."

"If I find her sharp tongue too much of an irritant and cannae beat it out of her, I will simply cut it out. Did that with my first wife."

Walter stared at Henry as the man watered his

mount at the small burn and then got back in the saddle. He hurried to do the same but he could not shake something Ilsabeth had said out of his head. She had warned him that Henry would get what he wanted and then kill him. Walter had scoffed at such a foolish statement but he did not feel like scoffing anymore.

Chapter 16

He thinks I can give him a son.

Simon growled as those words slithered through his mind yet again. He could not shake free of them or the power they had to make him angry. Not even reminding himself that Ilsabeth was right, that she was safe where she was, helped him regain the calm he needed to do his work. Henry could not reach her in her prison cell, he kept telling himself, but himself was not listening too closely. The fact that Henry had tried to return to the dungeons was enough, however, to make him eager to put an end to his brother's freedom and traitorous games as soon as possible.

"Here comes Wallace," said Peter, looking toward the line of trees to their left. "Ye were right about him. He is an excellent tracker."

"He has always had the skill," Simon replied. "I think he was born with it."

"Aye. I had feared we had lost our prey when they had escaped the trap at the dungeons, but this lad will sniff them out." Peter smiled faintly as he studied Simon. "Calm yourself, Simon. Ye are pacing like a mon awaiting his firstborn. This will be over soon."

"Ye feel it, too? Feel that the end is close?"

"Aye. I do and verra strongly. The others involved in this plot are being quietly collected up so that their compatriots arenae warned that they have been discovered too quickly and then flee. Although I suspect a few will escape. Cannae help that, and Gowan has our men starting at the top of the list so that we can be sure to bring in the ones who had the most important part in all this. Nay your list, either. Gowan's list."

"Gowan had his own list made?" Simon began to wonder if Gowan had his eye on Simon's place in the king's household and then decided that he really did not care. "How did Gowan list everyone?"

"By the value of their lands, property, or purse. Our Gowan kens weel what the king is most interested in. Aye, the king wants the traitors, but he also wants the riches he will be confiscating from them. Gowan kens that giving the king the wealthiest of the lot will be enough to satisfy the mon so that we willnae be made to suffer for any who get away. Gowan means to better himself and weel he deserves to. Just nay sure the king will want to lose such a fine captain of his guard."

"Would ye be willing to work with Gowan?"

"Ye mean when ye move on to became a laird?"

" 'Tis a possibility."

" 'Tis more than that. Lochancorrie will be yours after today."

"Is that a prophecy, old friend?"

"Nay, but ye can take it as one if ye like. 'Tis time ye left the king's service. Mon like ye has choices that me and Gowan dinnae and ne'er will have. Ye dinnae have to remain at the king's beck and call."

Simon smiled fleetingly. "We are all at his beck and call, Peter. 'Tis part of him being the king and all."

"Was that a jest?" Peter met Simon's narrow-eyed gaze with a grin but quickly grew serious again. "I ken that ye dinnae like it said, but ye have a great heart. Ye feel things too deeply at times. Naught wrong with that. Wheesht, it has made ye an excellent hunter of the truth and a lot of innocents have been saved and a lot of the guilty duly punished. But, it also means that by doing what ye do, seeing all the rot that ye must see, leaves its mark. If ye have a chance to be a laird, take it and leave the dark work to men like Gowan."

"And ye?"

"Aye, and me, though I will sorely miss having ye about. Ah, here's our lad."

Wallace arrived with Gowan only one step behind him. Simon studied Gowan closely and decided he was right to think that Gowan had his eye on Simon's job. When Simon still felt no qualms about that at all, he also decided that Peter was right. It was time to leave his post as the king's hound. He was tired of the hunt and the ugliness he saw all too often.

"The mon is but a mile away, mayhap less," said Wallace, pointing toward the trees he had just emerged from. "The laird and the mon with him paused at a wee burn to water their mounts. I think there may have been an argument for one of them was sent to the ground. Hard. Wee bit of blood on the ground, nay much, so I think it was nay more than a slap or the like."

"So, Henry hasnae killed his lackey Walter yet," murmured Simon, "but he is obviously not verra pleased with the mon."

"Nay," agreed Wallace, "and nay doubt it was Sir Walter who went down. There was no other sign to tell me there was more fighting and the laird wouldnae let anyone put him on the ground without making the one who did it pay a verra dear price."

"A verra dear price indeed. Do ye think they are going to make a stand then?"

Wallace nodded. "I do. I circled round and there are a lot of signs showing that men are gathering nay so far ahead of where the laird and Sir Walter stopped. If ye think it wise or helpful, I could draw closer, see how many men the laird has, how the land lies all about where they mean to make a stand. I kenned ye were eager to learn where they were so I thought I had best tell ye that and ask if ye want me to go back and find out anything else."

"And I will go with him, Sir Simon."

"Aye, Gowan, I think that would be a good idea." Simon looked at Wallace. "How long have ye been a soldier for the laird?"

"Nay long, but I can handle a sword weel enough to stay alive until I can run." Wallace blushed when the others laughed, but their good humor brought a faint smile to his face. "I was set to farm my wife's father's land, wasnae I. But, for this madness, the laird grabbed every mon who wasnae too old or too lame and yanked them into his army. I wouldnae be surprised if half the people in Lochancorrie have a knife at their throats, on them or on one of the ones they love."

"Which makes for a verra weak army," said Gowan.

"Aye and nay," said Simon. "It all depends on how deeply the mon concerned believes Henry can reach those the poor sod loves even though Henry is here, about to face us in battle."

Wallace nodded. "There are some at Lochancorrie who think the laird has sold his verra soul to the devil and that gives him power."

"Henry is just a mon. He may be evil, cruel, and all of that, but he is still just a mon. Go with Gowan, Wallace, and see what can be seen. We dinnae want to lead our men in blind. We will wait here until we ken something, e'en if all ye can discern is that some of Henry's men wait for us just beyond the trees. My hope is that, since ye have already begun to arrest men, Gowan, the army that could have been mustered will have already begun to shrink. I dinnae think many men will want to risk being taken up for treason if their laird isnae pushing them into it."

"That was my hope, too, Sir Simon," Gowan said, and then started off toward the line of trees. "Come along, Wallace. Show me this trail."

"It will be easier to do so if ye would be a bit more careful where ye are putting those big feet of yours," muttered Wallace as he hurried after Gowan.

Simon could tell by the hint of a smile on Gowan's face that the man had heard that impertinence but had taken no offense, simply pretended that he had not heard a word. It was one of the things that made Gowan such an excellent leader of men. He allowed the men to grumble as men would, and needed to, so long as they continued to do the job they were supposed to. That understanding and the fact that Gowan did all he could to make certain his men had food, clothing, and the best of weaponry was what kept his men so loyal to him. Peter was right. If Gowan decided to become the king's hound instead of just the captain of the king's guard, he would be missed.

"I was right," Simon murmured. "Gowan has grown a wee bit more ambitious."

" 'Tis a good ambition," said Peter. "Gowan wants to marry a lass but her family sits higher at the table than he does. To become the king's hound would change that."

"Ah, so ambition has a bonnie face," said Tormand as he stepped up beside Simon and then grinned at Simon's surprise.

"How did ye get past the king's guards?" demanded Simon. "Especially since ye arenae wearing one of your ridiculous disguises."

"I ken most of these men, dinnae I. And those disguises I wore were verra weel thought out."

Simon snorted in derision, Peter echoing the sound. "Honestly now, Tormand. Tell me what ye are doing here. Has Morainn had another vision?" he asked quietly, not wanting any of the other men standing around to hear him for what Morainn could do unsettled too many, raising whispers of witches.

"Nay. I am but here to collect my due, get a few answers," Tormand replied. "I have been tripping along the edges of all this for weeks. I want to see it ended, if I am allowed, mayhap even take a small part in the ending of it." He patted the sword hung at his side, a weapon Simon knew could be wielded with awe-inspiring precision by his friend. "I will leave ye the honor of doing in Henry as ye please but, if ye mean to kill him here, I would like a word with him first."

"Why?"

"Nothing verra important. Just a need to satisfy my curiosity."

Simon did not believe that for a moment, but he did not press Tormand for more information. "How are the children behaving? I hope Morainn isnae troubled too much by their presence."

"Nay, the children help her as weel as they can and she enjoys them. After I see the end of this, I will take them with me to collect Ilsabeth. They will be letting her out of prison, aye?"

There was no mistaking the steel behind Tormand's question, a force that made it more of an order than a question. "I plan to see to that as soon as I present the king with the true traitors and the leaders of the plot."

Tormand looked as if he wanted to argue but was stopped from doing so by the return of Wallace and Gowan. It took several rounds of discussion to decide what to do next. Simon mused that it was fortunate Henry and Walter were waiting for their allies to appear or there would be no one to battle with if the king's men continued to just discuss fighting and not actually do it, and Simon said as much. Within moments they were creeping through the wood, planning to move around Walter and Henry until they encircled them.

When Simon finally saw his brother, Walter, and the men they had with him, he knew they could win this fight. It was the first moment since they had sprung the trap in the dungeons and caught only soldiers that he had felt so confident. Some of the men looked tough, confident, and ready to fight. Simon suspected they were swordsmen for hire, men long overdue for a hanging who would rather die by the sword than be taken prisoner. There were about a dozen men from Lochancorrie, Walter had said, and Simon suspected they were the ones huddled together looking as if they wanted to be anywhere but there. Even better, Henry and Walter were arguing. The alliance they had made was shattering. Simon drew his sword and prepared to face his elder brother on an even footing for the first time in his life.

"They have deserted us," said Walter, looking at what was not even half of the army they had been promised. "We have verra few o'er what we gathered ourselves."

"Aye, I think my wee brother has been verra busy," Henry murmured.

"What do ye mean?"

"I believe our allies in this are now a wee bit busy trying to protect their own necks."

"They have been arrested?!"

Henry looked at Walter, who had gone pale and was beginning to sweat. "That would be my guess, aye. I suspect we can thank your cousin for that. He probably squealed like a pig on the butchering block. I told ye that ye should have killed the fool but ye believed David would ne'er betray ye, e'en though ye betrayed him by tossing him to the wolves."

"Then we should be fleeing this place, nay standing here ready to face the king's men. We dinnae have enough soldiers for a fight like that. We should be headed for the coast and hie ourselves off to France until we can face Simon and Gowan and their men."

"I hadnae realized what a coward ye are."

"Nay a coward. A mon who can see that we arenae ready yet. We need more men, more power, more money. In France we would be safe and could make new plans."

"This is my new plan. We stand and fight and take down the best men the king has to offer. Then we take the king."

"Ye are still thinking Simon is the lad ye bullied and drove from home years ago. He isnae that boy anymore. He is a mon many fear and he has brought many a mon to the gallows. The king listens to him. He willnae heed us if we try to say Sir Simon is wrong. Sir Simon is never wrong. If we lose this battle and he drags us afore the king, we had best say our prayers for we are naught but dead men."

"Walter, I am going to give you two choices." Henry looked at Walter and nodded when the man paled even more, so much so that he looked ready to faint. "Ye can stand and fight like a mon or ye can have me cut your cursed throat to stop your whining. 'Tis a boring way to shut the mouth of a coward but I havenae the time to do it as I wish, and to use ye to show these men that cowardice willnae be tolerated."

Walter opened his mouth to respond only to squeak out a warning. "They are here. 'Tis too late to do anything to save ourselves."

Simon stepped out into the clearing where his brother and Walter stood with their small army. He was not surprised when the men from Lochancorrie immediately dropped their weapons and surrendered. It was possible that the sight of Wallace alive and fighting on the side of the king's men made them see a chance to get out of the trap Henry had put them in. Once the men from Lochancorrie surrendered, a great many others did as well. Simon left Gowan, Peter, and Tormand to deal with the others while he stepped up to face Henry.

Henry smiled and Simon had to fight a fear left from a childhood scarred by this man. Walter had warned Henry that he mistook Simon for the boy he had been the last time Henry had seen him, but Simon knew he suffered something similar. He, too, saw himself as that boy, the one who had never been able to get the best of Henry. He stiffened his spine as he reminded himself of all he had accomplished in the years since Henry had left him broken and bloodied to die on the bed where he had been caught lying with Henry's wife.

"Weel met, little brother," drawled Henry, and drew his sword.

"I am going to ask ye to surrender to the king's justice, Henry," Simon said as he and his brother began to circle each other in preparation for a fight that Simon knew would be to the death unless he could bring Henry down in a way that allowed capture instead of immediate execution.

"Aye, ye would, wouldnae ye?" Henry chuckled and it was not a pleasant sound. "Ye may get my cowardly partner Walter to do so, but I have nay wish to hand myself o'er to the verra king I meant to kill. If I must die, I will do so by your sword. Here. Now."

Henry had barely finished speaking when he lunged. Simon parried the attack and the fight began in earnest. He did his best to keep from getting wounded by his brother, knowing that Henry would move in for the kill as quickly as any adder. Henry would not be held back by the fact that they were of the same blood, born of the same mother. It soon became evident, however, that, like so many who depended on fear and intimidation, Henry had not honed his skills with a sword over the years. Simon had.

It was not until he was soaked in sweat and growing concerned that he might tire before Henry when luck gave Simon the chance he had been waiting for. Henry stumbled over a collapsed Walter, who was sprawled in the dirt whimpering over a badly wounded arm. Simon struck swiftly, knocking the sword from Henry's hand. Before he could secure the man and take him prisoner, however, Henry pulled a dagger from his boot and attacked again.

They wrestled across the clearing that had been chosen as the battlefield. Henry scored Simon with the dagger several times, but Simon realized he had more strength than Henry. Pushing aside all doubt of his ability to beat the man who had terrorized him for so long, Simon soon had the man pinned beneath him. Tormand moved in quickly to help Simon tie his brother's hands behind his back.

As Simon stood up, all too aware of his bruises and bleeding wounds, he looked down at Henry. He felt no triumph, no sense of a job well done. All he felt was weary and resigned. He had beaten Henry but that meant that he would be taking his own brother to the king for a hasty trial and a horrific execution. He would have his own brother's blood on his hands.

"I was pulled into this against my will!" cried Walter, dragging Simon from his dark thoughts, and he looked over at the trussed up Walter. "He threatened my own mother! What choice did I have?" Walter did not seem to notice that Peter, who stood by him, was paying no attention to his pleas and excuses.

" 'Tis no wonder I have lost this battle," Henry said, staring at Walter in a way that told Simon his brother was envisioning all the vicious ways he would like to kill the man. "I depended too much on a fool and a coward."

"I cannae understand why ye even started it," said Simon, grunting softly in pain when Wallace began to tend to his wounds. "Ye have no claim to the throne."

Henry shrugged. "As much claim as the mon sitting on it now. I would ken how to rule this land. The king is too weak, too merciful. It takes a strong hand to rule a country and make it great."

Staring into Henry's face, Simon could see the madness clearly now. "Ye dinnae even think ye have a rightful claim, do ye. Ye just wanted to be king."

"Aye. I have been the laird of a small holding for nigh on to fifteen years. It was time to better myself."

"Is that why ye killed our father? Because ye felt it was time?"

"Aye. The fool had ruled long enough but he wouldnae name me his heir, wouldnae step aside. He was so strong, so cursed healthy, I would have been an old mon myself ere he died and the laird's chair was empty."

"What do ye mean, name ye his heir? Ye were always his heir."

"Nay after the fool looked around and realized I was the only son left. He kenned it was me who had gotten rid of all of ye. It was then that he began to talk of making ye his heir. Weel, that wouldnae be right. I was the firstborn, after all. Since ye didnae have the decency to draw near enough for me to be rid of ye as I was rid of the others, the only other way to see that ye didnae get what was mine, was to be rid of the laird. When ye were eighteen, I thought I had finally rid myself of ye as weel, but ye lived."

"Are ye saying that ye killed our brothers? Nay, ye cannae have for I am certain I have been hearing of them from time to time. I was told they had all been fostered out."

"I dinnae ken how ye could have heard about them as I tied them up, put them in a wee boat that wouldnae stay afloat for verra long and set them adrift on a very big, very deep loch. E'en if they got themselves free of the ropes, they couldnae swim, could they."

"They didnae have to," said Tormand, his quiet, deep voice cutting through Simon's shock. "They were picked up out of the water ere they drowned by a passing fishermon."

Henry cursed and shook his head. "I cannae believe how impossible it was to get rid of ye. Ye would think I would have succeeded in but one of my attempts."

"Ye ken where my other brothers are?" Simon asked Tormand.

"Aye, and they are all healthy. They are also good men although they are swords for hire from time to time." He glanced at the ones Simon and Gowan's men had defeated. "Nay like these fools who dinnae have the sense to ken that they were accepting the coin of a madmon." Tormand looked back at Henry as if fascinated. "Ye should have waited to see if they truly did drown. Just curious as to how ye thought to explain that they were all tied."

"I assumed they would sink to the bottom of that verra deep loch and ne'er trouble me again. But, ye are right. I should have waited about to make certain of it."

Simon felt an urge to be sick. "They were little more than bairns."

"They were a threat, as ye were. And the one thing I wanted of ye, ye couldnae even give me that. A son. Nay, I got just another wee, puling girl child. I kenned she would have your eyes and she would be staring at me, judging me, so I rid myself of her as weel." He smiled coldly at Simon. "It wasnae hard because she was sickly and I had already had some practice at that with my other children."

Simon staggered a little and Wallace caught him, steadying him. The madness in Henry was so clear, so chilling, as he spoke of killing children. Of killing Simon's child, his young brothers, their father, and even his own children. For reasons of his own Henry felt like talking and every word out of his mouth was horrifying.

"Weel, ye failed to rid yourself of your brothers," Tormand said. "They havenae been dead all these years, just wise enough to stay so hidden away that ye would think them dead. They may even come and watch your execution so ye may get another chance to see them as ye are made to pay for your treason."

"Where are my brothers?" demanded Simon, unable to stomach listening to any more of what Henry was spewing out.

"Ye will see them soon. I was but curious as to why this madmon would do such a thing. As ye said, your brothers were just bairns."

Simon looked at Walter, who stared at Henry as if he had never seen the man before. "Seeing more clearly, Hepbourn? Seeing that ye gave up all ye had for the sake of a madmon?"

"I am nay mad," Henry said, acting highly insulted. "I am but logical and do what is necessary to stay the laird and keep Lochancorrie safe and the people fed."

Wallace's snort of derision told Simon that Henry was seeing only what he wished to. Simon could not bear to hear any more. He had known that Henry killed easily and that he was one of the most brutal men he had ever met, but the coldness with which he spoke of killing so many of their own blood terrified Simon.

"Time to take him to the king to be judged," said Gowan as he stepped up to Henry, grabbed his bound arms and yanked him to his feet.

"Do I ken who ye are?" asked Henry. "There is something verra familiar about you."

"I suspicion I look like my cousin," Gowan said as he roughly dragged Henry along the rocky ground.

"Your cousin?"

"Aye. She was your first wife's maid. We were all set to bring her home, kenning that she wasnae happy, that she was afraid. When we got there all we found was her body after ye were done with her. E'er since that day my family has sworn to make ye pay despite the fact that they are poor and powerless. Weel, ye may soon die for other reasons than the rape and murder of a wee lass of barely fifteen, but it will do. Aye, it will do verra fine indeed."

"Weel, that was interesting," murmured Tormand as the men that had come with Simon and Gowan began to take the prisoners away.

"He kills like a child who sees a toy he wants and just takes it," Simon said. "Henry sees what he wants, and if someone stands in the way, he kills them."

"Aye and that is his madness."

"And my brothers are alive?"

"Verra much so but it took telling them that Henry was about to meet his much delayed fate to get them to come out of hiding. Ye will see them soon. Best go with the others and take the prisoners to the king." He nodded toward the small group of men from Lochancorrie who were talking to Wallace. "Save for them. Gowan didnae think they were any trouble and left them for ye to see to. Let the others who so hastily dropped their swords escape as weel. Good mon, Gowan."

"A verra good mon," Simon murmured, "who is eyeing my place as the king's hound."

"I heard. Ye willnae be able to do it as ye have been for ye are now a laird. There is a clan and lands that need you."

"But will the people of Lochancorrie want another from that family of brutes and madmen to rule over them?"

"Ye arenae your father or Henry."

Simon prayed he was not, but a knot of fear had formed in his belly. He instructed Wallace to take the Lochancorrie men to his home while he went to the king along with the prisoners. Tormand ambled along at his side and Simon knew it was so that he could take Ilsabeth with him when she was free.

That was for the best, he told himself. He was about to turn his brother over to the king, a traitor and a madman. He had three other brothers who might be untainted but he could not know until he met them. He had had a child with his brother's wife and that child had been murdered. No matter how much Henry deserved his fate, it was going to be Simon who handed him over to it, so he would soon have his own brother's blood on his hands. There was so much wrong with him and his family he could not see making any woman accept him, especially the one who had suffered so much from the crimes of his own brother.

He had to let her go, he decided. Had to let her find a man who was not weighted down as he was.

Or a man who might well have the seed of madness in him, a seed that could be given to any child they might have together. Nor could he make her turn her back on her family, who would undoubtedly hate him for his family's part in causing them to spend the last few weeks hiding as soldiers ransacked their home.

"Ye have a look on your face, friend, that tells me ye are thinking hard," said Tormand. "Why do I think that is a verra bad idea?"

" 'Tis always best to think things over when one is about to hand one's mad brother over to the king to be tried, convicted, and executed. I am about to stain my hands with my brother's blood. And ye are about to take Ilsabeth back to her family where she belongs."

"Jesu, I kenned I wasnae going to like how ye were thinking."

Chapter 17

Her cell was seventeen paces wide and one and thirty paces deep. It was rather roomy for a prison cell, she thought, as she paced back toward the cell door. Ilsabeth knew the battle with Henry would not end with some quick, simple sword fight, but she did think it had been too long since Simon, Gowan, and the others had finally gone looking for Simon's brother. She certainly doubted it was civilized debate that was keeping everyone away for so very long.

Despite her efforts not to put Simon and Henry together in her mind, as brothers, Ilsabeth found she could not fully control her own thoughts. Simon and Henry shared a look about them and she had to wonder if any of Simon's other siblings had that look as well. Perhaps she would look into his bloodlines, she mused, and hastily shook the idea away. Simon had to know his own bloodlines, had to know which relatives, if any, he had who might shelter his younger brothers. And his brothers had to have heard at least one tale about Simon yet they had made no effort to get to know him, talk to him, or even just go to Simon's house to see what he looked like.

She did not understand families like that. Ilsabeth knew Henry had to have been a source of the poison that had torn apart the family, but why had the ones Henry tormented and hurt never banded together against him? It made no sense to her. It was as if the other three brothers had escaped and made no effort to see if Simon had managed to do the same.

"Bastards," she muttered as she began to stomp back and forth across her cell, pleased to have some target to hurl her anger at. "Simon has been a king's mon for years. It wouldnae have taken his younger brothers much effort to just open their eyes and look about a little to find him."

"But we did."

Ilsabeth was surprised that the screech that escaped her had not brought every guard in the area rushing to her cell. Then she remembered that every guard around, except for a few hand-chosen ones left to keep the king surrounded and protected, was hunting down Henry Innes of Lochancorrie and stupid Walter. She felt a pinch of fear over the fact that she was unguarded and there was a stranger there, but calmed herself with the knowledge that she was safe where she was.

"Who are ye?" she demanded, edging close enough to the cell door to get a better look yet staying out of reach of whoever was standing there watching her.

There were three of them. The tallest of the

three leaned against the bars of her cell and replied, "I am Malcolm Innes. This is my younger brother, Kenneth." He pointed to the one standing by his right shoulder. "And this is my youngest brother, Ruari," he added, and pointed to the young man standing on his left. "I believe ye are acquainted with our brother Simon and, sad to say, our eldest brother, Henry."

"How did ye come here? Now? Today instead of years ago?"

"We have come because your cousin Sir Tormand Murray told us that Henry will soon be gone. He was why we stayed in hiding. He tried to kill us."

"But, ye would have been nay more than bairns," she said.

"Aye. He tied us up and tossed us in a wee boat that had a lot of small holes in it. Then he pushed it out onto the waters of a verra large loch. I recall him telling us that it was also verra deep and no one would e'er find our bodies."

Ilsabeth could see it all too clearly and she pressed her hands over her mouth for a moment, before removing them enough to whisper, "How did ye survive?"

"A fishermon from the clan that lived across the loch. He pulled us from the water just before the boat finished sinking. I told him we could ne'er go home, nay as long as Henry lived or before we were big enough, strong enough, and powerful enough to kill him. So he took us to his laird. His laird decided his lands were too close to Henry's for our safety and so he sent us to his brother who had married a laird's daughter far up into the Highlands. That is where we have grown and learned to

wield a sword, daggers, our fists." He shrugged.
"Sometimes we sell those skills to ones who need
them. It helps the clan, which is poor and small."

"But, Simon would have helped ye. He has been
one of the king's men for years now and he has
both power and skill. If ye had come and told him
what Henry had done, he might have been able to
rid Lochancorrie of that madmon ere now."

"Mayhap. I ken that we hid longer than we
needed to, but ye werenae stuck in that boat, tied,
unable to swim even if ye kenned how, and kenning
that ye will die and have to watch your brothers die,
too."

"True. I wasnae. 'Tis hard to understand a mon
who would so easily kill wee lads, especially when
they are of his own blood. Wasnae your father still
alive then? He wouldnae have wanted ye all dead,
would he?"

"I dinnae ken what our father thought when we
all disappeared but he didnae come looking for us,
did he. Nay, father wasnae like Henry, but he was a
brutish mon. If he thought we had been killed, 'tis
plain to see that he didnae look to the one who did
it or why."

"So why are ye here now?"

"To see Simon and, mayhap, return to Lochancorrie. I have ne'er forgotten our home for all that
it wasnae a verra happy place for us as children."

Ilsabeth stepped a little closer to the bars to
study the three young men. They all held the look
of Simon although Ruari was of a larger build, like
Henry. The gray eyes were the same, just different
shades of the same color. If Henry were defeated,
Lochancorrie would have need of such men.

"They went to hunt down Henry and his fool, Walter. I dinnae think it will be all that hard to find them. 'Tis evident ye ran into no trouble in getting inside the keep."

Ruari grinned and Ilsabeth could see even more of Simon in the youth's face. "Only the king himself is heavily guarded today."

She nodded. "I recalled that when I screeched after Malcolm spoke. That should have brought a few guards running. Of course, ye shouldnae have been able to come in here without a guard, either."

"Tell us about Simon," said Kenneth. "We need to ken the mon we are about to see."

That made sense and might even ease what could be a very awkward meeting. Ilsabeth did her best to tell them all she knew about Simon, including all they had been doing to get proof about Henry's treasonous activities. By the time she had finished, all three brothers were looking at her with faint smiles.

"I dinnae think I told ye anything funny," she murmured.

"Ye love him," said Malcolm.

She felt a blush sting her cheeks and glared at him. "I do not recall saying so."

"Ye didnae have to say. We all heard it. 'Tis clear ye havenae told our brother so dinnae fear we will." He stepped back and looked at her prison. "I suspect that, if all ye said about Simon was true, he will have ye out of here verra soon."

"I am praying for that."

They said their farewells, a subtle promise to see her again underlying each one. Ilsabeth sighed, wishing she were free so that she could see that reunion. Even though they had never had a real chance to be brothers because of Henry, it was never too late to try. She would just have to be satisfied with the fact that something she had said while talking of Simon had convinced them to search him out. She grimaced as she looked around her prison. And she also hoped they did not get so caught up in it that they forgot she was still down here.

Ilsabeth was beginning to get worried that she had been forgotten when she heard someone approaching. The quick stab of anticipation that quickened her heart faded abruptly when David Hepbourn stopped in front of her cell. He looked worn, tired, and as if he was grieving for someone. She quickly pushed down the twinge of sympathy that softened her anger and stared at him.

"What are ye doing here?" she asked.

" 'Tis over, ye ken," he said. "Walter and Henry Innes are being taken to the king."

"So, 'tis all over," she murmured, and wondered why she was not free yet. "My family can go home."

"Aye. Ilsabeth, I have come here to beg for your forgiveness."

"There is no need."

"Oh, aye, there is. I was a part of it all. I didnae feel it was right to place the blame for a murder on you but I did naught to stop it. I heeded every word Walter said and blindly followed. For that, I was willing to let ye pay for what he had done. I pushed away all doubts and heeded Walter's slander against your kinsmen."

"Nothing to fret about. They have been called worse."

His smile was faint and fleeting. "It still wasnae right. For that unkindness, and for this, I beg your forgiveness."

"Then ye have it. And, I am sorry about Walter, David. I ken that ye loved and trusted him. What will ye do now?"

"Weel, it seems that, because I turned him in as a traitor and helped them catch so many of the others, I will retain most of Walter's property. The king rather liked Walter's father and doesnae want it to leave the hands of a Hepbourn."

"Walter's mother must be stricken with grief."

"She is and she has already left for her sister's for she says she cannae stay here while they murder her son and she cannae stay in the same house with the mon who handed her bairn over to the king as I did. There are a great many things she said but a few made me certain she kenned exactly what Walter was doing and approved. She thought Walter deserved to be a king."

"But, it wasnae Walter who was to be the king, nor did he particularly wish to be."

"She willnae heed that and it doesnae truly matter." He glanced over his shoulder and then gave her a faint smile. "I had best go for they all ken where I am and someone may soon come hunting me down. I would prefer to return to where I am supposed to be without help or an escort."

"Did ye happen to see Simon?" she asked, inwardly cursing the weakness that made her utter the words.

"Aye, he has just met all three of his younger brothers. 'Tis quite a reunion, although they had to endure some verra harsh words from Henry. I think

I always kenned that there was something wrong with Sir Henry but I could ne'er decide. So, as always, I followed Walter's lead." He bowed to her. "Ye will be out of here soon and back with your family. I will see what I can do to send ye some reparations for all the trouble the Hepbourns caused."

Ilsabeth did her best to dissuade him of that but he would not listen. She decided he needed to do it for his own peace of mind. Although it was difficult to completely forgive him since he was one who helped put her in this cell and send her family into hiding, she did feel a little sorry for him. He had been Walter's pet and Walter had betrayed him. Not only had the man dragged David into something that would ruin the younger man if it did not kill him, he had turned his back on David in his time of need.

She started pacing again and wondered if she was suffering a like fate. The battle was obviously over, Walter and Henry had been sent to the king and would await judgment, and Simon was meeting his younger brothers for the first time since they had been children together. As far as Ilsabeth could see, she was the only one who was not doing anything. Was it not time for her to be released?

Simon winced as Henry scolded the king for harnessing a great man like himself. He had the feeling that Henry had finally taken that last step into a madness so deep it was no longer possible for him to hide it. It was both humiliating and frightening to watch.

Just as he was about to suggest gagging his brother, for he had already said more than enough to get himself convicted of treason three times over, three young men walked into the main hall. Simon stared at them, sensing that they were familiar, yet not recalling ever seeing them before. It was not until they stopped directly in front of him that he saw the familial resemblance. The gray eyes, the black hair, the bone structures were all Innes.

"Kenneth? Malcolm? Ruari?" When the three young men grinned and nodded, Simon ran his fingers through his hair and just kept staring at them in disbelief. "But Henry said he had killed ye. I began to think the occasional whisper of news about ye was actually about someone else."

Malcolm hastily told the tale, shocking the king and his ministers. "I confess, it bred a deep fear that we have only just been able to shake free of and come out of hiding."

"Ye should have stayed in hiding, ye miserable little bastards," said Henry.

"Nay more a bastard than ye are," murmured Ruari. "Ye dinnae look so verra threatening now. Dirty and chained, ye are, and I find that most soothing. E'en if we hadnae come looking for Simon and found ye here like this, once I heard of it I couldnae stay away."

Henry started cursing them and when the king reprimanded him, Henry returned to scolding the king again. Simon directed his brothers to his home for he knew they would not be able to have any sort of reunion with Henry there. As soon as his newfound brothers left, Simon turned his attention back to Henry and vainly tried to shut the man's mouth. The king finally signaled for the prisoners to be removed.

When a weeping Walter and a still scolding Henry were taken away, the king waved Simon over. In the man's eyes, Simon could see the same unease, even fear, that he suspected was lurking in his own. There was something about looking into the face of such madness that had one wondering how easily it could affect oneself.

"He made no attempt to deny what he had planned," the king said.

"Nay, for he thinks he had the right and that we should all see that."

"That is what is so puzzling. How can he think that? That is where the madness is, isnae it?"

"Some of it, aye. As I think on it, Henry has always been that way, always felt that he was right and everyone else should understand that or be made to. The brutality may come from that, too. I dinnae ken. All I do ken is that he has taken that last step into utter, easily seen madness."

"He will be punished as the traitor he is despite that. He wasnae always this clearly insane so one cannae say he didnae ken what he was doing. Walter is a different matter. His mother has already begun petitioning the court. She doesnae openly ask for the property back, but makes some wild accusations about David Hepbourn plotting all this so that her poor son would suffer and David would get everything."

"David couldnae plot his way down the street," muttered Simon, and the king grinned.

"Nay, he couldnae. He is a follower. I shall just make sure he has the right mon to follow now. And, now, let us speak on the men with Henry and Walter. We didnae get all of them, did we?"

"Nay, sire." Simon did not really like this particular line of questioning. "Some escaped."

"Because of the lax attitude of three of my best men?"

"Nay, sire. We were all verra busy subduing Walter and Henry."

"Of course ye were." The king sighed. "I am pleased with the ending of this even if I think mercy may have been taken too far. But, the common soldier pulled along into the wrong battle because his laird has ordered it is of no real importance to me. And set that poor lass free."

"Of course. And her family, the Armstrongs of Aigballa? Their names, and to some extent that of the Murrays, have been damaged by all of this."

"I ken it and the word has already begun to spread that they were just the pawns in another's game. The soldiers will be leaving as soon as they get the message I just sent them and they, too, have sworn to spread the word. It will take a while for we both ken that once a stain has been put upon one's honor, 'tis a verra difficult thing to wash away. I have great faith that Ilsabeth's people will manage."

Simon nodded, biting his tongue against the words he wanted to say. A family forced to run and hide, branded traitors, their home taken and treated roughly by soldiers, and a few of their oldest clan members killed in the taking of the keep did not equal a "stain" on the family honors. Simon would not press now for the reparations the king had spoken of early in this deadly game, but he would not forget them, either.

The king should be pleased with the traitors that were caught, he mused. There were eight men, not including Walter and Henry. Eight men of good blood, wealth, and property who would soon be tried and, undoubtedly, proven guilty of treason. Simon decided he would do his best to be somewhere far away when the executions began. Even Henry's. Lochancorrie needed him. Wallace had already reminded him of that several times. He now had brothers who might be willing to return home and make Lochancorrie the place it should have been before the darkness of Henry's madness had descended upon it.

He was tired. Tired, heartsore, and, at the thought of losing Ilsabeth, feeling very empty inside. He was going to set Ilsabeth free and not just from prison. Simon could not hold her to a man who came from such a troubled family, the hint of madness always there. She needed a brighter future.

Simon finally excused himself from the king's presence and started to make his way to the prison. He met a very solemn Tormand and the children at the door that led down into the dungeons. The realization that he would be losing the children, too, nearly brought him to his knees. He stiffened his spine and greeted them with the cool indifference he was hoping to perfect soon.

"He is setting her free?" asked Tormand as they started down the stairs.

Picking up Elen, who had stood before him with

her arms stretched out to him, Simon nodded. "He has also begun to spread the word that the Armstrongs of Aigballa were no traitors, just victims of the real traitors' attempts to hide their trail."

"We both ken that willnae clear away the mark left on them," said Tormand. "The whispers will always be there. That is the way of it when 'tis bad news, aye?"

"Aye, but we can do what little we can and hope."

"True. Now open the door so I can let the children go and greet her and then mayhap ye will tell me what has ye looking as if your dog Bonegnasher has just died."

"I dinnae ken what ye are talking about," he muttered as he set Elen down and opened the door to Ilsabeth's cell.

He was about to turn back to Tormand when Ilsabeth hurled herself into his arms and kissed both his cheeks. For one brief, heady moment he held her close for the last time. Then he released her to greet the children. He stepped back, fighting the temptation to join them in the happy reunion and then looked to see Tormand at his side staring at him.

"Ye are making the painful choice, arenae ye?" said Tormand. "The one Morainn spoke about."

"There is no choice about it. Ye saw Henry; ye saw what lurks in my blood."

"I thought ye didnae believe in that."

"I didnae until I saw the madness in Henry, until I felt the unreasoning rage he could stir within me. And I have lands now but from what Wallace says, they will need a great deal of work to get them to produce a goodly supply of food again."

"Ye are making excuses."

"They arenae excuses, they are reasons."

Tormand made a mocking noise deep in his throat. "Ye keep telling yourself that. Mayhap it will work. Just remember that changes cannae always be fixed."

"Oh, Simon, I am so sorry for ye, for what ye are having to deal with with that brother of yours." Ilsabeth walked over and hugged him.

Simon stepped back again, gently but firmly pulling her arms away from his body. If she kept touching him, he would never be able to let her go. He fought to ignore the hurt that flared in her beautiful eyes. It was better to hurt her now than to condemn her to a life where there might still lurk madness and despair.

Ilsabeth thought her heart would shatter. There was no welcome light in Simon's eyes.

He had pushed her out of his arms as if he could not bear to have her touch him. That caused her so much pain she nearly cried out from the sharpness of it.

He was leaving her. She could see it in his eyes. The gray was as cold and penetrating as it had been the first day she had met him. What Ilsabeth did not understand was why he was doing it.

"Simon?" She reached out to him and he stepped back.

" 'Tis time for ye to go home, Ilsabeth," he said. "Your family will be anxious to see that ye are unharmed by your ordeal. They will soon be returning to their home and that is where ye should be."

"If that is what ye truly wish," she whispered, determined not to cry in front of him even though her eyes felt full of tears.

"It is what must be."

Ilsabeth watched him walk away and knew he was taking her heart with him. She did not understand. The last time he had visited her in her prison his words had been tender, his touch even more so. Now it was like hugging a stone. She looked at Tormand, who just shrugged.

"A mon can be a fool sometimes," Tormand said.

"He can change so in but one night?"

"If he has come to a decision, aye."

She thought about it for a moment and then sighed. "It has to do with Henry's madness, doesnae it?"

"I think so. Give him time. Seeing it so clearly has overset him. Ye didnae see it but Henry lost what little grip he had on sanity right there in front of the crown. It wasnae a pretty sight. He also boasted of all he had done whilst still out on the battlefield."

"Time, is it? We shall see."

Now she was growing angry. Simon had questioned the belief that such sicknesses of the mind crop up within families. Obviously when it appeared in his own, he lost all of his former doubts of such beliefs and suffered fears for himself and his children

The thought of children caused her to place her hand on her belly. It was too soon to know but considering how often she and Simon had made love, it was a possibility that she already carried his child. She searched her heart for a fear of the insanity that had taken Henry and felt none. Her family was not free of that problem yet it did not run rampant in the bloodlines. Henry was twisted in some way from the day he was born; she was certain of it. She had also seen none of it in Simon or his brothers. She just wondered how long it would take Simon to see it, too.

"Are ye going to be all right?"

She managed a smile for her cousin. "Aye. I willnae say that I willnae hold out a hope that he will come to his senses, but aye, I shall be fine. It has been a terrible time for him."

"Where Simon?" demanded Elen.

"Simon has gone home, love," Ilsabeth said, and gently brushed some of the thick curls off Elen's face as the child began to scowl.

"He left us," said Reid.

"Now, ye dinnae ken that for certain," Ilsabeth began to protest.

"I do ken it. He didnae e'en want to smash his mouth on yours."

"Smash his mouth on yours?" muttered Tormand. "I would have thought Simon had more finesse than that."

Ilsabeth elbowed her cousin in the stomach and he grunted before he laughed. "Reid, Simon is a grown mon and he can do as he pleases. We may nay agree with what he is doing, but 'tis his right to do it."

"Then why do ye look so sad?"

"Weel, I didnae say I had to like what he was doing."

Reid stood up very straight. "If he has hurt your feelings then I will go and punch him in the nose."

"Thank ye, Reid, but, nay, dinnae do that. Ye

must understand that adults can decide that they cannae be together even if they have been, er, smashing mouths." She tried to elbow Tormand in the stomach again when he snickered but he nimbly eluded it.

"Does that mean he cannae be with us, either?"

"I fear so, although if he e'er asks for ye to visit I willnae say nay."

"Where Simon?"

"Simon had to leave, love," she said again, and had the feeling she was going to have to repeat herself on that matter more times than she wanted to deal with.

"Simon stay."

"Oh, dear." Ilsabeth could see that look of stubbornness forming on Elen's angelic face and prepared for what could become a glorious fit of rage. "Simon cannae stay, dear."

"Where Simon?" Elen bellowed, her small hands clenched in front of her. "Want Simon now."

"Elen, we cannae always have what we want," Ilsabeth said, and thought to herself that that was sadly true even for adults who ought to have better control over their lives.

"Si . . . mon!!!"

Simon halted on the steps out of the dungeon as that childish bellow resounded off the walls of the cool, damp stone. He closed his eyes and fought the urge to go back to the child. It was best for Elen if he did not waver. She would get over needing to see him.

"Si . . . mon!!"

He hesitated another moment and then bolted up the stairs, the sound of Elen bellowing his name following him every step of the way. Selfish bastard that he was, he had not even considered the children's feelings. It was too late to back down now. Repeating the words that it was better for them all if he left, he slammed the door to the dungeons behind him, cutting off that bellow. He knew though, that he would be hearing the angry pain in it for a long time.

Chapter 18

Simon studied the lands of Lochancorrie closely as he, his brothers, and the men Henry had dragged from their homes all rode toward the huge keep that dominated the hillside in front of them. Not many of the fields were planted and there appeared to be few livestock grazing on the low, rolling hills around them. He had to wonder what Henry had done in his time as laird aside from abusing the people who depended upon him.

"Is it all like this?" he asked Wallace, thinking that winter could prove to be very harsh if they did not get in some supplies.

"Aye," replied Wallace as he looked around. "'Tisnae as bad as I thought it would be in truth. Seen it worse. Henry wasnae here much after the spring rains ended, ye ken, for he was off plotting with those others. I think the people here must have used his absence to get some work done. But, Henry did take a lot of men from the fields to train them for his war. He was also fond of large feasts.

He would have his friends round, snatch a few lasses, and do naught but eat, drink, and wench for days."

"Weel, we shall have to think of some way to build up the supplies or it shall be a dangerously lean winter. Now, do ye think Henry's guard is still here?"

"Nay, for the gates to the keep are open."

"It could be a trap," said Malcolm, and drew his sword, Kenneth and Ruari quickly doing the same. "If Henry's guard was loyal to him I wouldnae trust them as far as I can spit."

"They were loyal enough," said Wallace, "for they got all the food and wenches they wanted when he was here."

"Wallace, am I going to find a keep full of Henry's bastards and poor abused lassies who cower at every shadow?" asked Simon.

"I fear there are some bastards. Henry didnae pay much attention unless they were the children of his wives and I fear the poor lassies he bred didnae live long. There are some, as I said, and all are lassies. So ye dinnae need to worry that there will be anyone challenging ye for the laird's seat."

"I wasnae worried about that so much as I was worried that Henry didnae take care of the children he bred."

"He didnae but those ones were luckier than the ones bred under his own roof."

Simon shook his head as they cautiously rode into the inner bailey. All that waited for them were a few women and children and a half dozen soldiers who showed no sign of attacking them. Simon got the bad feeling that Henry had stripped the place bare in his quest to be a king.

He turned to ask Wallace to introduce him only

to see that man leaping from his mount and running toward a slender red-haired girl with a plump baby in her arms. Most of the other men from Lochancorrie were doing the same and the bailey was filled with the glad cries of welcome. Simon experienced a distinct stab of envy.

He dismounted and climbed up the steps to the front door. Turning, with his brothers flanking him, he called for the attention of those gathered in the bailey. The moment they were all looking at him with a mix of anticipation, hope, and resignation, he struggled to think of what he needed to say.

"Your laird, Henry Innes, is dead. He was executed last week for the crime of treason against the crown." Someone cheered and Simon ignored it. "I am Simon Innes, the new laird of Lochancorrie, and these are my brothers." He introduced his brothers in order of their age and noticed how the curiosity of the people began to overcome the wariness. "We need to get to work. From what I have seen, we have a lot of hard work ahead of us if we dinnae all want to starve this winter.

"I will take an hour now to clean up and eat and then I want anyone who has something to say to come to me in the great hall. That should also give ye time to tell the others, such as the people in the village. We shall all have to work together if we are to make this place what it was in my grandfather's time. While I am certain some of the tales of the bounty and beauty of this place at that time are just that—tales—I suspect that with some efforts we can do it or come close. Go and spread the word about the meeting and think of what is important to ye that ye feel must be attended to."

"Weel, at least they havenae run screaming from the keep at the thought of four Innes men here," murmured Malcolm.

"They were a wee bit wary to start but I think the return of their men, hale and weel fed, helped ease things," Simon said as he opened the door to the keep and came face-to-face with a plump woman of about thirty years holding the hand of a pretty dark-haired girl. "May I help ye?"

"Aye, I be Annie. I do most of the ordering of the household. The laird thought this child to be mine."

"And she isnae?"

"Nay, m'laird, she is yours."

Simon looked at the little girl again. There was no question she was of Innes blood with her thick black hair and clear gray eyes, but he could see nothing to tell him she was his child. He looked back at Annie. "Are ye certain?"

"She be born of Mary, the laird's third wife, nine months after ye were beaten nigh unto death. Mary didnae want her"—Annie kissed the child on the cheek—"and we all ken what the laird did to his girl babies, so I took over the whole care of her."

"But he said he had killed my child."

"He thought he had. There was another bairn born that night, another wee lass, but I kenned that one wouldnae be living for long. The breathing was all wrong, ye ken, and the skin was yellow. I switched the bairns. When the other poor lass died, I claimed the bairn everyone thought was Mary's and have raised her. She is yours, laird. Nay question of it."

He looked at the little girl. "What is your name, loving?"

"Marion."

"A fine name. Weel, when I have bathed and eaten, ye may sit with me in the hall if ye wish. There is going to be a meeting and we are all going to talk about what needs to be done here to make it a better place."

"May I think of some things, too, and speak?"

"Aye, ye may. Now, we shall meet in the hall in an hour." He held out his hand to her. "Agreed?"

"Agreed." Marion shook his hand.

Annie suddenly smiled at him, revealing that she had been a very pretty young woman at some time. "Ye will do, laddie. Ye will do."

"I suppose that was a compliment," said Kenneth as they all gathered in the laird's bedchamber while several serving girls ran back and forth with water to help the men bathe.

"I think so," Simon murmured, and found himself wondering what Ilsabeth would think of his child.

"Do we wish to ken how it is ye had a child with Mary?" asked Malcolm, and there was a thread of anger in his voice.

"In a moment." Seeing that the tub was full as was the washbasin, he ordered the serving girls away and shut the door behind them. " 'Tis a long and sordid tale. I was eighteen and a wee bit naïve when it came to women," he began, undressing as he spoke.

He had reached the part where he had heard Henry and Mary discussing him as if he were a stud bull and then took off his shirt. The looks of horrified shock on their faces made him wince a little. He had become accustomed to the feel of the scars and Ilsabeth's acceptance of them had made him forget how they looked.

"Why are ye nay dead?" asked Ruari.

"My foster father said he decided I was too stubborn to succumb to it or the fevers that wracked me for days afterward. This is what I was still all too painfully aware of, despite the fact that it was healed, when I arrived to rescue a bitch who didnae need rescuing."

"Has Ilsabeth seen those?"

"Aye," Simon replied with a hint of wariness behind his reply.

"And she stayed. Weel, until ye threw her away."

Simon gave his youngest brother a scowl and then climbed into the tub. "I believed, and still do, that she deserved better than the brother of a madmon and a traitor, or the laird of a keep that will need years of work and a lot of money to see life improve here. Now, let us speak of any ideas ye might have for making this land one that can be lived off, and lived off weel."

By the time Simon went down to the hall to start the meeting, his mind was swimming with ideas. He took little Marion by the hand and seated her in the chair at his right hand. A grin from Malcolm told him his brother was not insulted, willingly giving up his rightful seat to the little girl. To his amusement he noticed that Marion held a small chalkboard with several things listed on it.

The meeting began cautiously, all those who had gathered to say their piece doing so with some trepidation. Simon could only imagine how Henry would have taken some farmer or cottager trying to give him a suggestion. As he listened and responded with quiet, thoughtful answers, people began to relax and he knew he was now hearing the true concerns of Lochancorrie's people. And then Marion raised her hand.

"What is it, loving?" he asked her.

"I think we need to mend the stables and keep them nice and clean so that, if I get a new pony, it will have a nice home."

Simon noticed that he was not the only one who had to bite back a laugh over that very clever way of asking for a pony. "Ye need a pony, do ye?" He frowned when her bottom lip wobbled in a way he recognized from Elen.

"I had a pony but the laird saw me playing with it and he hit it because it wouldnae let him near and that made him mad and he decided he needed meat for the table and he killed my pony and had Cook make a stew and he made me eat some."

Simon pulled her into his arms and sat her on his lap, rubbing her back as she sniffled into his shirt. "Then we shall fix the stables and get a pony. Now, dinnae we need a fine place for our horses, too?" He felt her nod against his chest. "It was a fine suggestion. I can see that Malcolm has already added it to his list of what must be done."

She leaned back and looked at him as she wiped her tears away on her sleeve. "I have another one."

Simon was terrified to ask what it was, but he forced himself to smile. "Tell us then." He was a little startled when she gave him what he could only describe as a mean look. "Marion?"

"I want a rule saying that men cannae hit ladies and make them cry."

"Done," said Malcolm before Simon could find

the words to answer what was yet another horrifying insight to the life this child had led.

It was late before everyone left and Malcolm had several sheets of suggestions before him. Simon sipped at his ale and stared around the great hall. There was little left of the grandeur that had once existed. Between his father and Henry, it had been stripped of all its fine tapestries and carpets as well as many of the old weapons.

"When Marion said that about her pony," began Ruari, and then he just shook his head. "I think we will be hearing of our brother's cruelty for a long time."

" 'Tis astonishing that she is still such a sweet lass." Malcolm suddenly grinned. "Weel, maybe nay so sweet for that was one mean look she gave ye when she wanted that rule about hitting ladies."

"Aye, it was. Reminded me of the one wee Elen gets on her angelic wee face when she is ready to bellow in temper."

He suddenly heard that last bellow, the one that had echoed in the dungeons. There had been more than anger in that sound. There had been a lot of hurt.

"Ye, brother, are an idiot," said Ruari.

"Why do ye keep prying at me about it?" snapped Simon. "Look at this place. We will be lucky to find clean linen and a blanket for the nights when it is cold."

"That isnae why ye walked away. Ye think ye might go mad like Henry."

"And what is wrong with worrying about that?"

"Because he is the only one who went mad. Nay, he was born mad. I am not, neither are Malcolm or

Kenneth. Neither are ye. Father was a brutal bastard but he wasnae mad. It doesnae always run in the blood. I think sometimes it is something wrong in the head. It was there in Henry from the moment he first opened his eyes. We all ken the tale of how he butchered a poor cat when he was but four years old. That isnae right. Henry was ne'er right."

Simon rubbed at his temples. "I ken it, yet, how can one be certain that fault willnae show up again? In a child? In a grandchild?"

"Ye cannae. Just as ye cannae be sure a child ye breed doesnae come out with its breathing wrong and all yellow, barely living long enough to cry the once to say it is alive."

That made so much sense that Simon felt like punching his youngest brother in the mouth. As the days had passed, filled with dealing with Henry's trial and execution, and then the ride to Lochancorrie, Simon had mulled over the matter of Henry's madness so often that he had wondered if he could go mad just from thinking about it so much. He had begun to waver in his fear. It was strong one day, such as when he heard Marion's story of her ill-fated pony, and then it would fade and he would feel a fool for allowing that fear to rule him.

He was afraid that he would let his need for Ilsabeth make him cast aside all good sense and just reach out for her. He would wake up in the night and reach for her, then groan from the weight of the loss when he found his bed empty. Simon was beginning to think he should have heeded Morainn's words more carefully, however. He had made the painful choice and it certainly felt as if it was the wrong one.

"I will take some time to work on bettering this place and promise to think on the matter," he finally said, as much to himself as to his brothers.

"Weel, dinnae ponder it too long. A lass like that doesnae need to sit about waiting for a fool."

Ilsabeth wiped the sweat from her brow and looked about the bedchamber with a sense of satisfaction. It was finally clean. The soldiers had been swine in their habits and she wondered if she was insulting the swine. Everyone was working day and night to clean up Aigballa. The only good news was that the men had not stolen anything. They had the coin to make up for the loss in supplies and some of the linens and things that would never be good for anything but rags now.

She flopped down on the clean bed and breathed in the crisp scent of clean linen. As always, the moment she stopped working, her thoughts went to Simon. It had been almost two months since she had seen him and there had not been any word from him either. Ilsabeth knew she had to accept the fact that he had left her.

Placing a hand over her still flat belly, she grimaced. Her mother was too busy to notice yet, but Ilsabeth was sure that soon her mother would know that her daughter was with child. The problem she faced now was whether she should tell Simon.

And just how did one do that? she wondered. Send a polite letter? Send her brothers to beat him into the mud and then, while he lay there bleeding and groaning, congratulate him on his upcoming fatherhood? Maybe she should just wait until her belly was huge and then ride out to Lochancorrie. That might be entertaining if only to see his face when he caught sight of her belly.

"Moping again?" asked her sister Finella as she walked in and sat on the bed by Ilsabeth's feet.

"I am nay moping," protested Ilsabeth.

"Oh, aye, ye are, Two."

"Ilsabeth," she said through tightly gritted teeth. "I was but thinking for a wee while ere I go and start to clean another room."

"Ye shouldnae do so much heavy work."

"Why not?" Ilsabeth slowly sat up and eyed her sister with a touch of apprehension.

"Ye could hurt the bairn." Finella grinned.

"There is no bairn. Ye are just imagining things."

Finella made a rude noise that would have gotten her soundly rebuked if their mother had been near. "Ye are with bairn. I cannae say how I ken it, but I do. I can see it in women who have only that night conceived. Ye are going to have to tell Maman and Papa soon."

"Why, are they planning to conceive tonight?" She grinned when Finella blushed for, at sixteen, she still refused to accept that their parents made love.

"Ilsabeth, it was Simon Innes, wasnae it?"

She sighed and flopped back down on the bed. "Aye. I love him although I am trying verra hard to make that I *loved* him."

"But, if he wished to bed ye, why didnae he ask ye to marry him?"

"I think it was because his brother was utterly

mad, viciously mad, and now he fears that will happen to him. He always said it wasnae something one could catch and he didnae believe it could run in the blood, nay for all madness leastwise, but then he watched Henry rant and rave and a fear set in his heart."

"Oh, and he feared he would go mad and didnae want ye to be with him when he did."

"That is what I think and, if I am right, there is naught I can do. The cure for that fear must come from him."

"Elen still misses him. So does Reid, I think, but he is already such a little mon, he hides it."

Ilsabeth nodded. She had seen Reid up on the walls at times, just staring out into the distance. She knew he was hoping to see Simon ride up. What Reid did not know was that, if that happened now after two months with no word, she would have the doors locked against him. A simple change of his mind was not enough to make up for the pain he had caused her and the utter silence she had endured for two months.

"Ah, there are my girls," said Elspeth as she hurried into the room with some flowers in a jug. "Something to sweeten the air."

"But, it doesnae need sweetening. I just cleaned in here," protested Ilsabeth.

"Aye, but it takes a wee bit more to fully get rid of the scent of a woman getting sick every morning."

It took Ilsabeth a full minute to understand what her mother had just said. "Oh, bollocks." She was certain she heard her mother laugh, but the face the woman turned toward her was an utterly serious one. "It was something I ate." She frowned in confusion. Had her mother just said *lucky Simon*?

Elspeth sat on the edge of the bed and stroked Ilsabeth's tangled hair. "Ye need to cease working so hard. Whate'er else happens or is said, there is one thing that must concern ye above all others— the health of the bairn ye carry. It was Simon Innes, wasnae it?"

"Aye." There was no point in lying to her mother. "I love him. He might love me, but he fears he will go raving mad just like his brother."

"Are ye sure he is the one?"

"I was sure the moment I saw him and felt the fire in my blood. He was trying to brush cat hair off himself. He has a cat he hasnae named yet. A stray he fed who refuses to leave the house. I thought that was a good sign although a better one would be if he named the poor beastie. He also had no trouble taking in Elen and Reid.

"And yet where is my perfect man? At Lochancorrie worrying that he will catch his brother's madness."

"That will pass, dear, and 'tis no small worry. We have had a few in our family and I am sure your father can tell ye a tale or two of some in his. Not all madness comes down through the blood. In truth, I am nay sure all that many do. But, nay matter how sensible a person, the mere thought of being inflicted by madness can terrify him. It is a frightening thing to see and I heard that Henry Innes's was terrifying."

"Aye, it was that. Such viciousness and all done just because he wanted to do it, enjoyed it. Somehow that type of brutality when there isnae really anger there, that calm, cold butchery, is more terrifying than rants and rages. And, he made Simon so enraged that I fear Simon saw that as a bad sign instead of a sign that he had never resolved things from his past, and I dinnae ken how one talks a mon out of such thoughts." She scowled. "Especially when said mon is staying verra far away."

Elspeth nodded and stood up, then leaned down and kissed Ilsabeth on the cheek. "I am going to tell your father. . . ."

"Oh, nay, Maman."

"Oh, aye, daughter. So if ye hear a lot of yelling, cries of *I will kill the rutting bastard* and the like, just ignore them. I will get him settled and then we can talk about this like sensible people."

Several hours later, Ilsabeth sat in the great hall with just her parents and watched her father pace the room muttering dire threats against Simon Innes. He did not look very settled or sensible to her. Her mother, however, just sat in a chair near the fire and did her mending.

"I think it is a little late to be lopping off that part of the mon, my heart," murmured Elspeth when Cormac Armstrong muttered a particularly bloodthirsty threat against Simon. "And, just think, if she and the fool do get married as I think they ought and really want to, she will miss it."

The look of horror on her father's face at the thought of her enjoying that part of Simon made Ilsabeth giggle. She hastily swallowed the sound when he glared at her. No, her father was not feeling very sensible and settled at all.

"They will be married," he said firmly. "I willnae have any grandchild of mine marked as a bastard."

" 'Tis still early days yet," said Elspeth.

"How early?" he asked, and stared at Ilsabeth's stomach.

"Two months." Ilsabeth suddenly recalled exactly where she was two months ago.

Elspeth sat up straight and frowned at her daughter. "What is that strange look on your face? Ye look absolutely horrified."

Ilsabeth refused to believe that her child had been conceived in a prison cell so she frantically counted back several times. Each time the answer came out the same. Her baby had been conceived in the dungeons at the king's keep.

"Oh, bollocks." This time Ilsabeth was certain she heard her father choke on a laugh but when she looked at him, his expression was one of the utmost seriousness.

"Something wrong?" he asked. "Might it be exactly where ye were when the child was conceived?"

She had the sinking feeling her father knew. "It might be."

"Such as in the king's dungeons?"

Ilsabeth was not sure why her father was sounding angrier but she nodded. "It appears so." There was a red flush spreading over his face and she hastily said, "I was verra afraid. I was all alone there and I didnae ken whether I would be tried as a traitor or—" The rest of her words were smothered by her father's broad chest.

"He didnae take advantage of that, did he?"

"Nay. Simon is an honorable mon. I just think that he is a wee bit confused."

Cormac stepped back and stared at his daughter. "Sir Simon Innes, the king's hound? Confused?"

Ilsabeth took a deep breath and told her father about Simon's life, from his childhood through to the betrayal by Mary and right up to finding out Henry had tried to kill his three younger brothers when they were just bairns. "Ye see? Henry tainted every part of their lives. Every part. And o'er it all is that taint of madness. I just hope I am right and that is what made him suddenly walk away. Then again, if it is that he fears the madness is the sort that could touch him or any child he bears, he may ne'er shake free of that fear."

"The mon butchered the child's dog?" Cormac shook his head. "Someone should have killed Henry the moment he slid out of his mother's womb."

"True," Ilsabeth said. "He has ruined so many lives and there was so much blood on his hands. Simon cannae see that he could ne'er be like that. He is too honorable. He has an ugly stray cat who sits on his lap and eats roasted chicken." She smiled at her mother when Elspeth laughed. "And he thinks it is cute when Elen bellows his name."

"We have a month or two before we risk bad weather for travel. I will give him that time to come to his senses." He smiled when Ilsabeth hugged him, kissed his cheek and skipped out of the room, and then he looked at his wife. "I was right."

"Aye, ye were and I will allow ye to gloat about it for a wee while and then we must think of a way to knock some sense into the lad."

"He is missing her right now. Let that work its magic."

Chapter 19

"I believe all is looking weel here now," said Ruari as he moved to stand beside Simon on the parapets.

Simon rolled his eyes, knowing that Ruari was yet again urging him to go after Ilsabeth. "We will survive a hard winter, aye."

"Still concerned about going mad?"

"Nay, the more time passes between seeing the true insanity of Henry and being with my brothers, the more that fear eases. We have no taint. I can see that now. Neither did our father. Nay, Father was just an arse." He grinned when Ruari laughed. "Nay, I dinnae think I have madness lurking in my blood. The rage is gone," he murmured.

"What rage?"

"The nearly uncontrollable rage I would go into when Henry did something. I realized recently that I felt it when I was young, too, but was too small to do anything about it."

"It was the injustice of so much of what Henry did. Ye have that need for justice that made ye such a good king's mon. It was probably there at an early age and all ye kept seeing was Henry doing his worse and never being called to account for it."

"Aye, that is what I am deciding. I also recalled that I ne'er even put a bruise on Ilsabeth when I was in one of those rages. E'en tried to get her to leave because I feared I would be too rough."

"So? Are ye going after her?"

"I hurt her and I have left her alone for two long months. I dinnae think she will welcome me with open arms."

"Nay, I suspect ye will have to work for her forgiveness. She is worth it."

"Why are ye so certain of that? Ye only met her once and had a short talk with her."

"We asked her to tell us about you. Every word she said revealed how she felt about you, brother. Every little word. And anyone who listened to her kenned that he had better not question your honor or honesty or near anything else about you or she would tear your tongue out. That is what I urge ye to go after." He suddenly grinned and winked. "And she is a verra bonnie wee lass."

"So, ye think she loves me?"

Ruari rolled his eyes. "Please, God, dinnae let me be such an idiot when I find the right woman. Aye, idiot, I think she loves ye. Nay, not think, she *does* love ye. No doubt about it."

"Weel, then, I had best go and try to get her to forgive me for my idiocy." Simon started down the steps from the parapet.

Hurrying after him, Ruari said, "Bastard. Ye had already decided to go."

"Aye, when I was abed last night and realized I was beginning to allow Bonegnasher and Cat to sleep on my bed because I didnae like to be alone in it anymore." He ignored Ruari's laughter and went to pack what he needed for a journey to Aigballa.

Simon tried smiling sweetly at Morainn and it did not work. The woman scowled at him. He had spent a fortnight doing all he could to reach Ilsabeth but she was ignoring him. She sent back his letters, his gifts, and tossed his flowers over the walls. Still in the vase. He was sure that that time she had been aiming at his head.

"Ye made the wrong choice and after I had warned ye," said Morainn.

"I was just finished with fighting my brother and taking him before the king to be tried as a traitor," Simon said. "All I could see was his madness and I had to protect her from that. Aye, a part of me still believed that ye cannae get madness like ye do the ague and it doesnae have to run in the blood. But then I would see Henry calmly speaking of how he tied up my three younger brothers, put them in a leaky boat, and pushed them out into the loch. Or how he killed his wife and near every girl bairn his wives gave him. 'Tis a madness so big, so cold and terrifying, that, aye, I was frightened."

Morainn took him by the hand and drew him into the little cottage she and Tormand used when visiting with the Armstrongs. "Come and have some of my mead. Ye are being very boldly ignored in your attempts at wooing, I hear."

He sat down at the table and dragged his hands through his hair. "Thoroughly ignored and I have run out of ideas on how to get her to notice me."

"Oh, she is noticing ye. Ne'er doubt that."

"She isnae noticing me in the way I want her to. I just need to talk to her. I tried writing out what I wanted to say but she willnae read the letters. I havenae e'en seen the children," he added quietly, a little hurt that the children also ignored him. "But, they have at least kept the wee gifts I bought them."

"They will come round, too. Right now I suspect they are following Ilsabeth's lead."

"Weel, I am running out of patience."

"So, what? Ye will tuck tail and run home?" said Tormand as he walked over to the table and kissed the top of Morainn's head.

"Nay. I will kidnap her and make her listen to me." He frowned when Morainn started to giggle so hard, Tormand had to steady her in her chair. "It wasnae that funny."

"Nay, but 'tis exactly what ye must do." Morainn grinned at him. "Give her one more week to come round, then whisk her off to some place secluded. Aye, that will work."

"So, here he is. The bastard that seduced my daughter."

Simon slowly stood up to look at Cormac Armstrong. For a man his age he was still fit and strong enough for Simon to wonder if he could win in a fight. Then he saw the glint in the man's eyes. He, too, was laughing. Simon idly wondered when the man who had struck fear into people's hearts as the king's hound had begun to become a source of amusement to everyone.

"I didnae really seduce her," he started to say, and then grimaced. The manner in which a man took another man's daughter's virginity was not something to discuss, especially with that father.

"Aye, best ye stop right there." He smiled at Morainn when she served him some mead. "Thank ye, love. Whenever ye realize what a mistake ye made in wedding this rogue, ye just let me ken it. I have a bevy of sons who need good wives."

"That make a fine mead?" she asked.

"That would be a good thing to add to the clan." He looked back at Simon, who was just finishing a fortifying drink of Morainn's mead. "Ye are doing a verra good job of wooing her."

"Ye wouldnae be able to tell that by the way she receives my gifts and letters."

"Ye ignored her for two months."

"I had a keep stripped of all that was valuable, three brothers whom I hadnae seen since they were bairns, and a terror of becoming a madmon. I was a wee bit busy."

"Getting irritable, too. The true sign of a mon bent on wooing a difficult woman."

"I just ne'er thought she would be this difficult. I thought that, at the verra least, she would wish to yell at me. The only true show of temper she has revealed was when she threw the flowers at me, still in the pitcher."

Cormac chuckled. "Aye, that was a good toss and ye jumped right quick. I think she was even madder that ye managed to get out of the way in time."

Simon looked at the grinning Cormac, Tormand, and Morainn and slowly shook his head. "And to think I spent weeks tortured about the insanity in my family."

"Wheesht, wait until ye spend some time with the women in the clan."

"Ahem. I am nay sure if I should feel insulted or nay," said Morainn.

"Ye are the exception, sweet Morainn," said Cormac.

"Because of my mead."

"Nay, that but adds to the wonder of your presence."

"Oh, husband, that was groveling if I have ever heard any and I have." Elspeth looked at Simon and smiled in a way that reminded him all too strongly of her daughter. "I have been trying to sneak o'er here for days just to meet ye." She smiled even more at his elegant bow and the kiss on her hand. "Verra nice. Courtly manners. Are ye still involved with the court?"

"Only when directly asked because Gowan cannae figure out whatever the puzzle is," Simon replied, and then he took a deep breath. "There is one thing I have been trying to get your daughter to hear or read. 'Tis something I feel must be told before we can deal with all else between us. I have a daughter."

"He didnae kill her?" said Tormand, and then hastily explained Henry's tendency to kill off his daughters, leaving both women pale and Cormac scowling at him. "Apologies."

"Nay," said Elspeth. "None needed."

Morainn murmured an agreement. "Ye just spoke the truth." She looked at Simon. "When we were quite angry at Ilsabeth and ye because we, er, guessed that ye did a wee bit more than protecting her, and were wondering why ye werenae here to ask for her hand, she defended ye in the only way she kenned how. She told us some things about ye. The child is Mary's?"

Simon blushed and wondered why Elspeth nodded approvingly over that. "Aye." He took a deep breath and told them all about Marion, including the horrible things Henry had done to her, then sighed when both women cried and both men glared at him. "It is important that Ilsabeth kens what the child has suffered. She is a sweet child although there are times she can make a face so fierce I can think of naught but wee Elen." He was glad when both women laughed and nodded. "Yet, she has to be different in some ways from a child who grew up, say, here. I just havenae really seen it yet. Annie loves her and mayhap that helped."

Elspeth hugged him and patted his back. "It did. Oh, aye, it did, for it let her see the good." She stepped back. "This has gone on long enough anyway. A fortnight of throwing all ye offer in your face is quite enough. The child needs ye back home, I am certain, and we begin to get too close to the weather making travel dangerous." Elspeth tapped her fingers on her chin. "I think that, if she doesnae soften in a week's time, ye will have to kidnap her." She looked around when everyone laughed and then grinned. "Already thought of that, I see." She rubbed her hands together. "Then since we have all had the same idea, let us plot out just how to do it."

Ilsabeth yawned and stretched out in the sun just a little more, careful not to fall off the bench she was sprawled out on. Simon had sent her another letter and she was still holding it, debating with herself on whether she should read this one or not. He had been unwavering in his attempts to woo her for three long weeks. She was tired of her own temper, tired of the way she kept recalling how he hurt her and then getting mad at him because he had. It was as if she was caught on some millstone grinding away at the same old anger over and over and yet never turning it into anything that could be blown away on the wind. She was beginning to bore herself.

Then, abruptly, the sun faded. Ilsabeth opened her eyes and stared up into three pairs of gray eyes. Who had let Simon's brothers in? Even more important, was Simon lurking somewhere in amongst them. She struggled to sit up, scowling at the three men who just stood there with their arms across their chests.

"What are ye doing here?" she asked as she finally sat up and brushed her skirts down. "Did Simon send ye?"

"A better question is what are ye still doing here?" asked Ruari. "Why are ye nay riding back to Lochancorrie with Simon?"

"Simon and I are discussing things."

"Nay, ye arenae. By the looks of it ye arenae even reading his letters."

"I was thinking about reading this one."

"How many have ye not read?"

"About fourteen," she muttered, and glared at them when all three shook their heads in disgust. "Ye werenae there when he set me aside so dinnae ye go judging me and my anger."

It pleased her to see them all take a step back, but Ruari said, "I would think ye would want to ken what he had to say. Mayhap an explanation about why he did what he did, why he regrets it, why he wants to speak to ye."

Ilsabeth sighed and waved the letter in front of her face. They were right and that was probably why she wished she could hit them. She did not wish to lose Simon but she was certainly doing her best to send him far, far away. It was hard to understand why except that what he had done when he had turned from her had hurt so badly, she did not wish to risk feeling that hurt again. And that, she mused, was utter cowardice.

One glance told her Simon's brothers were not going to leave until she read the letter. Sighing, she sat down and opened the letter. The first line was not very soothing. He had a daughter? She read on, cried a little, and then smiled, but if he thought this tale of the little girl would make her run to him with open arms, he needed to sit down and think that out again.

"Weel? What did he say?" demanded Kenneth.

"The letter was to me, nay you. But, if ye must ken, it was all about Marion."

"A sweet lass who has seen too much for her tender years," murmured Malcolm.

And a lass in danger of being severely spoiled by four men hoping to make up for the dark things she had seen and suffered, Ilsabeth thought. Annie, she thought, was an angel. Marion had been lucky to have the woman to shelter with during her life at Lochancorrie.

"This is indeed something to think about, but it doesnae excuse him forgetting about me for two months."

"Forgetting about you?" Ruari shook his head. "Where did ye get that foolish idea? The mon has started to let the cat and dog sleep on the bed with him."

Ilsabeth could not help it, she laughed. Ruari had told that little tale as if he was confessing that his brother was doing something unnatural. Ilsabeth understood that need for warmth. She had a cat or two on her bed at night as well. And two people who had so enjoyed sleeping curled up together now being reduced to sleeping with cats for some warmth was just very sad.

"Have ye come to take him back to Lochancorrie?" she asked, unable to hide all the concern she felt, a little leaking into her voice.

"Nay, that is, not unless he wishes to go," said Kenneth. "We came to find Marion a new pony."

"Oh, how lovely. Old Gregor just down the road sells the most beautiful Highland ponies. They are perfect mounts for children. I have been meaning to get one for Reid." She frowned. "And if I get one for him, I suppose I shall have to get one for Elen or she will bellow."

"Then come and help us choose one for Marion on the morrow."

She studied them closely for a moment. "This isnae a trick, is it? Ye arenae trying to get me out of here and force me to meet with Simon, are ye?"

"Nay. When Simon saw us coming here, he made us swear to stay out of what is between just the two of you." Both Ruari and Malcolm nodded vigorously in agreement with Kenneth. "I ask because I ken nothing about the ponies. Horses, aye, but nay ponies. Ne'er had one when I was small, either. Ye seem to ken something about them and it would be a help. And ye ken the mon selling them, aye?"

Ilsabeth had to admit that she was very tired of lurking inside the walls of Aigballa. A little visit to Old Gregor to look at his ponies would be nice. She nodded and they smiled. Ilsabeth felt a pang of guilt for mistrusting them so as they arranged a time for the trip.

"Did she agree?" asked Simon the moment his brothers joined him at the inn for an ale and a few meat pies.

"She did after a wee hesitation and accusing us of tricking her," answered Kenneth. "She will be there after midday on the morrow. We take her to Old Gregor's down the road to look at his Highland ponies. I felt that since we really are going to buy some, it wasnae a complete lie."

Malcolm nodded. "Felt bad for tricking her until I saw she hadnae even opened your last letter and then she confessed to nay having opened the fourteen before that. She isnae being reasonable."

"Nay, and that isnae like Ilsabeth," Simon said, and sipped at his ale. "She was ne'er coy and this seems a bit like coy to me."

"She mentioned that ye had forgotten about her for two months and how ye set her aside that day. Seems those wounds cut a wee bit deeper than ye realized."

Simon nodded. "I was afraid of that. I panicked when she hugged me that day. Kenned that, if I didnae get her away from me, I would weaken and toss aside all worry about madness and that didnae seem wise at that time. So, aye, I cut away from her as if she was something dangerous or even unpleasant. As for two months of forgetting her?" Simon snorted. "As if I could. And, as if Ruari would let me if I tried."

The brothers all laughed when Ruari blushed faintly, but he put up his chin and said, "Ye were tossing aside something good and I didnae want to see ye do that. 'Tisnae often a mon has a chance like ye have."

"Ruari, have ye made a mess of such a thing before?" Simon asked quietly, although thinking that, at only two and twenty, Ruari was a little young for such a thing.

"Nay, but a verra good friend of mine did. He did what all wanted him to instead of what his heart ached for and he is the most miserable bastard now. He hates the wife he was told was perfect and has to watch the one he loved go about with her husband and children. It eats at him every day and I fear he will grow bitter beyond fixing."

"Sad to say, he just might. I have seen the same. 'Tis my opinion that such arrangements for land or bloodlines or property should be banned. We have enough miserable bastards without making more through bad marriages."

His brothers laughed and soon the talk turned to what to look for in the ponies they would buy tomorrow. It was late by the time Simon sought his bed. His empty, lonely bed, he thought as he slid in between the cool linen sheets. He had to be at his best on the morrow. He needed Ilsabeth and he had to get past her anger and hurt to the heart he was sure she had given him.

The fact that she had been hurt by his cold turning away from her and then two months of silence troubled him, and not only because he had hurt her. He was going to have to explain himself with the utmost care. Simon knew he would also have to be completely open and honest about all he felt for her. He knew he held to his privacy and controlled his emotions a little too tightly, but baring his soul felt like a giant step in the opposite direction.

As he sprawled on his back and stared up at the ceiling, he went over everything in his mind. With himself he could be utterly honest about what he felt for Ilsabeth. Somehow he was going to have to get those words out of his mouth. He would only have one chance because, even though her family was helping him to kidnap her, he knew they would come looking for her if he kept her too long.

"Tomorrow, Ilsabeth, please be in a mood to open your heart to an idiot with a tongue that has ne'er been smooth."

*   *   *

Ilsabeth winced as she climbed into bed. She has spent too much time on her hands and knees weeding the garden. Her mother was right. She had to stop trying to work until her mind was too tired to think of Simon. Nothing was worth putting her child at risk.

Her child who had been conceived in a dungeon, she thought, and grimaced. Ilsabeth was not sure that was a story she wanted to tell her child later in life. In fact, considering all the bad things, the chilling things concerning Henry, that had happened, it might be best to forget the whole matter. She could always make up a story if her child was ever curious but the idea of lying to a child was an uncomfortable one.

And why am I worrying about things that are not even close to happening yet? she asked herself. It was because she did not want to think about Simon. In truth, she sighed, she did not wish to look at how she was acting toward Simon. Ilsabeth was beginning to feel a little ashamed of herself.

A soft rap at the door promised a welcome distraction and she sat up as she told the visitor to come in. Her mother came in and sat down on the edge of the bed and Ilsabeth became immediately nervous. Her mother had that look on her face that promised a lecture. The true problem with her mother's lectures were that they were cleverly disguised, forcing the one hearing them to answer questions that invariably made them see some fault in themselves. Since Ilsabeth was beginning to see one already, she did not really want her mother to have seen it as well.

"Weel, that isnae a particularly welcoming look for your old mother," said Elspeth.

Ilsabeth laughed. "Ye arenae old and weel ye ken it. I confess, the face was because I ken ye are here to give me one of your talks where ye get me to see that I am nay behaving verra weel."

"Beginning to see it yourself already, are ye?"

"Aye, but I am having so much trouble getting beyond the hurt. In the beginning I tried so hard to be understanding. Henry was an evil beyond explaining. It was only reasonable that Simon would fear such evil could be a part of his whole family, that he needed time to see that he had none of that in him and ne'er could. But two months?"

"Men can be slow, love. And"—she patted Ilsabeth's clenched fist—"he had a lot to deal with aside from his own confused feelings, didnae he. Then, too, he was trying to put ye aside for what he thought was your own good."

"And just what gave him the right to think he kenned what was for my own good?"

"His being a mon."

Ilsabeth's temper faded and she laughed. "Aye, and 'tis his nature. He protects and defends those who cannae do it themselves or those so caught up in another's tangled web that they cannae get free without help. And I was both to him. I think that is what troubles me. Does he truly see me or does he see just another wounded innocent who needs his protection?"

"Only he can answer that, love, and ye are nay even reading his letters."

"I ken it. I have been behaving badly. Oh, a week

mayhap, of sulking and pouting, but I have gone way beyond that." She frowned. "I find that I am afraid of being hurt again."

Elspeth hugged her. " 'Tis a common fear of women in love. But, sweetheart, a mon in love suffers as weel and 'tis often harder for them to express what they are feeling. Just think on this. This proud mon, this mon ye say keeps himself in control, has been lurking about here for three weeks sending ye gifts and letters. Even when he kens ye are refusing to accept any of them, he is still here."

Ilsabeth felt an urge to cry. "I have been unkind."

"Nay, ye have been afraid. He hurt ye and I think he hurt ye more than his poor monly brain can understand." She smiled when Ilsabeth gave a watery giggle. "But, how can he ever understand enough to ne'er do it again if ye willnae even talk to him?"

"I ken it. I have to get rid of the fear, dinnae I?"

"Nay so much get rid of it as push it aside long enough to listen. What he wants to tell ye may well mend the wound."

"Ye dinnae think it will just add to it, make it deeper?" she asked in a near whisper.

"Nay. Ye may curse me if I am wrong, but I truly dinnae believe a mon hangs about getting rejected for three long weeks unless he feels something verra deep and strong." She placed her hand on Ilsabeth's stomach. "And, ye have a piece of him inside ye now. Ye have that child to think on. Is it just your heart that was bruised, or your pride as weel?" She kissed her on the cheek and started out of the room. "Just try, lass. Even a mon desperately in love can only abide so many nays before he gives up. He has his pride, too."

Ilsabeth settled back down and stared up at the ceiling. Her mother was right. It was not just her heart that was bruised, but her pride. She had given Simon everything and he had turned from her, rejected it all. It had broken her heart but it had also lacerated her pride. The two of them together had kept her from forgiving Simon.

And Simon did have his pride. She had seen it. Thinking over how she had treated him for the last three weeks, she was astonished that he was still here, still trying. She had certainly paid him back in kind and she was not very proud of that.

She would go with the brothers and pick out some ponies on the morrow and then she would invite Simon to a private dinner here at Aigballa. The two of them would talk as she had not allowed him to talk before while she was still nursing her wounds. There would be some things she would insist upon before she gave in to him and the very first was to know exactly how he felt about her. Now that she had had a taste of how it felt to have her love rejected, she was not going to go anywhere with him until she was sure he returned it.

A small smile curved her mouth. It would be so nice to see him again, to touch him even in the polite confines of a shared meal. Now that she had seen how she was acting and why, she could admit to how desperately she had missed him. His brothers claimed Simon missed her, too. It was foolish for two people to miss each other if there was no true reason for them to be apart. On the morrow she would put an end to this game one way or the other.

Chapter 20

Ilsabeth frowned as the three brothers herded into the barn. The best ponies were out in the little corral, but they had only glanced over them and then insisted upon looking in the little barn. Even Old Gregor had insisted. She wrinkled her nose at the smell of horse droppings and hay. Her stomach curled in revulsion and Ilsabeth decided her child did not like that scent.

"I think I had best go outside," she said. "I am feeling a wee bit unweel."

"Why?" Kenneth sniffed. "Old Gregor keeps a verra clean barn."

She was about to tell him that no matter how clean a barn, once a horse or pony was put inside the smells began when someone slipped a linen sheet over her. Two strong arms were wrapped around her and she was carried off. For one brief moment she was terrified but then, as the outside air cleared her nose of the smell of the barn, she smelled a very familiar scent.

Why was Simon spiriting her away? Because she had refused to speak to him. Ilsabeth sighed as she thought of the lovely romantic setting she had planned for their meal together. She hoped he had remembered to bring food and wine to wherever he was taking her.

It was not long before being wrapped in a linen sheet and carried over a broad shoulder was not comfortable and Ilsabeth complained. The sheet muffled her words and all she got was a mumbled apology in what Simon must have thought was a disguised voice and a pat on the backside. After the first pat, there was a moment's hesitation, and then another pat that was much more like a caress. There was obviously one particular thing Simon was missing, she thought, and had to admit that she was missing it, too. Even her awkward position could not dispel the warmth that slight caress sent through her body.

When he ran his hand up and down her leg, she decided a true kidnap victim would protest so she screeched a little. Simon obviously was not thinking clearly if he thought all kidnap victims were so complacent. Then she had a wicked thought and turned her head to the side in the hope that she would be somewhat more understandable when she spoke.

"Ye had best put me down and run for your life," she said. "Ye willnae get away with this. This place is swarming with my kinsmen and kinswomen and they will hunt ye down like a mad dog when they discover what ye have done."

He mumbled something that sounded like assurances that she would come to no harm. Then he began to caress her leg again as if he could not help himself.

"I am warning ye . . . Oh. Oh. My. Do that again," she said as she heard a door open. "Oh, that feels so verra fine."

She screeched when she was suddenly dropped on a bed. Ilsabeth tore the sheet off her head to find Simon staring down at her, his hands fisted on his hips and a look of pure jealous anger on his face. She could not help it, she started to laugh.

Simon looked down at the giggling woman he had carried all the way from Old Gregor's and shook his head, a reluctant smile pulling at his lips. She had not been fooled for long. And all that ooh and aahing had certainly caused him a moment of alarm. One did not like to think that one's woman would ooh and ahh at just any touch. And the wretch had known that, too.

"That was a mean trick ye just played," he said.

"Me? I wasnae the one who ran off with ye wrapped in a sheet. And, I need to speak to your brothers about the sin of lying." She sat up and swung her legs over the side of the bed, recognizing one of the many little cottages her family kept for guests, a necessity when one had a family as large as hers. "Weel, this was fun, but I need to go and get a pony."

"My brothers are buying the ponies. One for Marion, one for Reid, and one for Elen."

"Because they ken exactly what they are looking for."

"Aye, one of the people they lived with raised them."

"Lies, lies and more lies."

"I was desperate," he said, and hurried to securely latch the door when he saw her eyeing it consideringly. "I need ye to speak to me. I would stay here until ye do but I have to return to Lochancorrie soon. The harvest and all, ye ken." He went back to stand at the side of the bed.

"Simon, I will say that I have acted badly." She held up her hand when he began to protest. "I have. I cannae say whether I was trying to punish ye or just sulking, but it was unkind and many other wee sins I am sure my mother could enumerate, to just keep ignoring ye."

"Then why did ye do it?"

"Ye hurt me when ye pushed me away so coldly, so abruptly and completely that day in the dungeons. It also hurt more because I was free, and all we had done to prove who the real traitors were was at an end. I wished to share that success with ye and, aye, even the sad part of it since it was your own blood involved. And then it seemed like ye and I were at an end as weel and it made me feel as if I was naught but another innocent ye work hard to protect."

He sat down and pulled her into his arms, ignoring the faint hint of tension in her lithe body. "Nay, ye were never just a puzzle to me, something to solve, toss aside, and go on to the next. Never. I had to make the cut quick and sharp for I was weak. I wanted to stay there and hold ye and let ye comfort me o'er the idiocy of my mad brother."

"But why did ye have to go at all, Simon?" She tried to catch him by the hand when he stood up and began to pace.

"This isnae easy to explain," he said. "I was a

craven coward. I had just watched my eldest brother, my laird, lose his last grip on his sanity. The things he said were still sitting in my head proving his insanity nay matter how I looked at things. It was terrifying to watch that last thread snap and hear him talk of all the killing he had done and why, and who are we to judge. I was reeling with it. It was as if he had somehow tainted me with it.

"All I could think of was how ye deserved better than to become tied to a mon who could turn into what Henry did at the end."

"But, Simon . . ."

"Nay, I ken now that I am nay like Henry. Ne'er was; ne'er will be. But it took a while for me to see that. Those bouts of rage I suffered didnae help me see clearly, either, for I was certain they were a sign of something wrong. And they were, but nay what I thought. They were a sign of years of built up anger o'er all the bad things Henry had done to good people."

"Simon, I told ye that ye werenae like him," she said. "I told ye that. Why couldnae ye believe me?"

"Because ye were my lover," he answered as he sat down beside her. "My lover and my confidante and I dared not accept your opinion. I think ye would tell me the truth, but it was always possible ye would lie or soften the truth to spare my feelings."

"Oh. That makes sense in some ways. But why did ye stay away for two months, Simon? Two months without sight or word. Did ye ne'er think I might do my best to forget ye?"

"That was what I told myself I wanted ye to do— forget me. I wanted ye to find happiness with a mon who didnae have madness and a traitor in his family." He lightly kissed her frowning mouth, fighting against the urge to ravish that beautiful mouth until neither of them could breathe right. "And I would think of that and then I would hate the mon ye found who didnae have a problem with such things as madmen, treason, illegitimate children, and three brothers now living with him."

"Simon, if ye hadnae thrust me away so coldly, if ye had told me that ye needed to think, that ye were worried about the insanity, I would have waited."

"Would have waited?" He frowned. "Are ye telling me that ye didnae wait for me?"

"Bad choice of words. I would have waited for ye because ye asked, instead of waiting for ye and doing naught but hoping ye would come back, that mayhap I mistook what had happened, and then hating myself for that weakness."

"Ah, Ilsabeth, I was unkind. Nay. E'en worse, I was so lost in what troubled me I ne'er gave a thought to what it was all doing to ye." He pulled her into his arms. "I was a confused idiot. I kenned that madness doesnae have to be in the blood, have seen that with my own eyes, but then I would fear that what ailed Henry was one of the ones that can be in the blood."

He gently pushed her down onto the bed. "I wanted to do what was right for ye and yet I didnae want ye to leave me. I feared the insanity yet kenned that I couldnae have it. I think I drove my brothers to distraction with my own confusion."

"And when did ye ken that they werenae worried about the madness?"

He kissed the side of her neck and then grinned. "That did take a wee while to sink in to my mind. I needed some time and distance from all Henry was and had done. I think I was shamed by him as weel," he admitted softly. "Shamed that such a creature shared a family tie with me."

"That is verra understandable. Despite what he was and all the cruelties he had inflicted upon his own family, 'tis always difficult to, weel, disown the one doing them." She slowly began to unlace his shirt.

"And all the while I was sorting through my wee troubles ye were thinking I had tossed ye aside just because I was done with ye?" The ways she blushed was all the answer he needed.

"I cannae apologize enough for that. I hurt ye and I kenned I had when I walked away that day. I have ne'er been able to shake the look on your face from my mind. Each time I saw it I wanted to come and beg your forgiveness." He unlaced her bodice and kissed the soft swell of one breast. "I also kept hearing Elen's bellow, hearing the pain beneath the fury. I hurt her, too."

She placed her hands over his to stop the undoing of her clothing. "Simon, I do need to ken something. I need to ken that ye willnae just walk away from me like that again. It felt as if something broke inside me and I cannae bear to ever feel that again. The fear of feeling that again is one reason I have been so unkind, pushing ye away again and again."

He framed her face with his hands and looked into her eyes. She had not said the words but he could read them in her eyes, hear them in how she spoke of her pain. Simon touched his mouth to hers in soft apology.

"Never again, Ilsabeth. I cut out my own heart when I walked away. I love ye," he whispered and, with a soft cry, she flung her arms around his neck and kissed him in a way that thrust all other thoughts from his head but the taste of her.

"Simon, I have missed ye so," she said as they both began to rapidly unlace each other's clothing, desperate to feel skin against skin.

The moment she bared his chest, Ilsabeth covered the warm expanse with kisses, shifting her body to help him as he pulled at her clothes. He kissed her again and she could sense the desperate hunger in him, one she shared. When they were both finally naked, she moaned with delight as their skin finally touched. She nearly purred as she rubbed her body against his, savoring the difference in the textures and the way the rough tickle of his body hair made her feel.

He began to caress her with his hands and mouth all over her body. He devoured her breasts as he slid his hand between her legs to drive her wild with need. Ilsabeth struggled to return the pleasure stroke for stroke and kiss for kiss but her need to feel him inside her was growing so strong, so swiftly, she knew the time for slow loving would have to come later.

"Now, Simon," she said as she grasped him by the hips and rubbed herself against him. "I need to feel ye deep inside me right now. I have been empty for too long."

With a soft growl of need, he gave her what she wanted, plunging deep inside with a single thrust. Ilsabeth cried out from the force of the pleasure that tore through her. She clung to him as he rode her hard, all the while muttering words of love and sweet flattering nonsense against her skin. When her body tightened and the wave of delight crested, she wrapped herself around him as tightly as she could and cried out her love for him. Through the roar of passion in her ears she heard him cry out *mine* and nearly laughed with joy at the rough possessiveness behind the word. When he thrust inside her as deep as he could and spilled his seed inside her, her desire soared to the heights yet again and she nearly wept from the joy of it.

Simon slowly rolled onto his back and pulled her on top of him. He did not think he could let her go again for at least a week and then he might go and get them some food. She loved him, he thought, and grinned. She had yelled it out as her body had tightened around him, clenching until she held him tightly inside while he gifted her with his seed.

He felt her move and opened his eyes to catch her looking at him, frowning despite the laughter in her eyes. "Frowning? Did I do it wrong?"

"Nay and weel ye ken it, rogue. Nay, I just thought ye were looking verra smug there for a moment."

"I probably was." He kissed her nose. "Ye bellowed out that ye love me."

"Ladies dinnae bellow."

He laughed and lightly bit her neck. "Ye did and I would wager I could make ye do it again."

"I told ye, ladies dinnae bellow."

He rolled her over onto her back and grinned at her. Ilsabeth always made him feel as if he was the most skilled of lovers when he knew full well he did not have the experience to claim that he was. He was going to make her bellow out her love for him again and take full delight in the double pleasure offered. Her passion and her love.

Ilsabeth gritted her teeth as he licked and sucked at her nipples and knew he was going to win the wager. He kissed his way down her body and she was panting with anticipation and desire before he even kissed the inside of her thighs. The moment his tongue touched the heated skin between her thighs she lost what little control she had. He brought her to completion twice before he joined their bodies and took them both to the heights, together, one more time. Ilsabeth knew she had bellowed out her love for him more than once, but such rich pleasure deserved such a reward.

"If ye gloat or say ye won, when I have the strength again, I will have to hit ye," she said as she lay sprawled across his chest, both of them breathing as heavily as if they had run for miles. She smiled when he laughed and she bounced up and down on his chest.

"Marry me, Ilsabeth," he said, and kissed the top of her head because it was the only place he could reach and he was still too weak to even reach down and tilt her chin up.

It was a struggle, but Ilsabeth lifted her head and looked into his eyes. He spoke calmly and the hand he idly smoothed up and down her back was steady, but there in his eyes she saw that touch of vulnerability. Despite the way she bellowed out her love when passion conquered her, Simon was still not sure she would take him to her side for life. She brushed a kiss over his mouth.

"Aye, Simon, I will marry ye." She laughed softly

when he hugged her so hard she grunted a little. "When do ye want to get married?"

"As soon as possible but I ken that women like to have their celebrations. We could wait a few weeks if ye want to have one."

The tone of his voice when he spoke of waiting held all the joy of a man saying he wanted a tooth pulled. "Nay, Simon, we can marry as soon as ye wish. There are so many of my family here now and more to come in the next few days that we can have quite a large celebration without much planning. The only thing that needs to be sorted out is the priest and what he may ask."

"I will see to that."

She sat up, straddling his hips, and studied him for a moment. It was time to tell him about the baby and yet she was suddenly nervous. That made no sense for they had both declared their love and they had certainly consummated those vows with vigor. When his eyes narrowed and his hands tightened slightly on her hips she knew he had sensed her unease.

"What is wrong, Ilsabeth?" he asked, and brushed a lock of hair back over her shoulder.

"Ye do realize we will be starting this marriage with three children, aye?"

"Aye. Elen, Reid, and Marion. Ye arenae saying that troubles ye, are ye?"

"Nay. I just wondered how ye would feel if we started the marriage with four." She grimaced even as the words left her mouth for it was a poor way to tell the man the news.

Simon stared at her, watching the blush rise up from the tops of her breasts and into her cheeks. It took a full moment for his pleasure-soaked mind to grasp what she was saying. He looked down at her belly, even though he knew it was too soon for her to show, but her long hair was covering it.

"Ye are carrying my child?" he asked, not surprised to hear a faint tremble in his voice for the emotions tearing through him at the thought of her giving him a child were too strong to control. "When did ye ken it?"

"Weel, if ye dinnae count the time I was sure but denying it until my eyes crossed, a few weeks." She slowly stroked his chest, aware of the strength of his emotions through the faint tremor in his body and the pounding of his heart.

"Were ye going to tell me if I hadnae come to ye?"

"Simon, that is a verra hard question to answer. The way I felt until a wee while ago, I cannae say what I would do. I was still so angry and hurt. Yet, everything in me cried out that ye are the father and whate'er was wrong with us, ye would be a good father. If ye had decided nay to come back to me, I believe I would have told ye eventually, simply because I could ne'er keep a child from his father if that father was as good as ye would be."

He held her close and slipped his hand down between them until his palm rested over her womb. "Thank ye for that."

"Weel, is that too much? Three children already and now another to come?"

"Nay, ye can fill my keep with children. Lost ones like Reid and Elen or our own. I will take as many as ye can give me and consider each the greatest of blessings."

"There is one wee thing that ye ought ken about this bairn." Ilsabeth felt him tense and decided she should have spoken with more care.

"Do ye think something is wrong already?"

"Nay. Not a thing. I was referring to the conception of this child. I am almost certain this bairn was conceived in the dungeons." She narrowed her eyes at him when his mouth started to twitch into a smile. "Ye think that is funny?"

"A wee bit. Aye." He kissed her and rubbed his nose against hers. "Just a wee bit. 'Tis a monly thing." As he expected, she just rolled her eyes and shrugged it off. He promised himself, however, that if the child was a son, it was going to be a story they would enjoy when the boy was old enough.

"What do ye wish?" she asked as she rubbed her cheek against his chest. "A son?"

"I dinnae care so long as the bairn is healthy and ye dinnae have any trouble." The thought of all that could go wrong in a childbirth went through his mind and he trembled with fear, his grip on her tightening. "Ye will nay have any trouble."

"I dinnae think I will, Simon, but dinnae fear for me. There are many, many skilled midwives and healers in my clan. The skill of them all has kept many a Murray woman safe during that dangerous time."

"Thank God. Then mayhap we ought to stay here until the bairn comes."

"Nay, Simon, we will head to Lochancorrie ere the weather turns and makes travel difficult. Someone from the clan will get to us when my time nears. 'Tis how we do it."

He nodded. It eased some of his worries but not

all of them. Simon had the feeling he was going to
be a very protective husband at least until the baby
came. There might be a few arguments ahead for
he doubted Ilsabeth would take kindly to being
watched as closely as he would be watching her. She
could argue all she wanted, however. It would not
stop him.

"Damn, Ilsabeth, the way we were just romping
around, I could have hurt ye."

"Nay, ye couldnae have."

"How can ye be so certain? Ye havenae had a
bairn before."

She laughed and kissed his frowning mouth. "I
havenae but, Simon, both the Armstrongs and the
Murrays are a very prolific clan. Breed like rabbits
is what they say of us. And, for your peace of mind,
I can tell ye that so few of us have trouble birthing a
child, it isnae worth the worry ye are beginning to
take on."

"Aye, ye are right, but I doubt I will heed that
good advice for very long so ye will no doubt be
tired of giving it to me."

Ilsabeth laughed and kissed him.

"We shall have to tell Elen and Reid," he said a
moment later. "Do ye think they will speak to me
now?"

Ilsabeth pressed her forehead against his. "I am
so verra sorry that they havenae welcomed ye. They
follow me and I was sulking and ignoring ye. I think
we shall wander back to Aigballa from here and tell
them tonight. They have missed ye, Simon. Ne'er
doubt that."

"It was funny in a way. I hadnae realized how
much they had come to mean to me until they left

my house. It was so quiet and empty. No running feet, no bellows, no running through the house with Bonegnasher in pursuit and Cat getting up as high as it could to be out of the way. Suddenly it was silent and I couldnae bear it. When I turned away from ye, I realized I was losing the children, too, and the double strike nearly brought me to my knees. I cannae wait to introduce them to Marion."

Even though he wanted to spend the rest of the night, and a few more, just making love to Ilsabeth, Simon allowed himself only one more taste of the passion she gave him without reserve. Then they got up, dressed, and he gave her a small engagement ring of garnets that had been his mother's. He barely recalled the woman's name, but the tale was that she had received it from her lover. Ilsabeth laughed, loving the slightly scandalous tale that went with the ring.

Pandemonium reigned after they entered the great hall at Aigballa and announced their betrothal. It was not until a full round of congratulations had been endured that she noticed Reid and Elen sat off in a corner watching everything with very solemn faces. She took a few honied oatcakes off a tray and went to talk to the children.

"Why are ye hiding o'er here?" she asked as she forced herself between them and offered them each an oatcake. "I thought ye would like to go and say hello to Simon. He has missed ye." She ignored Reid's snort of disbelief and looked at Elen's sad little face.

"Do ye have to marry him?" Reid asked even as he picked up an oatcake and started eating it.

"I want bairns, Reid, and, anyway, I love him."

"Can we stay here then? Will these people let us stay here? I will work hard."

"Reid, love, ye will come to Lochancorrie with us."

She could see the doubt in his little face, as well as the fear in Elen's, and looked around until she saw Simon clapping her cousin the priest on the back in a way that indicated a deal had been struck. When he glanced her way with a smug grin on his face revealing his victory, she waved him over. Perhaps Reid would take Simon's word for it. One day she fully intended to have cured Reid and Elen of this fear of being left somewhere. Simon kissed her hand and then smiled at the children.

"Simon, tell them where they are going to live," she said, and put her arm around Elen to hug the little girl close. Ilsabeth could tell by the look on Simon's face that he quickly understood why she had asked and what needed to be said. "Why, with us of course. As soon as Ilsabeth and I are married, we will ride to Lochancorrie."

"That is a funny name," said Reid, but Ilsabeth noticed that the boy had moved closer to Simon.

" 'Tis a place near a loch, a lake. Ye will see. 'Tis beautiful. And ye will meet my lass Marion."

"Ye have a daughter?"

"I do. A wee lass a few years older than ye, Reid. She waits for us and a pony at Lochancorrie. I will send a messenger there on the morrow so that they will have the news of our arrival and be all ready for us."

"So we will be a true family?" Reid asked so softly that Simon had to lean very close to the boy's mouth to hear.

"Aye, we will, and to make it even more special, Ilsabeth is already carrying my child, so we will soon be a family of six."

Reid grinned and Elen, seeing that her brother was no longer nervous, hopped down and started to climb up Simon's leg. She kissed him on the cheek, then demanded to get back down so she could run and get some food. Reid sat quietly beside them eating his oatcake and Ilsabeth could almost feel the peace that had come over him. The boy knew he had a home for him and his sister now.

"Weel, what did ye talk the priest into?"

"Tomorrow afternoon. I offered him a new window."

"Simon! A new window is too much money."

"Nay, I ken a mon who can make beautiful ones for nowhere near what others make ye pay. And it doesnae matter for it is worth it to marry ye as quickly as possible and get our family back to Lochancorrie." Simon saw Reid grin and reached over to tousle the boy's hair. "And ye should go and meet your new uncles. See them o'er there?"

Reid nodded and Simon gave him a little nudge in the direction of his brothers. Simon watched the meeting carefully but within moments, Reid was laughing and acting silly as only a child can do. My family, Simon thought, and the word filled him with contentment. He put his arm around Ilsabeth when she leaned up against him.

"Ye are looking verra pleased with yourself," she said.

"I am. I have a beautiful woman and will soon claim her as mine. She loves me and makes my eyes roll back in my head when we make love. I have my home, the fields and livestock are better than they were so we willnae starve this winter, and I am about to marry into a verra large family who stays together. Oh, and I have a fine new son." He nodded toward Reid, who was obviously in a face-making contest with Ruari, and then touched her stomach. "And a child on the way. Brothers returned to the lands made for us, and a wee daughter and"—he glanced toward where Elen was looking for him—"I ken I have forgotten something but I wonder what it is."

"Si—mon!"

Ilsabeth laughed as Simon grinned at her and then caught Elen up in his arms.